"I was thinking."

"About what?" Mara asked.

"You." Reed faced her. He had to stop talking like this. Otherwise everything might pour out of him.

Mara leaned her head against his shoulder, her sleep-warmed body reminding him yet again of why he'd left her on the couch.

She was an incredible woman. Brave and competent. She'd taken steps to put her attack behind her. She'd moved back into her home. But there was still a criminal on the loose. Every time Reed thought about Mara—which seemed to be all the time—he slammed up against that.

For Mara, that was yesterday....

ABOUT THE AUTHOR

Vella Munn is a strong believer in focusing on the future—that people can take control of their lives and overcome anything. *That Was Yesterday* embodies that belief for her, and she hopes her readers will enjoy sharing the powerful discoveries that are so much a part of Mara and Reed's story. Vella Munn lives and works in Jacksonville, Oregon.

Books by Vella Munn
HARLEQUIN AMERICAN ROMANCE

115–WANDERLUST
164–BLACK MAGIC
184–WILD AND FREE
264–FIREDANCE
308–WHITE MOON
332–MEMORY LANE

VELLA MUNN

THAT WAS YESTERDAY

Harlequin Books

TORONTO • NEW YORK • LONDON
AMSTERDAM • PARIS • SYDNEY • HAMBURG
STOCKHOLM • ATHENS • TOKYO • MILAN

To Natasha Kern,
agent and friend
support system and frank, knowledgeable critic.
Finally, it came together.

Published August 1991

ISBN 0-373-16404-1

THAT WAS YESTERDAY

Chapter One

If the moon hadn't been full, Mara Curtis might have stayed in her beloved home at the edge of the desert. But the warm southern California night called. She was out of ice cream; that was enough reason for her to go for a drive. After giving her doberman, Lobo, fresh water, she slid behind the wheel of her Corvette, rolled down the window to let in the breeze and brought the powerful vehicle to life. San Diego lay ahead.

The Corvette responded, sharing its energy with her. Mara inserted an easy rock tape and cranked up the sound. Salt-tinged air teased her senses and danced over her bare arms, making her feel like a sixteen-year-old with a brand-new driver's license. How could anyone not love life!

Thirty minutes later, mindful of her gas bill, she pulled into a nearly empty supermarket parking lot. After wandering up and down the frozen-food aisle twice before selecting double chocolate with nuts, Mara walked back outside. As she passed from the supermarket's neon light into the shadows that separated her from her car, she sent out a silent message to her family. She hoped they could take a minute from the pace of hitting five races in a little over a week to simply smell the air too, to acknowledge the moon.

Someone, a man, was collecting abandoned shopping carts. Mara tucked her purchase in the crook of her arm and stabbed at her back pocket for her car keys.

The man lunged. Mara sensed the movement, but even her quick reflexes were no defense against the suddenness of the attack. Before she could do anything except draw a half breath, his arm cinched around her neck, hauling her tight against him. She felt sharp metal against her cheek.

"Not a sound, lady. Got me? Not a sound."

Mara finished inhaling, a natural movement, a pocket of sanity in a suddenly insane world. He had a knife. He was powerful. Her ice cream lay at her feet. Those things she could concentrate on.

"Good. Nice and quiet. You want to live, don't you?"

What? Mara waited, her mind and muscles leached of every strength they'd ever known. She couldn't remember how to make another breath come on the tail of the last one.

"I asked you something. You wanna live, don't you?"

They were alone; there wasn't another soul in the parking lot. "Y-yes."

"Yeah. Yeah. That's right, sweetheart. Nice car you've got there. I've been watching it for you. Keeping it safe." The man laughed. "You and me, we're going for a ride."

No!

He had to push her to get her started toward the Corvette. Off balance, Mara stumbled, taking a breath in the process. The night air felt hot in her lungs. The man's belt buckle poked her. A scream clawed at her throat. This wasn't happening. Not on a July night in sprawling San Diego. Any moment now the theater lights would go on and the movie would be over.

"You drive."

That Mara could do. In her sleep. Or she could have if the man didn't still have his arm locked against her throat, forcing her to grip his knotted forearm to keep herself from falling. The knife—she could see its hazy outline—was huge...something Daniel Boone would use to battle a bear.

"Where's your keys?"

Keys? Why wasn't her brain working? "In my pocket," she muttered after what seemed like a lifetime.

"Then get them out." The arm around her neck tightened. Somehow Mara managed to obey. The key almost slipped from her numb fingers. For an instant white-hot fury exploded through her, but she killed the useless emotion.

"Sweet car you got there, lady. Your boyfriend give it to you?"

Before Mara could decide whether the man expected an answer, he'd opened the passenger door, shoved her in and followed so close there wasn't a half second in which to plan an escape. Mara dumped her lean frame in her bucket seat, pulling her legs over the gearshift on the floor. She stared ahead, hands on the wheel. The wheel represented strength and untapped power. Next to her the man laughed.

"I watched you." His voice sounded as if he'd been abusing his lungs with cigarettes for years. "Watched you drive in here. This is one sweet car. I figured only a fox would be driving it. I was right."

"What—what do you want?"

"To go for a ride." The man drew the knife slowly from Mara's ear down to her elbow and then up again. He stopped with the tip poking against her sleeveless T-shirt. "For starters."

If only she could stop shaking. If only she could think.

"You know how to drive. Do it."

The Corvette's masterful hum soothed her. This was right; she belonged behind the wheel of a car. With its power at her fingertips, she could make a stab at thinking. Mara pulled out of the parking lot and onto the road. Because the man hadn't said where he wanted to go, and she wasn't going to speak to him any more than she had to, she headed west. Aimlessly.

The man amused himself by running the knife tip from her elbow to her shoulder and back again. Tickling. An agony of sensation. An invitation to madness. As each stroke was completed, Mara prayed. This time he would stop. This time he wouldn't begin the terrifying upward swipe again.

But he always did. And Mara jumped each time the knife touched her flesh.

She felt fear. And hate. A hate she could taste.

What did he look like? She would get away. When he was done with her, she would run to the police and tell them— Mara started to turn toward him. Before the gesture was finished, he slammed his fist into the side of her jaw. "No you don't, lady. I'm the one who'll do the looking."

The lesson stuck. Mara would stare out at the night. And she wouldn't let him know he'd made her bite her tongue.

"Hot these days, isn't it. Makes a person want to go without clothes." The knife dipped lower. Touched Mara's thigh. Made her jump despite the layer of denim. "I bet a lady like you . . . I bet you sleep in the raw."

Mara didn't have to look at the man to know he was staring at her breasts. She clenched her teeth until her jaw ached, despising him. If they were in traffic she could run a red light, maybe catch the attention of a policeman. But they had the quiet residential streets to themselves. No matter what she made the car do, only she would know. She and this animal.

"Where do you live?"

Mara hauled her mind back to the man sitting next to her. "What?"

"I said, where do you live? You got a roommate?"

Think. Damn it, think! "A husband. My husband's waiting for me."

"Liar. You aren't married."

With the knife against her thigh, Mara could do nothing except keep her eyes on where she was going. That and plan how she was going to stay alive. "Yes I am."

"No, you aren't. No man would let his woman drive around like this at night. You're cruising, lady. Married broads don't cruise."

"I went after ice cream." Why was she saying anything?

"But you got me instead." The man laughed. "Yeah, this is some fine car. Who bought it? Your sugar daddy?"

Mara clenched her jaws. "No."

"Who then? Maybe your pimp. Is that it?" The knife was no longer poking into Mara's thigh. He began inching it upward, this time running the weapon along her rib cage, over her right breast. Mara's vision dimmed and a scream threatened to escape. But the last time she'd screamed was five years ago; she wouldn't start again tonight.

"Nah," the man amended. "Woman who looks like you. She doesn't spend her days sleeping 'cause she worked all night. You know what you look like?" The knife made another circle. "A lifeguard. That's it. They sure as hell must pay lifeguards more than I thought they did."

Mara dismissed the words. If she wanted to get out of this alive, she would have to act.

Soon.

"Tell you what." Another circle with the knife. "A little later, you're going to open up this baby and show me what it can do. But now—" The man laughed; Mara smelled stale cigarette smoke. "Now it's time for us to get to know each other."

He's going to rape me. Just like that.

"You'd like that, wouldn't you?"

Lights. Lights from approaching cars. She could swerve into one of them. They weren't going that fast; no one would be killed. She would sacrifice the Corvette. If the knife was wrenched from the man, if she braced herself and he slammed against the dash, she would be free.

No. She couldn't risk anyone's life. A telephone pole? Maybe a tree. Why couldn't she think?

"I asked you a question. You'd like that, wouldn't you?"

"What?"

"What are you? Stupid? If you want to get through this alive, you're going to give me the answer I want." The knife tip was at the base of her throat putting an end to thoughts of swerving. Any move he didn't expect and he would plunge the knife into her. "I said—you'd like crawling between the sheets with me, wouldn't you?"

No!

He was applying pressure. "Wouldn't you?"

"Y-yes." Revulsion turned her sweat to ice. This wasn't her. She would never agree to anything like that, but she wanted to go on living. "Yes."

"That's what I thought." He backed off on the pressure. Not enough to allow Mara any sense of freedom, but enough that she could believe she hadn't, yet, come to the end of her life. "There's a place. Yeah. There's a place."

As the man gave directions, Mara fought down the bile that rose on the tail of the words she'd been forced to say. He ordered her to drive out of the city and head toward Sunset Cliffs. It would be desolate out there.

Silent.

Mara's thoughts raced in one direction and then another, bashing against dead ends. She could reach out, grab the door handle, leap out despite the speed—and splatter her body against the unyielding pavement. She could wait until they came to another stop and then, before he could prevent her, bolt into the night. No. At every intersection he pressed the knife into her ribs.

"You're going to like this," he was saying. "I know how to make things right for a woman. You tell me what you like. I'll—"

Mara shut down; she wasn't going to listen. She could, if she had no choice, pretend to go along with him. He might grow careless. He might put down his weapon. If she could reach it, she would use it.

"I'm talking to you." The knife broke through the thin layer of nylon and nicked the skin over Mara's rib cage.

"I—I didn't hear you."

"Damn you! I'm offering you the best night of your life, but you don't even know it."

"Why? What have I—"

"What have you done? Right place at the right time, lady. Plus, you turn me on, and I turn you on. I want to hear you say it."

"You want what?"

The knife found its previous home at the base of Mara's throat. "I want you to say I turn you on. Say it."

Not again! She couldn't say those things again!

"I won't ask again," he rasped.

There was pressure. Pressure and pain and blood trickling downward. It was a nick, just enough to let her know he wasn't going to accept silence. "You—" No. She couldn't jerk away. If she did, she might lose control of the car and they were going too fast for that now. "You turn me on."

"And tonight's going to be the best night of your life."

With the knife tip against her flesh, Mara managed the hated words. "Tonight's going to be the best night of my life."

The man laughed as the Corvette cut through the night. He continued to talk, now about other women he'd done this to. How they all had loved it. How Mara was going to have a night to remember. How the only way for her to come out of it alive was to make him happy.

Mara understood one thing—unless she found a way to gain control, tonight she was going to be raped and perhaps murdered. Strangely she was grateful now that the rules were clear-cut. It was her against this man who clung to the shadows. Only her. Only him.

"There. Pull over there."

Mara jumped. Barren rocks surrounded the deserted road. How had they gotten away from civilization so quickly? But maybe she'd been driving for hours. Mara did as she was told and waited for the half second that was all she wanted out of life.

"Party time." The man reached out, gripped Mara's jaw and pulled her head around. His hands felt like neglected leather; his features were cloaked in shadows. "You want to party, don't you?"

Mara knew what he wanted to hear; she couldn't give it to him.

The hand holding her jaw turned into a weapon, fast and decisive. When he hit her, Mara again bit her tongue. Her cheek flamed and went numb. "This is party time, bitch. I do what I want, when I want." He held the knife in front of her, bringing it first within a whisper of her face and then lower. Mara thought he was going to touch her throat or breast again. Instead he slipped hot steel under the shirt at the shoulder and pulled upward, slicing the fabric in two. "Party time."

He was leaning away, reaching for the door handle, holding the knife in the air. Laughing. Mara stared into the night. Thinking. Death now or when he was done with her. Everything boiled down to that.

The hell it did! The moment she heard his door open, Mara gathered herself, wrenched her own door handle, and rammed her body against the barrier.

She landed on her shoulder and arm on the ground but sprang to her feet before the pain registered. She ran into the night, embracing it, needing it as she'd never needed anything in life. He was only a few steps behind, his voice ragged and hard as he screamed obscenities. She could sense him clawing his way after her, feel the horror he represented. If she stumbled— No! She wouldn't fall, not if she wanted to live.

Thirty seconds passed, then a minute as Mara ran. Her heart pounded; her breath came in terrified gasps. She couldn't see where she was going, but that didn't matter. Nothing did except pitting her long legs against that animal's rage. Was he gaining? Was the noise she was making blocking out what she needed to know? After another minute, Mara ordered herself to hold her breath, to simply listen.

For the first time she heard the ocean, only the ocean.

Chapter Two

Reed Steward sat in the Harbor Island Police Department. According to what he'd been told, the Harbor Island department was tightly run. Much of that reputation was due to the tenacity of the man sitting across from him.

Captain Bistron hung up the phone for the second time since Reed walked in. "It's crazy, I tell you. I don't care what anyone says. The moon brings them out of the woodwork."

Reed smiled, at least as much of a smile as was in him. Inside he was knotted with concern, but he knew better than to let it show. Tonight was for collecting facts. Tomorrow was for action, for putting out for the man who'd done so much for him. Reed shifted position, accepting that his 198 pounds and six-feet, one-inch frame didn't comfortably fit into molded plastic chairs. "You're sure it's organized crime?"

"You aren't?"

"Right now I'm leaving every option open."

"Hmm. What happened to Jack Weston last week, is this a first for you people?"

"It's the first time we've had an attempted murder." Reed ground out the words. The National Automotive Theft Bureau which paid Reed's salary had given the San Diego police his file. What the captain didn't know was that because it was Jack who was trapped in a hospital, this wasn't just another assignment for him. His best friend—his only true friend—had almost been killed.

"Attempted murder. Yeah. We can't call it anything else, can we? Will you tell me why a Lotus Turbo is worth a man's life?"

Reed shook his head, his stomach knotted. "What we're up against is more than just stealing a car. The Lotus was hauled out of a locked garage. And unloading one of those takes specialized contacts. That means organization and ruthlessness."

"Bingo. Like I said, we're not talking kids on a lark here." Captain Bistron ignored the buzzing intercom. "Look. About what happened. I'm sorry. Weston's car being rammed—"

"Jack was hurt because something went wrong."

"And you want to make sure it doesn't happen again."

Reed leaned forward, his entire being focused on this moment. He needed the captain to understand that this was something he couldn't and wouldn't walk away from. "Jack and I go back a long way. That stubborn old man took an angry, confused kid and pointed him in the right direction. I owe him more than I'll ever be able to repay."

"But finding out who tried to kill him and putting that person or persons out of business is one way of evening the score. That's what you're saying, isn't it?"

Reed nodded, then glanced out at what he could see of the police station beyond the glass walls. The booking sergeant was talking to a bail bondsman. Next to him a police-woman hung on to a phone. Two policemen were hunched over forms. Five or six citizens waited their turn to talk. To an outsider, the scene would probably be both fascinating and foreign. To Reed, it represented nothing more than a starting point for his own agenda.

"Don't let dedication get in the way of good sense," the captain said. "I need you doing your job, not in the hospital next to your friend."

"I won't. I've been at this business long enough to know better," Reed said as a young man and a disheveled woman entered the station. "What can you give me?"

"Not much, I'm afraid," Captain Bistron said, following the unmatched couple's progress. "Mostly opinions and a handful of facts you might already know."

The words registered on an unconscious level but the newcomers commanding the captain's attention held Reed's interest as well. The woman was struggling to hold her sleeveless top together. The teenager near her looked as if he wanted desperately to walk back out the way he'd come.

A glass wall and a closed door separated Reed from the action, but he sensed drama. The woman with short, dark, tangled hair stood almost as tall as the teenager holding on to his motorcycle helmet. Her shoulders were broad, her legs long enough for a marathon runner. Yet there was a sunken quality to her, and she seemed incredibly alone in the crowded room. "Tough," he said.

"What?"

"That woman. She looks like she's had a rough time."

"It happens every day around here. Sometimes more times than I can keep track of, unfortunately." The captain upended the soft drink can he'd been sipping. "Would you like to take a drive? I thought we'd start by getting you oriented. I'll show you where Weston was found."

Despite the reference to Jack, Reed didn't take his eyes off the woman. He made note of the small wound at the base of her throat. Her left arm and elbow were scraped. She shivered. The policewoman put her arm around her shoulders, and the victim, if that's what she was, leaned into the woman in uniform as if desperate for comfort. "It's a place to start," Reed remembered to say. "You said you've heard rumors?"

"Maybe." Captain Bistron frowned at his empty can. "What we're guessing is that most of the cars are being shipped out of the area. Probably in the back of some rig after they've been altered. But without a vehicle identification number, tracing them is all but impossible. We can't stop every truck that leaves the area.''

''We need to put out some bait.''

''That's what Weston said. You know how to do that?'' The captain started to say more, but was distracted as the policewoman poked her head into his office.

''It's too soon to be sure,'' she said, ''but it might be that slime with the knife. The supermarket abductor. I need to get more from our victim, but I thought you'd like to know.''

Captain Bistron nodded. ''How's she doing?''

''Scared.''

''Does she need someone from rape counseling?''

''It sounds as if she got away before that happened.'' The policewoman glanced back to where the woman with the torn shirt and big, wounded eyes waited. ''That's one gutsy lady. She wasn't going to go down without a fight.''

''That or get herself killed.'' As the intercom buzzed again, Captain Bistron dismissed the policewoman and turned toward Reed. ''I'll be right with you. Damn phones. I hate the things.''

The call, Reed gathered, was a personal one. Partly because he wanted to give the captain privacy and partly because he was drawn to the newcomer, Reed left Bistron's office. The woman was still shaking and speaking in the carefully measured tones of someone who had to take self-control one breath at a time.

''I don't know what I would have done if this young man hadn't come along.'' She nodded at the teenage motorcyclist. ''I know I scared him the way I ran toward him. But I had to get out of there.''

''I'm just glad I was around,'' the teenager said.

''Me too.'' The woman's laugh was unnaturally loud. She held out hands that contrasted with her soft curves. The fingers were sinew and bone; rangy muscle stood out on her scraped forearm. ''I haven't felt this way since I couldn't find my mother at Indy.''

"Indy? What were you doing there?" the policewoman asked as she touched a dampened paper towel to the mark at the other woman's throat.

"My father was racing there. You said you had questions. Are there photographs I should be looking at?"

"We'll get to that. Don't put any more pressure on yourself than necessary right now. Is there someone you'd like to have here? It might make this easier."

"I can't think. Maybe— Can I make a call?"

Captain Bistron was still busy on the phone. Reed stepped closer, pulling change from his pocket so he'd have a reason to go to the soft-drink machine the woman was leaning against. Her long arms were now wrapped around her slender middle. Someone had given her a safety pin to hold her top together. The fabric hung submissively. She was tall enough that the word fragile shouldn't describe her, and yet this jean-clad woman, standing in the middle of a police station, carried an air of delicacy. A quick movement, a sudden sound might strip her of what self-control she'd managed to hold on to. The look she gave Reed as he dropped coins into the machine was guarded.

Reed doubted she would remember him. But he wouldn't forget. For one of the few times in his life, he wouldn't be able to shake off someone else's emotion. Her eyes were green, without end to their depth. He doubted that they'd ever exposed that much before.

"If you're up to it, I'd like to start getting this down now," the policewoman said. "While everything's fresh in your mind. I know you're concerned about your car, but it's not your job to look for it. We'll dispatch a unit."

"If he's done anything to it—" The woman ran her hand over her tangled hair. "He wouldn't let me look at him. The things he said. His voice—"

"You remember his voice?"

"For the rest of my life. It was dark. I didn't see him clearly. But his voice..."

"Good. That might help." The policewoman indicated a nearby chair and waited until the woman sank into it. "Look, what happened to you tonight makes *Friday the 13th* look like a Disney movie. We'll go at your pace. I'll ask questions. If there's one you don't feel ready to answer, or you want to wait until you get someone here, we'll come back to it. I just want you to understand that it's natural to be afraid, even in here."

"Afraid? I'm mad, but I'm not scared."

She was lying. How he knew that, Reed couldn't say. He understood procedure. Steps. Logic. Intuition wasn't part of his nature; he'd never allowed it to be. It wasn't dependable. But tonight it was as if he was being allowed access to this woman's thoughts. "Don't fight what you're feeling," the policewoman was saying. "Accept your emotions."

"I just want to do what needs doing. Try to remember everything. Help solve... And then I want to go home."

"Are you sure?"

"Sure?"

The policewoman explained. "What I'm saying is, there's a certain sense of security that comes from being surrounded by cops. When you go home that's going to change. You're going to feel vulnerable and exposed. You should let people know what you're going through. Don't be afraid to admit what you're feeling."

"If he's done anything to the Corvette—"

"Then we'll go after him together," the policewoman said, smiling ruefully. "I've always wanted a sports car. I could die for something that'd make every other car in the road eat my dust. But when there's an orthodontist to support... Look. I don't know if you've thought about this yet, but—"

"What?"

"He got more than your car. He has your purse."

"I don't care about the money."

"I'm not talking money," the policewoman said softly, gently, as she stretched out her hand. "He knows your name now. Your address."

The muscles in the woman's neck became taut cords, and when she swallowed, Reed both saw and sensed the effort it took. He wanted to say something, anything, but he didn't have the words. All he had was a feeling. A need to stay here, until he could no longer detect what was pooling up inside her and threatening to spill over. Until he thought of something that might help.

By the time the captain joined him, Reed had remembered his soft drink. He shook off the sound of the woman's voice as she responded to the policewoman's questions. Still, her body language continued to send out messages. She was feeling things she'd never felt before and trying not to acknowledge them. Gut-level fear was still ricochetting through her. She wouldn't get over it soon.

Reed wished he could be the one to help her understand that, and to regain the strength he could sense was usually as natural to her as breathing. He longed to see her whole.

"MISSION BAY has been particularly hard hit," Captain Bistron explained as they left the police parking lot. "That and the shopping centers where we're headed. People with money come to those places in cars that cost more than I make in a year. And when they're ripped off, believe me, we hear about it. Look, the average family loses the old station wagon, and they turn it over to their insurance company. They file a report, and we add the wagon to the hot sheet. Sometimes we get lucky, but most people eventually reconcile themselves to the fact that having a car stolen is part of life. But when a professional ballplayer or bank president or high-priced engineer has fifty-thousand dollars' worth of status stolen, he demands action. That's why we alerted your bureau. Facts are, we don't have the necessary manpower for this kind of investigation, and there's no putting this on the back burner."

Despite his long day, Reed was alert. Nothing had been said, but he understood. Like the local police, Jack had felt the pressure. That's why he'd put his life on the line, and almost lost it. "You're getting a lot of heat?"

"Plenty. That sort of thing makes the papers. And makes us look bad."

"Yeah. I guess it does. People expect miracles when there aren't any to be had. Look, like I said earlier, I need everything you can give me. I'm starting almost at point zero."

"I know, and I wish there was more. One thing I can tell you, they sure as hell know what they're doing. Right now I wouldn't trust anyone who's in any way involved with automobiles around here. Sales, bodywork, detailing, anything."

Reed glanced over at the captain, nodding agreement. "Whoever we're up against is after cars that can be sold black-market. Cars that bring in big money and can't be traced."

"Exactly. You want the facts? In the past thirty days, seventeen automobiles worth at least thirty thousand dollars each have disappeared."

Reed whistled. "You said you knew a few things."

"Damn few, mostly conjecture. We figure this ring is new. We've had surveillance on the usual places. Wrecking yards, parts shops. If any of them are involved, we haven't been able to make the connection. I've heard a few rumors about connections that go beyond San Diego. That doesn't surprise me. I passed that on to your co-worker. Nothing specific, I'm afraid." The captain put on his signal, then turned down a side street. "Like I told him, right now I suspect everyone and anyone connected with autos."

Reed tried to digest that particular piece of information. Certainly what the captain said made sense. However, there weren't enough lights on this narrow street. The dark reached out, touched him, reminded him of eyes without end to their depth.

"Can I ask you something?" Reed asked. "About what happened with that woman earlier tonight. The one who came into the station just before we left. Something was said about a supermarket abductor."

"For lack of a better name. If that's who grabbed her, that makes her the fourth. The other three didn't get off as easily."

Reed's stomach knotted. "They were killed?"

"Raped. And pretty badly beaten. They were all attacked at night and so scared we haven't gotten much of a description. The man's pretty good at intimidating. Hopefully, because this one got away before any physical damage was done, she'll be able to help us. Either way, it shouldn't affect your job...."

"But there is something you do need to know," Captain Bistron went on. "Night before last, one of our squad cars happened on what could have been one of the thefts. Two of my men observed someone jimmying the door on a new Caddy. Before they could make a move, whoever it was jumped in the car and took off. My men pursued. They were shot at."

Reed grunted. "Anyone hurt?"

"The suspects put a hole in the squad car's front windshield. Missed one of my men by inches. They got away. What I'm saying is, that's the way these guys operate. Forcing Weston off the road, running him into that telephone pole, they knew exactly what they were doing."

What did his superiors at the bureau call him? A pro. A trained operative. Reed was those things all right. This time, because of Jack, he was also a man with a debt to pay. "I'm going to be taking precautions."

"What kind?"

"If I get into the same situation Jack did, I'm planning to come out on top. Starting Monday I'm taking lessons in survival driving. I've already signed up at an advanced driving skills school."

"You have? You do move fast." Captain Bistron nodded. "Yeah. If it was me, I'd want that edge myself. Look, these thefts have to stop."

"That's the other reason I'm taking the course. There's always the possibility I'll hear something while I'm there. Whoever is running this driving program must know the local auto scene." Reed winced as the captain ground through gears.

"Damn. Looks like another transmission shot. You have a point about that school maybe being a contact. You know, in a way I envy you. You don't have the public looking over your shoulder telling you how to do your job, do you? You call your own shots. Do what you know needs doing without having to have a summit conference about every move you make. Of course, there's an element of danger."

"What happened to Jack—it's a first for the bureau."

"That's what you said. Look, do you want to see where we found him?"

"No. I don't want to. But I think I have to." Reed clenched his jaw, adding to the tension already in his body. He had to concentrate, learn, start formulating plans. He would bury himself in this case, for Jack.

That was the only thing that mattered.

Chapter Three

"Are you all right?"

Mara stared out her kitchen window at the desert where she both lived and worked. The plants nestled in their pottery and wicker baskets along the sill cut down on her view, but Mara had never denied her need for greenery, for a feeling of life within her home. Before long, the Curtis School of High-Performance Driving would come to life, but for a few minutes more only the wind kept her and Clint Archer company.

"Better. Much better," she told him.

"Yeah? You aren't getting any backlash?"

"It's my home, Clint. Nothing's going to change the way I feel about it."

"I hope not. You might not want me to say it. I know I don't. But you aren't going to feel as secure in it now."

It was hard to remember that Clint was only twenty-two. He'd signed on with Mara right after high school and weathered the early days of the business with her. She might pay his salary, but they were close friends, too. "Maybe not right now. But soon. Clint, all I want is for things to get back to normal. Thank you for coming out here with me."

"No more *thank you*'s. I've heard that about a hundred times."

"I'm sure you have." She remembered how to smile. It didn't come easy, and it might not fool Clint, but she gave it a try. "Being able to stay with you— It kept me from going crazy."

"I know you, boss. You would have survived. I just wish we could get a locksmith out here before tomorrow. Your wallet. House keys. When I think of that creep having them, it gives me the chills. Listen to me. I'm shook, and it didn't happen to me. If you think you have to explain what you're going through, you're crazy."

Clint was wrong; he didn't understand everything because she hadn't told him more than she needed to to keep him around. There was absolutely no way she could have repeated the things she'd been forced to say to appease that monster. The degradation that had caused preyed on her as much as knowing the man could find her and, until the new locks were put in, might walk in her door. That was what they were doing here this morning, making sure he hadn't done that over the weekend while she was staying with Clint.

Normal? She wasn't sure what that meant, only that, somehow, she had to find it again. "I did act a little crazy."

"You acted human."

"I don't think I've talked so much in my entire life. I must have told you the story a hundred times."

"Five hundred and three, but who's counting? Look, that detective they've assigned to the case? When you go back to talk to him, I'm going with you."

"You don't—"

"No arguments." Clint planted his hands on Mara's shoulders. The touch made her feel five years old. She wished she were.

"All right." She remembered how, at the police station, with a roomful of people watching, Clint had held out his hand and waited for her to come to him. She'd done that gladly, gratefully. And once the police were finished, he'd told her to get in his car and put on her seat belt, and she'd obeyed. Once they reached his apartment, he'd told her to take a shower while he made hot chocolate, and she'd done that, too. Then she had sat on his couch, with his robe wrapped around her, and started talking while he applied antiseptic to the cut on her throat. He'd told her it was all right if she cried, and she had almost done that, too.

Mostly she had talked. All night. About everything and anything that might hold the horror at bay.

The next morning they'd driven out to her place so she could feed Lobo. Clint had unlocked the front door of her mobile home and walked in while Mara held back. When he'd told her it didn't look as if anyone had been inside, she'd walked as far as the living room with its new blue-gray carpet, clean wicker furniture, and the sunlight streaming through the oversize window. The large, misted painting of the ocean at dawn, hanging over the cushioned sofa, had always drawn a response from Mara. But on Saturday morning she'd barely noticed it. She'd been too concerned with absorbing the essence of her home and trying to draw strength from it.

The plants hadn't needed watering. She hadn't needed to stay. If Clint didn't mind— And he'd said he didn't. Except for going back to the police station once and coming back out on Sunday to care for her doberman, she'd spent the weekend at his place.

Her Corvette had been found, out of gas, on I-5 heading north. It had been stripped of all personal possessions. The police weren't done with it yet. When they were, she would scour it inside and out, a dozen times if that's what it took. Then she would take it onto the oval track and drive and drive until it felt as if it belonged to her again. Then—

"We talked about calling your folks."

"How?" Mara asked too quickly. "The way that bunch moves around—"

"You could find them if you tried. Just leave a message at one of the racetracks they're going to."

"What would I tell them? There's nothing they could do. And Mom would be on the next plane back here."

"Don't give me that, Mara," Clint interrupted. "You don't want to tell them because the Curtis family is supposed to personify the macho image, and you don't want to do anything to tarnish that. That's it, isn't it?"

Mara made no attempt to keep up her end of the conversation. She would tell her mother about her "adventure"— that's what she'd call it. But not yet. Not until the shadows no longer pressed around her. Not until the wound at her throat healed and she could speak without fear in her voice. "Speaking of parents, you're going to need your spare bedroom back."

"We'll worry about that when the time comes. In the meantime, I want you to go on staying with me." Clint turned away.

"I'm grateful. But Clint, this came at a bad time for you. Your dad's health—"

"Why don't you let me worry about that."

Mara nodded. The only thing she was capable of today was wandering through her rooms, running her fingers over vibrant ferns, fluffing a throw pillow, lingering at the bank of trophies that chronicled her father's racing career. She stopped at her answering machine and hit the Play button. Tucked into the middle of a half dozen messages for the racing school was her mother's voice.

"Sweden. It's Saturday so it must be Sweden. Wish you were with us, honey. The usual problems. There's something wrong with the ignition system in Matt's Beretta, and Steve's going through tires like there's no tomorrow, but they're both finishing in the money, and that's what counts. Steve says for you to build another shelf because he's got some trophies for you to store. I've been entering my share of races, but the less said about that the better. Your dad's back is giving him trouble, but he's too stubborn to admit it. I hate talking to this machine. I don't know when we'll be back your way, two months at least."

Two months. Two months without seeing her family. She should be used to this. Before the abduction, Mara would have simply accepted what made her different from her parents and brothers. But now her mother's voice, hollow from the long-distance call, brought her close to tears. She loved them. Just because she didn't want to bounce from one race to another and was exhausted from the effort of battling the tension that was part of watching her family compete, didn't mean she didn't love and miss them.

No! She wouldn't think about her parents and brothers. She wouldn't think about Friday night and the necessity of talking to a detective, and the question of when she'd be able to stand staying in her own home alone. Instead she would concentrate on making a living.

A minute later Mara led the way out of her mobile home and across the track she would be making payments on for longer than she wanted to think about. Her tennis shoes made a soft pad-pad sound on the already warm asphalt. There were no motors revving yet, and because Mara's only real neighbors were silent desert creatures, she caught the sound of the wind blowing over the flat acreage.

For the first time since she moved here Mara sensed, not her land around her, but isolation.

This week's students were waiting out by their cars, five men and a woman. The familiar routine claimed her. No matter what had happened, she had work to sustain her.

The woman looked to be in her late thirties, slim with small diamond earrings. She was standing beside her Alfa Romeo as if it was a wild stallion she'd just roped. Mara sized her up in a look. Money.

Two of the men, Mara remembered from their applications, came from the same high-tech company. Notes on their applications had said that taking the Curtis course was part of a confidence-building program for them. One man was barely out of his teens. His Mustang had gone through so many modifications that probably only the horse emblem was original. And the middle-aged gentleman standing next to him looked as if this was the last place he wanted to be. Mara guessed he'd racked up so many tickets that someone had put pressure on him to do something about his driving skills. He'd probably fight her every inch of the way.

The fifth man stood next to a bloodred Jaguar. His cobalt-blue eyes rested on her, and yet she sensed that he was testing, absorbing, appraising his surroundings. Mara understood, because in the space of a single evening, she had been taught to trust nothing and no one.

Without looking into the Jag, Mara knew the driver's seat would be pushed all the way back to accommodate his height. He wore jeans and a knit pullover. The wind whipped his dark-toasted hair. Despite the bright early-morning sun, he wasn't wearing sunglasses.

In his dark, deepset eyes Mara read recognition.

Her attacker! That was insane. Still, despite her angry denial, Mara remained tense. Maybe he'd seen her before, and maybe this was simply part of the insanity. Before Friday night, men had been friends or clients, fellow car enthusiasts or business associates. Now, thanks to a monster with a knife, a new element had been added. She wouldn't put a name to that element, just as she wouldn't lock eyes with the owner of the Jag. Whatever his message, and there was one, he could keep it to himself.

"First, to introduce myself, I'm Mara Curtis, owner, instructor, mechanic and anything else the job calls for," she began, taking comfort from words she'd spoken more times than she could remember. "I'm aware that it's quite a drive out here, but that's the only way I could provide the space needed for this operation."

Mara slipped into a sketchy history of the school's evolution, explaining that she had begun it four years ago. "I learned auto racing at my father's side. He taught me just about everything there is to know about controlling an automobile, no matter what the situation. That's what I'm committed to passing on to my students."

"Curtis?" the man with the Jag interrupted. "Your dad's Mark Curtis?"

Mara nodded. His voice. She'd never heard it before. That knowledge made it possible for her to relax. He was simply another student, not part of the nightmare.

"Then we are in good hands," the man told the others. "Miss Curtis's father is a professional driver. He's made a name for himself at the international raceways. He's still racing? Even after that crash?"

"It's his life," Mara said simply, and then took the kind of breath that had sustained her whenever she watched her father pull up to a starting line. It helped. A little. At least it allowed her to remember why she was here . . . and reject the big man's impact. "I want all of you to understand something," she said automatically. "From reading your applications, I know that each of you is here for a different reason. Although my personal background is the racing circuit, it doesn't hurt my ego that only one of you has such aspirations." She smiled at the young man with the modified Mustang. "I keep the classes small enough that each of you should be able to get the individualized instruction you need. We'll come back out here to work on practical applications. However, first we're going to go through a classroom experience. If you'll follow me . . ."

Mara started toward the small building which contained her driver-education classroom, grateful that she didn't have to get into a vehicle with any of the men, yet. Through the use of visual aids and driving simulators, she and Clint could handle the more elementary aspects of the course. After a break she launched into chapter two of her introduction. She noted that, except for the middle-aged businessman, her students all leaned forward, concentrating. She also noted that the man who knew about her father was watching, not the facts and figures she presented, but her.

She wished she could tell him to stop.

A little later Mara let Clint take over. He demonstrated the proper way to sit behind the wheel, upright, with one's back pressed against the seat so as to feel the car's response. "Hands at nine and three o'clock," Clint explained. "Nudge, don't grip the gearshift. And never stomp the brakes."

Mara's concentration faded. Something more essential than work reached out to her. Intrigued, wary, unnerved, she answered the call. The big man with the wind-touched hair wasn't listening to Clint, either. *"I know something,"* Mara read in his appraisal of her. *"Something no one else here knows."*

Although she remained convinced he wasn't her attacker, Mara still felt sick. Sick and hot and cold. She didn't risk another look at the man until the morning break. Then, while the woman with the earrings cornered Clint, and the two from the high-tech firm entertained themselves by slicing through a superior's reputation, she willed herself to remain where she was while the man, Reed Steward, joined her.

"Your father's practically an institution," he told her. "He did have a serious wreck, didn't he?"

"Yes."

"I admire anyone with the guts to get back on his feet after something like that. He wasn't able to race for about a year, was he?"

Mara fought off the impact of having a strange man this close to her. He couldn't know it, but he'd touched on a turning point in her life. "It was a long time ago."

"About five years. I saw a picture of what was left of his car. I don't know how he survived."

"My father's too tough to die. At least that's what he tells us."

"But he came close."

"Yes," Mara admitted. "He came close." Close enough that when the year of healing was over, Mara knew she couldn't sit through any more races if someone she loved was involved.

"That must have been hard on all of you. And he's still racing?"

"So are my brothers."

"Why?"

Why? "Because it's in their blood. Because they're crazy. Because that's the way they supported Mom and Dad while he was healing." The conversation wasn't going where she wanted... if she wanted a conversation at all. Where was Clint? No. She had to do this on her own. "That's quite a car you have, Mr. Steward. You don't see too many red Jags."

"That's what the guy who sold it to me said. That's how he tried to justify the price. Please." His voice slowed. "Call me Reed."

Why? I'm not going to see you after this week. "Have you had it long?"

"I just bought it. I had the engine modified to allow for the fastest acceleration possible. Maybe you'd like to look at it later. Take it through some curves."

"Maybe. What kind of business are you in?"

Reed shifted his weight. He could have used the gesture to bring himself closer, but he didn't. Despite her relief, Mara found she had to concentrate on the act of breathing. "I'm in the business of making money," he told her. "You see a lot of high-performance cars, don't you?"

"Yes."

"They fascinate me. Owning them, that is."

"That could turn out to be an expensive hobby."

"It could." Reed worked up a smile. Mara took note of the effort and wondered if their conversation came any easier to him than to her. "The thing is," he told her, "I don't like paying retail. There are other ways.... You really live out here?"

Cold touched her. Mara wasn't sure she could keep her reaction from him. "I hope we'll be able to live up to your expectations," she said, sidestepping. Where she lived was none of his business. "If there's anything you'd like covered that isn't part of the program, ask."

"Actually..." Reed's voice dropped. "If you aren't busy later, I'd like to discuss my situation."

There it was. The come-on. Mara had grown up around men who wore their masculinity like badges. The macho image—men dominating the world of fast cars—had been part of the fabric of her whole life. She should be immune by now.

But she wasn't. Not today. Not with this man.

"I'm going to be busy this evening," she told him. "I have loaner cars for students who don't have their own. One of them—the timing's off."

"You're not going to need them this week. We all have our own."

Reed was right. Working on a car wasn't how she expected to spend her evening. But Mara wasn't going to tell this stranger about her appointment with a police detective. "I've committed myself to something."

"Have you?" Reed nodded, then turned away and sat back down. It wasn't until Clint was five minutes into a discussion of the advantages of steering around a hazard versus using one's brakes that he pulled himself back to why he was here.

No matter what his reaction to finding out his instructor was the woman he'd seen Friday night—and there was a reaction—he would have to keep that fact separate and isolated from his job. She might have been a victim. She might have evoked emotions in him he didn't understand, emotions he wanted, yet at the same time didn't want. But right now the only thing he should be thinking about was that her work brought her in contact with the world of high-performance automobiles.

That world had almost killed Jack, and Reed's purpose here was to infiltrate it. Until and unless he knew Mara better, everything he said and did around her had to be calculated. His life depended on it. What he'd said to Mara Curtis about his interest in expensive automobiles had laid the groundwork. He would work from that base.

He wouldn't think about how much he'd wanted to comfort her Friday night, or how inept that emotion made him feel.

Reed sensed her incredible green eyes on him. He turned quickly, forcing the unspoken contact. For six, maybe seven seconds there was communication, vague and undefined. Then Mara pivoted away and he was left looking at her slim back.

Did she remember him? He didn't think so; there'd been nothing in her expression to indicate that. But maybe she, in the same way he did, knew what to reveal and what to keep hidden. He would be wise to remember that.

AT NOON Mara's secretary brought in sandwiches for the whole group and a message for Mara. "Detective Kline," she explained. "He wanted to know if you could come in this afternoon. I told him that wasn't possible. We settled on 6:00 p.m. if that's all right with you."

Mara nodded and placed the note with the telephone number on her desk. She'd go to the police station, but it would be a wasted trip. She had nothing left to tell him. Nothing more she remembered. "Did he say anything else?"

"Just that he thinks they'll be able to release your car soon. When I think of what you went through..."

Mara had told Diane only the bare details. As far as Diane understood, Mara's main concern was with getting her car back. "I just want to get this over. If it means a late dinner..."

Reed couldn't hear much of what the two women were saying—just the words *get this over* and a tone that shouldn't come from a woman who'd carved out her own business. He waited until Mara left her desk before walking over to it. The note gave a time, the name of a detective, a phone number. In a glance, Reed committed everything to memory. If he was here simply, as he'd told himself, to do a job, he wouldn't be concerned with what Mara might discuss with the detective. But he was curious. That's all, curious.

After lunch, classroom instruction gave way to behind-the-wheel experience. Mara explained that the first assignment would be driving through an obstacle course. "We'll start at twenty miles an hour and then increase the speed. Remember concentration, smoothness and consistency."

When Reed's turn came he found himself paired with Clint. At first Reed handled his assignment confidently. Gradually, however, Clint asked him to increase his speed until he was aware of nothing except gripping the wheel as he zipped around the barriers.

"Good reflexes," Clint acknowledged after Reed successfully held the needle at seventy-five. "You didn't allow yourself to be distracted. That's essential."

Reed took a deep breath. The exercise had left him tense and wondering what had gone through Jack's mind during those final seconds before the crash. However, what was important now was focusing on why he was here. "It's a good thing you're with me," he began, every word calculated. "I would have been distracted if you were Miss Curtis."

Clint didn't blink. "Not if you want to get your money's worth out of this course."

"Maybe. But a woman like that... She's like a fine car, if you know what I mean. There's not enough of them in this world."

"Yeah?"

Ignoring Clint's noncommittal grunt, Reed plunged on. "You know what I mean. Take this." He brought his hand down hard on the Jag's steering wheel. "This isn't just a car. It's a piece of me. Great cars, a truly fine woman... those are the kinds of things I'm after."

Clint reached for the door handle.

"Don't you agree?" Reed pressed. "Look, you gotta love speed as much as I do. Wouldn't you like to have the most beautiful woman in the city sitting next to you, cruising in a car that commands attention?''

"Maybe."

"No *maybe* about it. Look. I've got money. More money than I know what to do with." Reed nearly choked on the lie. Still, because it was necessary and he knew how to do the necessary, he went on. "For a lot of people, that'd be enough. But now that I've got the dough, what comes next? I look for ways to get what I want without having to put out a lot. There's more challenge in that."

"Whatever turns you on."

Reed was losing Clint. Although he was relieved the man hadn't bitten, Reed made one more stab. "I've got this thing about walking into a dealership and letting them take me to the cleaners. That's not the way I want to do business. If a man saw a car he liked and that car happened to belong to someone else—well, if he had the right connections, he could get his hands on it. If you know what I mean."

"That's talk. There's always talk."

"Talk nothing. It happens." Was he pushing things too far? Reed decided he had better change the subject. "How's Miss Curtis to work for? I mean, this isn't the kind of business where you usually find a woman running the show."

Clint opened the door. "Mara knows exactly what she's doing. She always has. That's why I work for her. We're going to be tackling skids next. Mara likes us to rotate. She'll be with you in a few minutes, Mr. Steward."

Reed leaned forward. Mara had just come back from a run with the businesswoman. Now the two of them stood next to the Alfa Romeo. Mara was perhaps four inches taller than the carefully dressed businesswoman. She exhibited a grace that the other woman with all her exercising and massages couldn't equal.

Mara stood with her weight settled over one hip, her free leg angled out, giving Reed a breath-stealing look at lean length. He remembered a white-faced woman with her arms wrapped around her middle but could make no connection between that image and the woman he saw today. Whatever had brought her into the police station the other night was under control. She could talk to Detective Kline without going back in time.

A woman like that could live alone out here.

After listening to the businesswoman explain that she could hardly wait to challenge a certain co-worker, Mara turned the conversation to what she needed to accomplish before the afternoon ended. She explained that as soon as Clint laid a layer of oil over the track, the students would put what they'd learned in the classroom about spin control to the test.

She had Reed wait until last. By then she'd forced herself to sit in a confined space with the other four men and resolutely kept herself from drawing comparisons between now and Friday night.

"I'm sorry," she said as she stared at the Jag's close bucket seats. "At least you've been able to watch the others. I hope you're not concerned about flipping."

"I'm working on it."

"That's half the battle." Reed Steward took up too much space inside the car. She told herself it didn't matter. She would deal with this emotion and master it. And she wouldn't let him know. "Whenever you're ready. We'll start at about forty miles an hour."

Mara strapped on her seat belt. Reed followed suit and then started the Jag. As he eased onto the track, he wondered what the bureau would say if they knew what he was doing to the expensive prop they'd leased for him. If he wrecked it—

The question didn't last. "Have any of your students lost it?"

"A few have come close, but there haven't been any accidents."

"So far."

Reed eased the Jag to forty miles per hour and headed for the oil slick. Just before the rear wheels lost traction, he glanced at the woman next to him. There weren't going to be any mistakes. Not with her life in his hands.

Reed didn't make the mistake of slamming the brake to the floor. Instead he shifted into neutral, keeping the front wheels straight as the car twisted 180 degrees, heading in the opposite direction. Then he went to work, cranking the wheel hard to the right to add momentum to the spin.

When the skid was over, the car once again pointed in the direction it had been going before it hit the oil. Reed nudged the gearshift and put the Jag into motion again. He was drenched in sweat.

"How do you feel?" Mara asked.

"You don't want to know." Reed shrugged his shoulders, forcing himself past the emotion that had knotted his hands, and went on. "But, like I said, I know my car. An automobile is more than a tool. If it's the right car, it becomes an extension of its driver."

"An extension?"

"Part of me."

The man's reactions were sharp, Mara thought. Despite his tension, Reed Steward had accomplished what was asked of him, and well. Whatever he needed from the Curtis School of Performance Driving, it wasn't the basic course. Why, then, was he putting himself through this? "You mentioned having some specialized needs?" Mara asked warily.

"Yeah. I do. But there isn't time to talk about that now, and you said you were busy tonight."

"I am. And I have to talk to Mr. Dixon. He's fighting this class every inch of the way."

"Of course."

Mara glanced over at Reed. He hadn't said anything about having seen her before. There'd been the time and opportunity for him to mention that she wasn't a stranger to him, but he hadn't done it. Maybe the flash of recognition she believed she'd seen had been nothing more than another layer of the insanity she was going through.

Maybe.

AN HOUR LATER Mara stood watching the last of her students leave. The red Jag was already nothing more than a blur of movement. With the echo of her conversation with Reed still nagging at her, she turned toward Clint. She felt hollowed out. "An interesting lot. Ms. Alsobrook likes you."

"Ms. Alsobrook likes anything in pants. I'd hate to be that desperate."

"Desperate? Did you see those earrings? She didn't get those at a dimestore."

"That's not what I'm talking about." Clint watched the aimless flight of a distant hawk. "So she's got more money than she knows what to do with. That money isn't buying her happiness."

Mara shifted her gaze to the hawk. "Do you feel sorry for her?"

"Yeah. I guess I do. She's trying to be something she isn't. But she didn't ask my opinion, and I'm not going to give it. What do you think of the guy with the Jag?"

"What?"

"He's a different one."

"Different?" Mara repeated.

"Let's just say he has some rather strange ideas. He doesn't fit in here."

"I know."

"He's a decent driver. But he isn't crazy about some of the things we've asked him to do."

"I'm aware of that."

"So why is he pushing himself?"

"I don't know. His application didn't say. But maybe I'm going to find out. He wants to talk to me."

"Yeah? About what?"

"I'm not sure. Clint, I have an appointment with the detective in an hour."

"I'll meet you there. Unless you want me to hang around here while you close up."

"No. Of course not. Honest. And you don't have to meet me there."

"Yeah, I do. I want to make sure they're taking this seriously."

"Do you think they aren't?" Mara asked.

"I wouldn't take anything for granted. We're talking about your safety. I don't want you getting lost in the shuffle, and I don't want to hear about lack of manpower or whatever excuses they might try to dump on you. In an hour. And then you're coming home with me."

Mara looked up at Clint, silent. She should tell him she no longer needed his protection, his spare bedroom. A woman who would turn twenty-nine next month was light years away from a six-year-old child crying for her parents at some massive, distant racetrack. But the words eluded her. She was frightened but determined. Reality was that in a minute Clint would leave and she would let him. She wouldn't see him again until they met at the police station.

In a minute she would have no one except a hawk and a watchdog to keep her company.

As soon as it got dark even the hawk would leave.

Chapter Four

The floors of hospitals squeaked. It didn't matter what kind of shoes a person wore, highly polished floors protested any contact. Reed pondered that, not because he cared about gleaming floors, but because right now the journey was easier to focus on than the goal.

But he couldn't put it off. He had no choice but to push open the door to room 312 and step into the gloom beyond. The room's amenities consisted of a single bed, a chair and a small, curtained window beyond the machinery that monitored Jack. His friend was covered by a faded pink coverlet. The smell of disinfectant pressed against Reed's senses and forced his mind back to other hospital visits when the patient had been his mother—when there'd been too many tears from her and not enough words inside him.

Jack wasn't moving. Damn it, he still wasn't going to be able to yank the man out of here.

"Jack? You awake?"

"Why? You taking a survey?"

"What if I am?" Even the undersized chair tucked in a corner of the room was pink. Reed decided that when and if he ever decorated a place, there wouldn't be a hint of that color in it. "Do you know what this place is costing the bureau? They want you out of here."

"Not near as much as I want out," Jack managed as Reed approached the bed.

Reed's mentor and only true friend seemed to have aged ten years. He tried to tell himself that any man stuck in a dark closet like this would look pretty bad, but that wasn't all. Jack had five broken ribs, a bruised kidney, a concussion and a lacerated forehead.

"At least you're talking," Reed said. He knew he should sit down, but going after the chair and dragging it beside the bed was beyond him, when the only thing he wanted was to pick Jack up and get both of them the hell out of here.

"What makes you think I wouldn't be?" Jack said, wheezing.

"Because the last time I saw you, you were a zombie."

"You were here before?"

"Three times." Should he take Jack's hand? Reed knew how to shake hands, slap another man on the back. He hadn't known what to say or do when his mother was the patient. And he didn't know how to give comfort to someone who'd never needed it before and might not want it now. "Do you remember how you got here?"

"Yeah." The word was hard-bitten. "I remember all right."

"They forced you off the road. They tried to kill you."

"I screwed up, Reed."

"No." The piercing depth in Jack's eyes might have intimidated someone else, but Reed had known it for more than half his life. He wasn't about to back down. "You don't screw up."

"If I didn't, I wouldn't be here. My cover? What a joke. I thought I had everything in place. I got ahead of myself. Started pushing before I knew what I was into. What are you doing here? I thought they'd sent you to Denver."

"I bailed out."

"Because you like hanging around hospitals." Jack coughed, his face contorting. "Don't kid me, Reed. I want to hear everything."

Reed rammed his hands in his back pockets and leaned his hip against the side of the bed. There was a gnawing sensation inside him, but he would do something about food later. It felt so good to hear Jack talking again. That first visit had come close to being the hardest thing Reed had ever done. Staring down at the bruised and misshapen features of the man who'd done so much for him was something he never wanted to repeat. "You weren't in any shape to complete your assignment," Reed said simply. "I figured I had to come pick up the slack."

"Yeah? Tell me something. If it was anyone but me, would you be here?"

Both men knew the answer to that. "The bureau's in an uproar," Reed said instead. "We've never had an agent almost killed before."

"Like I said, I screwed up."

"Come off it, Jack. Give yourself a break," Reed snapped. "I've been talking to the police. This isn't just big, it's well organized. And the operatives are ruthless."

"Still—" Jack coughed again. "There's no excuse for my getting into the mess I did."

"Why don't you let me be the judge of that." Reed didn't want Jack to exhaust himself talking, but it was the only way he'd learn the essentials. Briefly Reed explained the steps he'd already taken and that he knew he wasn't going to get far without Jack's help. Who had the older man contacted? What had Jack learned about the destination of the expensive automobiles being snatched?

Not enough, Jack admitted. What he did know was mostly what Reed had already deduced. Those behind the operation were determined enough that killing someone careless enough to be caught sniffing around wouldn't slow them. "You know what I'm going to say, don't you?"

Reed didn't.

"Don't do it. It isn't worth your life."

Jack Weston had given Reed direction when he hadn't known such a thing existed. Thanks to Jack, Reed wasn't sleeping on park benches or in prison. Jack had forced, encouraged, convinced him to take charge of his life and turn it into something worthwhile. It galled him to hear the desk jockeys at the bureau hinting that Jack had lost his edge. Damn it, no one was infallible. He'd like to see anyone else accomplish what Jack had during his thirty-year career.

But what Reed felt went deeper than just a commitment to Jack's reputation. Someone, or a number of someones, had tried to kill the man staring up at him. Reed wouldn't forget. Or forgive.

"I'm not going to get killed," Reed reassured his friend. "I'll get them, Jack. Put them out of business and behind bars. Then we'll tell the stuffed shirts at the bureau that we want and deserve raises, big ones. We'll get that sailboat we've been talking about. Head for the South Seas."

"I'm hanging it up, Reed."

"No." He should have been sitting. That way it wouldn't matter so much that Jack's words were making him light-headed.

"I mean it. It's time for me to get a desk job."

Men like Jack Weston didn't retreat behind desks. "Get yourself out of here," Reed said slowly. "Take time to heal. You'll see it differently then."

"I don't think so. I know I've been out of it a lot of the time, but I've been thinking. I remember..." Jack swallowed painfully. "I remember looking over at that damn truck coming at me. I knew there wasn't anything I could do about it. Not a thing. Then—I don't know if I'd crashed yet or not—it came to me."

"What came to you?" Reed asked, because not asking wouldn't stop the answer.

"That there's got to be more to life than this."

"There is," Reed countered. "There's...that sailboat."

"A sailboat. Come off it, Reed. Look at me. Look at yourself while you're at it. I've been in here for days, and do you know who's been here to see me? Doctors. Nurses. Some reporter I wouldn't talk to. Someone from the bureau trying to figure out how much it's going to cost them. And you."

"Three times," Reed pointed out, although he was beginning to understand.

"Wonderful. No family. No friends. Not even a bunch of flowers. Do you know why? Because I never stick around anywhere long enough to make friends. And because I don't have a family. Just a sister who hasn't heard from me since last Christmas and probably has no idea what's happened."

Reed wanted Jack to stop talking and get some rest. The older man might have been flat on his back for days, but he was still exhausted and understandably so. The drugs he'd been given were depressing his system. That's what it was. A drug-induced depression. That and his injuries.

"You want flowers, I'll get them. And I'll call your sister," Reed said, disturbed because he'd been so angry and worried that neither of those things had occurred to him. "I'll be back with something decent for you to eat. How about a pizza? You do what those doctors tell you and get yourself out of here. Go sit on the beach somewhere. I'll join you as soon as I can, and then we'll figure out how much of a raise we're going to hold out for."

"All I want is my retirement, Reed. I mean it." Jack ran dull eyes over the too-small room. "It might be too late for me. It probably is. But before I die I'd like to find out if there's more to life than this. More than just you giving a damn about me."

"What are you looking for? Sympathy?"

"You know better than that. Maybe running my head into a telephone pole woke me up. What's it all for, Reed?"

Reed opened his mouth. Nothing came out.

"That's what I thought. You should understand. There's no one who's going to send either of us flowers. Think about it."

Reed didn't remember reaching out. But somehow he wound up with his strong hands wrapped around Jack's limp ones. He squeezed, holding or until Jack focused on him. The wounded man's eyes were no longer dull. They glistened. When Reed blinked, he discovered that his own eyes were damp. "I won't let them get away with it," he whispered. It was a vow.

A HALF HOUR LATER Reed went back to the opulent, impersonal hotel room he'd set himself up in. Instead of going over what Jack had told him about the ring's operation, he stretched out on the firm bed with its crisp sheets and stared up at a white ceiling that was shot through with some sparkling stuff. Jack would bounce back, Reed tried to tell himself. He'd stop talking about wasted years, and Reed would no longer be forced to draw parallels between Jack's dark mood and the cloud permanently draped over his own mother.

Reed didn't blame Jack. He blamed those who'd almost killed him. Anyone who'd come face to face with death would have his underpinnings loosened. Jack couldn't honestly mean it about quitting the bureau. Retiring. Looking for something or someone else.

Someone. The thought stopped Reed. Except for him, all Jack had was a sister living in Portland.

Think about yourself, Jack had said. Reed did. For a half second. Just long enough to conjure forth an image of his parents. His father was painted in military blue, his mother in splotches of gray that faded off into nothing.

That was it. Except for Jack, that was it.

MARA'S PHONE RANG. She stared, willing it to be silent. Willing her heart to steady. "He has your phone number," the police had told her. "He might try to get in touch with you."

The phone rang again.

"It's Reed, Reed Steward," the man on the other end said in response to her numbed and hesitant hello. "Do you have a few minutes?"

"A few," Mara told him and took a deep breath. She still felt unsure, unbalanced. And yet somehow Reed Steward's voice took her beyond those emotions. "Did you forget something?"

"I mentioned I wanted to discuss a matter with you."

"I remember." Holding the remote phone against her ear, Mara wandered into the living room with its closed drapes and sank into her newly recaned recliner. Yes. Although it was a useless gesture since the locks hadn't yet been replaced, her doors were locked. And as soon as she checked on Lobo and grabbed a change of clothes, she'd be leaving for Clint's apartment. If she hadn't been so focused on her meeting with the detective, she wouldn't have had to come back tonight at all. She wouldn't be talking to this man.

"I don't think I want to wait until tomorrow," Reed was saying. "This needs to be private. We aren't going to have much privacy during class."

"You'd like to discuss this now?"

"Not over the phone."

"Oh."

"I'd like to come back out to your place, if you don't mind, Mara."

Mara. He'd spoken her name, giving it a timbre she'd never heard before. "Where are you?"

"At my hotel. It'll take me about a half hour to get out there."

"Oh," she repeated. Did she want someone, this someone, in her house? Did she want to put off going to Clint's cluttered but safe place long enough to, maybe, understand more than she did about the impact Reed Steward had on her senses? Angry, Mara stopped the questions. She'd spent years watching her family's raw brand of courage, learning that she wasn't enough like them. But she could wait in her own home to discuss a simple business arrangement with someone, couldn't she? Lobo would be there; she'd let Reed know Clint was expecting her. "It'll make a long day for you."

"I'm used to long days. Unless you're busy. . ."

"I'm not, but . . . are you sure this is necessary?"

"I think it's the only way."

Mara hung up, knowing not nearly enough. Although they had discussed a quiet route Reed could take from the city, she still didn't understand why he was coming, why he wouldn't talk over the phone. She should have pressed him about that, demanded an explanation. But she was afraid of revealing how exposed and unsure she was feeling. She had to get on with the day-to-day business of life.

While she waited, Mara threw together a simple meal and ate in front of the TV. She'd planned her living room with subdued lighting because it usually relaxed her. Now she was sorry she didn't have a bright overhead light. There were too many shadows in the room. Too many shadows everywhere. Mara felt clammy and picked up the unread newspaper to fan herself. No. She couldn't do that, either. Her father and mother and brothers took cars around hairpin turns at over a hundred miles an hour and didn't have to cool bodies heated by fear. She was putting the last of her dishes in the dishwasher when she heard the Jag.

Lobo announced the car's arrival. Mara jumped at his growl, but with a picture of her family on the coffee table acting as her anchor, she got up and opened the door. She called Lobo to her and waited with her hand on the dog's head for Reed to get out of the car. For a moment he was shadow. Then her outside light claimed him and Mara saw a man capable of both taming and appreciating a bloodred car meant for speed.

"I was curious about security," Reed remarked and nodded at the doberman. The night wind swirled the words, tossing them in Mara's direction. He stood with his hands hanging relaxed and yet not relaxed by his sides. He'd left enough distance between them for safety, and he was smiling, just a little. "I take it that dog isn't waiting for me to scratch behind his ears."

"I wouldn't recommend it." In Reed's smile and the end to Lobo's growl, Mara found her answer. Yes. She would let him inside. She stepped aside, the gesture serving as her invitation. He smelled of soap. He'd come close enough for her to know that. His eyes had acknowledged her, but now he was looking at her living room and doors leading to other rooms. She wondered what her house told him about her.

"Lobo tolerates people when I tell him to," she explained, hoping he understood what she was leaving unsaid, wishing this quiet warning wasn't necessary. "But I'm the only one he shows affection for."

"At least he does that." Reed was struck by the contrast between the stark landscape around the mobile home and its interior. He didn't know anything about interior decorating but doubted the place had been designed by a professional. There was a sense of belonging here, of warm, restful colors. An almost three-dimensional painting of the ocean claimed one wall, a picture of a smiling family in racing coveralls commanded another. The stack of magazines on the glass-topped coffee table ranged from *Sports Illustrated* to *Sunset*. A wicker couch was piled with throw pillows in muted tones of blue.

He didn't have to be here. True, he'd made a promise to Jack, to his employers, to himself. But he could have waited until tomorrow. Either that or he could have made this pitch over the phone.

No he couldn't. If he was going to sleep tonight, he had to know Mara Curtis was all right. It was the least he, a concerned citizen working with the police, could do. He indicated the animal leaning against his mistress's legs. "If I made a sudden move, what would he do?"

Mara's eyes went to Reed's throat. "If I screamed, you wouldn't do it again."

"Oh." She wasn't pulling her punches. Her honesty both established the ground rules and relaxed Reed. He was glad she wasn't as vulnerable here as he'd thought. When Mara sat, Reed settled himself nearby on the pillowed couch. He couldn't remember ever sitting in something that comfortable. As he watched, she curled her feet up under her. She wrapped her long fingers around her linen-encased knees. The gesture was casual, habitual. But the way she followed his every move and the lines of wariness in her body indicated otherwise. She'd invited him here, but she didn't trust him. There was nothing he could do about that, not if he was going to get his job done. "You live alone?" he asked.

"Is that why you're here?" she asked, tight-lipped. "To check out my living arrangements?"

"No." Reed turned his attention from her hands to her face, and in the movement nearly lost his concentration. Mara Curtis reminded him of an antelope he'd spotted while driving through Montana last fall. The antelope had been shy. Curious. Cautious. And breathtakingly graceful. Mara exhibited the same grace, the same easy acceptance of her body. And, like the antelope, she didn't trust. Had she always been like that, or had Friday night changed her? If it had, he would give a great deal to wipe the slate clean for her. "I was simply making an observation. I find it hard to believe there are parts of San Diego still undeveloped."

"I'm outside the city limits. The water system hasn't been expanded out here to the point it can support development."

"If it was me, I wouldn't be in a hurry to see that happen. You'll be surrounded by people, and property values will go through the roof."

"Exactly."

She wasn't making things easy for him. He had to work to keep the conversation going. Reed asked how long she'd been in business, how long she'd lived out here. Her short replies told him that the driving school had been in operation for four years and that the double-wide mobile home had been in place a little over a year. She didn't say why she'd chosen her career, or decided to live here.

When she sat silent and waiting, Reed tried something else. He again brought up that he was aware of her father's racing career and then, although she still hadn't relaxed, he took the conversation in the hard but necessary direction. "You know a lot of people who have more than a passing interest in automobiles."

"It goes with the territory."

"And you might have certain inside information."

"What are you getting at, Mr. Steward?"

"Reed. What I'm getting at is rather complicated."

"I guessed that." Mara was smiling with her mouth. Despite the half gesture, her smile stripped his mind of the comparisons he'd made between her and a wild creature. He wasn't sure what had taken its place. "You don't belong here, you know," she said.

"I beg your pardon?"

"You're a competent driver. Not Indy material, but there's no need for you to be. Working on skids wasn't what you wanted to do. You had to force yourself."

"And you'd like to know what my motives are if I, as you say, know the fundamentals and would rather not push myself any more."

"Exactly. Why are you here, Mr.—Reed?"

"To get to know you."

Something hot flashed in Mara's eyes. "That's not what you said earlier. I think you'd better leave."

"Leave? I'm sorry. I didn't phrase that well, did I? This is not what you think. I'm here to explore the possibilities of a business arrangement quite different from what we have now." Reed hated what he was doing; he wanted Mara to trust him. But he would harden himself to her vulnerability and do this job. For Jack. "A few minutes ago I made mention of your contacts within the automotive world."

"Yes."

"If I were to present you with adequate compensation, would you be able to satisfy my whim?"

"Your whim?"

"I'd like to own the first Lamborghini to come off the assembly line."

She laughed, a soft and light note capable of making a man forget a great deal. "So would a lot of people. If you're thinking of a Lamborghini as an assembly-line vehicle—"

"Poor choice of words," Reed amended. He wanted to hear her laugh again. He wasn't sure he dared. "Mara, I have a certain amount of money at my disposal. Unfortunately it takes more than money to make me happy."

"At least you're honest enough to admit that."

"Honesty has nothing to do with it."

"Would you like to explain?" This time there was nothing light or open in her voice.

"What's to explain? I was hoping you might have certain inside information."

"What kind of information?"

"Top dollar isn't enough to get certain valuable automobiles. One has to have certain contacts."

Mara shook her head, a resigned gesture. "Why don't you just go out and steal that damn Lamborghini?"

"Because that's not the way I operate."

"That's your decision. Why are you coming to me?"

"Because you're an insider."

"Not that kind of insider, Mr. Steward." Mara stood. Her fingers had become fists, and although he tried to deny it, Reed felt the impact of her silent blow. He'd failed her; she'd wanted something positive from him and he'd failed her. Her toes curled into the carpet as if seeking something to grip. "I consider this conversation finished."

"You aren't interested in supplementing your income?"

Mara shook her head. "Make your pitch to someone else."

"You wouldn't be willing or able to give me a name?" he asked, damning himself for being vulnerable to her gestures, her voice.

"No. If there's any part of that word you don't understand . . ."

Reed was silent for the better part of a minute, watching her, weathering her anger. He now saw the strength that had allowed her to run from her attacker instead of being over-whelmed by fear. Someday he'd like to be able to tell her of his admiration. "Mara," he said softly. "Please sit down."

"I told you. This conversation is finished."

Reed knew he was staring, but dropping his eyes from the graceful, angry woman was impossible. He wanted to touch her; he knew he shouldn't. He wanted to ask her forgive-ness for what he'd put her through. But he was sure that wasn't wise. Most of all he wished he understood what he was feeling. "I shocked you," he went on. "This wasn't what you expected to hear."

"Mr. Steward, I take pride in my business. I've worked hard at getting it off the ground. It's just now operating in the black. If I didn't have scruples, I would have consid-ered this particular option long before this."

"*Option,*" Reed repeated. "Is that how you see it?" It was then that the phone rang, a blurred sound coming from another room. Mara whipped her head around. "Are you going to answer it?" Reed asked when it rang for the sec-ond time.

"My recorder can— No. It might be my family."

Reed watched, absorbing the meaning behind her slow steps as Mara left the room. The phone stopped ringing. He heard Mara's voice but couldn't make out anything she said. After a moment, he no longer tried. A person, a man, could lose himself in a room like this. He felt somehow nestled in and remembered coming home one night to find that a cat had found its way into his house and had buried itself in his unmade bed. The landlord claimed the cat the next day, but Reed hadn't forgotten that look of utter feline content-ment. Funny he should think about that now.

"Bad news?" Reed asked when at last Mara was back in the room. She'd closed the door behind her but was hang-ing on to the knob with whitened knuckles. Her pale flesh wiped away the memory of a purring cat. "Something about your family?"

"No. A wrong number. I wish..."

Was there something he should be saying? A certain combination of words that would release the strain from her body? Damn it, he didn't know. "You were expecting something?"

"No. Mr. Steward, I'm going to be leaving soon. I want..."

This wasn't about her needing to leave and wanting him out of the house so she could do that. It wasn't late for the phone to be ringing; maybe her tension was nothing more than reaction to what he'd been saying. And maybe, like other times in his life, Reed simply had no idea what was going on inside another human being.

He didn't want it to be like that. He wanted... he wanted to be the kind of man who remembered to bring flowers to a friend in the hospital.

"This won't take long," Reed said softly, for one of the few times in his life going with his gut instead of his head. "I'd like to explain."

"I'm not interested."

"I understand. But I want to tell you something," he said. Her eyes and the tension in her graceful body combined with her strong refusal of his offer to guide his words. She'd been through so much; he wasn't going to add to her worries. "And then you can decide whether I should leave."

"I'd say I've already made my decision."

"I wish you'd sit down."

"Why?"

What was the word? *Instinct.* It grew within him, becoming powerful. He could trust her. "Because I need your help."

"Your help? I thought I'd made it clear. I'm not interested."

"I heard you. Believe me, I got that particular message. Hopefully I'll be able to explain eventually why I've been saying the things I have, deliberately misleading you."

"You've been misleading me?"

Hating the confusion in her eyes and his inability to touch her and thus wipe away what he'd done to her, Reed could only keep trying to explain. "I happen to be in a business which brings me in contact with people who have ulterior motives. Part of my job consists of uncovering those motives and dealing with them. As a consequence of that business, a certain cynicism has rubbed off on me."

Mara shrugged. "It happens."

"Yes. It does." Reed smiled, working at the gesture. He waited until he sensed a slight relaxation of her tension. If nothing else, he'd gotten her to listen to him. "I think we all go through a certain number of steps along the way from innocence to adulthood. We get stung a few times, and we learn from those lessons. We're no longer naive."

"No. We aren't."

"It can't be helped. Besides, I don't think any adult really wants to remain naive." Reed expanded his smile. "Being conned isn't much fun."

"No. It isn't."

"Exactly. Mara, I don't want to alarm you. I'm saying this because I hope it'll help to explain certain things." He paused, wishing he knew if he was handling this right or if everything would blow up in his face. "This isn't the first time we've met."

Instantly Mara's fingers were at her throat. He'd ignored her wound earlier today because it had been essential for him to focus on other things. That was impossible now. "What are you saying?" she asked.

"I'm saying we were both at the Harbor Island Police Department Friday night." She didn't back away. Taking that as his cue, Reed went on. "Me, because I had business there. You, because you'd been abducted."

"Ab— You were there?"

"On business. Legitimate."

"You saw me."

"I saw a great deal, Mara. You were grateful to be alive."

Reed knew more than she wanted him to. Almost more than she'd admitted to herself. "Oh" was all she could say.

"I'm bringing that up because I hope you'll believe, despite what I just said, that what I'm doing has the approval of local law-enforcement agencies. As I said, I'm in a business that doesn't encourage trust. I had to be sure of certain things about you before I played my hand, before I gave you certain information. Mara, I'm here tonight because I need you to teach me a number of specific driving skills."

"Teach? This doesn't make sense."

"Hear me out. I think it will. Are you all right?"

"All right?"

"I know where you went after work today."

Mara stared without blinking. This man had her off balance. Again. She wished he wasn't here. She wished he'd never come. Most of all she wished she could think around him. "How did you—"

"I overheard your conversation with your secretary. And I saw the note about Detective Kline."

"You went looking," Mara challenged. "That was none of your business."

"If it isn't, I'll apologize. Mara, I could ask the detective what the meeting was about, but I'd rather have you trust me enough to tell me. They haven't caught him, have they?"

Reed's questions were coming too fast for Mara to be able to deal with them. The only thing she understood was that the police knew what Reed Steward was doing. That helped. "No. It was dark. I didn't see him." Why was she telling him this? "But I won't forget his voice."

"I wish you could."

He sounded as if he wanted things to be easier for her. Mara reacted to that simple and necessary fact. She tried to tell herself it was the only thing she was reacting to. "Why?"

"Because that animal put you through hell."

A few minutes ago Reed had struck at her and her family and everything she'd spent her life building and committing herself to. She'd come close to hating him for that. She blamed him for her wild, frightened reaction to nothing more sinister than finding no one on the phone a minute ago. And yet he cared; she knew he cared. Suddenly she was a breath away from crying. "*Hell,*" Mara whispered. "That's one way of putting it."

"I think it's the only way. You were ragged around the edges."

"Maybe. I'm pulling myself back together." *Was she? Would he sense that she wasn't sure of her answer?*

"I'm glad to hear that."

"It was a shock. I won't deny that. But—" She was babbling, telling him too much. "So. What happens now?"

"What do you mean?"

Mara pulled her strength around her. She'd be spending the night with Clint. Safe, strong Clint who knew what she needed better than she did and made no demands on her. And, as soon as she'd put her "adventure" into perspective, she'd tell her family about it. If she could contemplate that, certainly she could continue this conversation. She would reclaim her equilibrium where Reed Steward was concerned.

Finally she did as he suggested and sat down. This was her turf. She could dictate what was said. And she wouldn't try to look below Reed's surface story. "I don't understand. First you ask me to get involved in something illegal. Then, when I threaten to throw you out, you change your tactics. You're telling me you had legitimate business with the police."

"Yes."

"*Yes* isn't enough."

"No. I don't imagine it is." When Reed leaned forward, Mara held her ground and stilled the impulse to touch Lobo. It wasn't that she feared Reed. But he was too masculine, too rough for the gentle surroundings she'd created. Everything he said, every gesture, left her feeling like a twig caught in an advancing tide. But certainly she could handle a simple conversation. "I'm in a sensitive position, Mara," he went on. "What I said about connections you might have—I had to feel you out."

"Why?"

"Because that's the nature of the investigation I'm involved in."

"Investigation?" A few nights ago she'd walked out of a grocery store and into a nightmare, and now a man had shown up asking bizarre questions and talking about investigations. If it weren't all so deadly serious, she would have laughed.

"If you want, I'll give you the name of a police captain. He'll vouch for me."

"Oh."

"Do you want his name?"

"I think you know the answer to that," Mara said. Her declaration was more to keep distance between them than to answer his question. "Are you going to continue taking my course?"

"Yes."

"Why?"

"Because I need your expertise."

"Even if you don't like skids?"

"It showed, did it? Mara, I'm hoping there are things you can teach me about evasive action. Survival tactics."

Mara hadn't been able to push her thoughts fast enough to anticipate anything, and yet now that Reed had said the words, they made sense. His cool, almost detached gaze took in a great deal more than it revealed. What little he did expose was calculated. He was telling her nearly nothing, only that to stay alive he needed certain cards stacked in his favor.

He'd told her only that there was a policeman who would vouch for him, and now he was asking her to assist him.

"I have to have more than that," she told him.

"I understand how you feel."

"I don't think you do, Reed. I run a legitimate business. If you won't tell me what this is about, then I don't want to work with you."

"You aren't making this easy for me."

Mara shrugged. It wasn't her job to drag more out of him or to make things easy for him. Her job, if it could be called that, was to try to absorb everything the man was throwing at her. Maybe she should thank him. If nothing else he was giving her more to think about than changing her locks, replacing her credit cards, getting a new driver's license, wondering when she'd live again in her own home.

"Mara. I'm not a policeman. I don't work for the FBI. Nothing that exciting. But—"

The mobile home creaked. Mara was used to the sound, but for a moment Reed paused. "I'm an investigator," he said. "I work with auto insurance companies. Something happened... A friend, a very good friend, was hurt. It was a pretty powerful message. It's possible that my staying alive will depend on my ability to get out of a tight situation. If I'm behind the wheel of a car and someone is after me, it's vital that I know what I'm doing."

Mara shivered. Five years ago she'd seen her father's car become crumpled tinfoil. Friday night she'd felt cold steel at her throat and thought nothing else could touch her in that way, and still she shivered. "You aren't joking, are you?"

"Did you think I was?"

"No."

"Have you changed your mind?"

She had. Professionally Mara felt challenged by what he was asking of her. And on a personal level... No. There was no personal level. She couldn't allow there to be. For reasons she now understood, he'd had to test her. It was essential that he know where she stood, whether she could be trusted. Now he wanted to employ her to provide him with certain skills. Those were the reasons the two of them were talking tonight. The only reasons.

For the next ten minutes they discussed specifics. What, Reed wanted to know, would Mara suggest if he was being forced off the road. Reed's eyes answered the question she couldn't bring herself to ask. He wasn't talking about remote possibilities. When she was done explaining that a combination of a firm grip on the steering wheel, pumping the brakes, and finally a quick steer back onto the road was his best and probably only recourse, Reed turned to questions about the various evasive actions he could take to avoid a collision.

"I'd use controlled braking, if I had no other choice." Mara's voice was flat. Businesslike. That wasn't what she was feeling. If she closed her eyes, her mind would settle on an image of Reed trapped behind the wheel of a wrecked car. She kept her eyes open and her mind, she hoped, on nothing. "But if you don't want to stop—if that constitutes another danger, you'll want to try a lateral evasive action. It all boils down to one thing. Control of your vehicle. You never want to lose control."

"I understand."

Mara took a deep breath. "Why are you doing this? You said you aren't a policeman. Why—"

"He's my friend. I owe him more than I can ever repay. He doesn't see it as a debt, but I do. Maybe this is my way of saying thank you."

She shook her head, not understanding, wishing she did. "What you owe him—that extends to risking your own life?"

"Maybe it does." Reed said the last so softly that Mara felt more than heard the words.

"Then I think I envy you. That kind of relationship is rare. Something to be savored."

"Yes. It is rare," Reed said softly. "He cared. That's what it all boils down to. He cared about me when I needed that."

Without asking if he wanted anything, Mara got up and went into the kitchen. She debated between iced tea and wine and settled on tea because they didn't know each other well enough to be sharing anything else. Still, she was glad they'd come far enough for this.

When she came back, Reed was looking out at the night. For a moment she simply looked at him, convincing herself that he was real. Then, wanting to be part of his reality, she stepped forward and handed him his glass. He turned and smiled a slow, almost shy smile. "Thank you," he said. "You didn't have to do that."

"I know."

"But you did it." His smile ebbed but didn't die. "I've been listening to the night. Silence," he said softly, indicating their surroundings. "Silence has a sound of its own."

His philosophical mood knocked Mara off balance. He was right, so right it was almost painful. She wanted to tell him she understood what he was saying, that she too had heard the silence, but if she did, she might reveal too much of herself. And until she understood who she'd become since Friday night, Mara would keep distance between herself and others. It might be hard, but it was better that way.

"Not having neighbors, that doesn't bother you?"

Mara worked on her smile. "It depends on what you mean by neighbors. There are more rabbits than I can count. So cute and curious. So destructive. They're always after my flowers."

"You dog doesn't chase them off?"

"He's about given up. Besides, I don't encourage that kind of behavior."

"Because he has a more important job. I noticed the picture of your family. Do they live nearby?"

Without, she hoped, making an issue of it, Mara took a backward step. She was no longer able to see out the window, but it didn't matter. She knew what black looked and felt like. "They don't really live anywhere," she told him. "Mom and Dad have an apartment in San Diego. My brothers have their own places. They share their apartments with a variety of roommates. But those are just places to store their belongings.''

"Then you're the one holding down the family fort."

"I guess." Was this what they should be talking about? And if it was, should she do more than give him this unfinished response? Mara found the answer in what little Reed revealed about himself. They had a business relationship, a short, focused business relationship. "They spend most of their time on the racing circuit. Competing the way they do is demanding. It doesn't make much sense to put a lot of money into a place they're seldom in."

"You don't race?"

"No." Mara wondered if he was going to ask her why. Instead he asked a few questions about the evolution of the school. She kept her answers brief, and he soon stopped.

"What happens now?" he asked.

"I don't understand." Reed was no longer looking out the window. He'd walked over to her seascape and spent several minutes studying it. Now he turned toward her.

"Are you going to spend the night here? I talked to the police about what happened. I'm sure you're aware they don't have the manpower necessary to turn this into a fortress."

Mara swallowed. "I know."

"Have you considered moving?"

"Moving? I'm not rich, Reed. I can't afford that. I'm having my locks changed tomorrow. I wanted to do it earlier, but I couldn't get anyone to come all the way out here over the weekend. There's my dog."

"That isn't enough."

"What else would you suggest?"

"A gun."

A gun. Guns were for killing. "I haven't thought—"

"Think about it. If you don't know how to use one, I'll show you."

This was insane. She didn't know who this man was, not really. Yet he was standing here telling her he'd teach her how to fire a weapon. She should tell him she wasn't interested. But a gun. Maybe, if she had one, she could sit in her house and not listen for the sound of glass breaking and the sight of a man climbing through a broken window. And maybe the act of reversing the pupil-teacher role would teach her something more about Reed Steward. "I don't know."

"Hopefully you'll never need it. Chances are you won't. But . . ."

You're scaring me. "I won't be staying here tonight," she told him. "Clint wants me—"

"Clint? Good. You should get there as soon as possible. We'll leave together."

"No. I'm— I have a few things I still need to do here."

"I'll wait."

"No," Mara repeated firmly. "I don't need a bodyguard. If I did, I would have asked a friend."

He wants to know something more, Mara thought. Whether it was about her relationship with Clint or if she'd come to a decision about a gun, she didn't know. But Reed didn't ask, and she didn't offer. When he got up and headed for the door, Mara followed. With Reed here, strangely, the night didn't touch her. For a moment that went on longer than it needed to, Reed stood with his hand on the car door and his back not quite to her. Then he slid into the Jag and brought it to life. "You won't be alone long?"

"Just a few minutes."

"Good. I'll see you tomorrow, then," he told her softly, simply.

"Yes. Tomorrow."

He was gone.

The effects of Reed's presence lasted while Mara grabbed clothes from her closet. She wished she could remember when she'd stopped wanting to throw him out and started believing he cared about her. The moment had been pivotal, essential. She was thankful he'd suggested she talk to a Captain Bistron. She still wanted to know more about

Reed, about the man he'd mentioned, named Jack Weston, and the bond between the two of them.

Then, without warning, Mara's thoughts turned to another recent conversation.

"He knows where you live," Detective Kline had said earlier, needlessly repeating what she already knew. "And he has your keys, which could give him a feeling of power. From what the other victims have told us, he fits the rapist profile. The man needs to be in control."

Mara wanted to crawl into bed and curl into a tight ball so she didn't have to step outside. She wanted to be a child again. If only she could call her family, run to them for safety. But those things were impossible. Instead she gathered what she'd come for and opened the front door, listening to the night. Trying to remember what Reed had said about silence having a sound of its own.

Then, with a scream trapped in her throat, Mara ran to the loaner car she'd left out front, with its stiff steering and the seat that didn't quite mold itself to her body.

REED REMAINED on the side of the county road until he saw Mara's headlights. He eased his car back onto the pavement ahead of her before she came close enough to be able to recognize him or his car. She hadn't wanted a bodyguard; she'd made it clear that she didn't need one. Fine. He would respect her wishes and admire her courage. Still, he felt better knowing she was no longer alone in her lonely place.

Chapter Five

A half hour after dawn, Clint and Mara returned to her place. Mara was relieved to see Lobo unruffled. If anyone had come onto her property last night, he would be agitated. Surely her attacker had better things to do than wait for a glimpse of a woman with a trained watchdog at her heels.

As he'd done before, Clint stepped inside the house first. Mara followed, walking over to the stereo system and turning it to an easy-listening radio station while Clint headed for the refrigerator. "You need to go to the grocery store if you're going to go on feeding me," he announced. "I wanted to tell you, I thought you handled yourself pretty well with that detective. He sure is a by-the-books cop. You haven't thought of anything else you should have told him, have you?"

Mara shook her head. "You heard him say he's told the police to step up their patrols out this way."

"What did you want him to say? That they weren't doing anything? I don't know. I guess I want them to pull out all the stops and get this joker."

"I haven't given them much to go on."

"You did the best you could. It's out of your hands now. Whew. It's starting to smell stuffy in here."

Mara had already noticed that. She went about opening a few windows, reminding herself to close them again before— No. She wasn't going to spend tonight with Clint. His parents would be in town this afternoon, and because the three of them needed to talk about Clint's father's heart problems, she'd told Clint she would be going to a motel.

A motel because, even with new locks, she wasn't yet ready to stay in her own home alone.

Clint went on talking about the meeting with the detective. "When I was a kid I thought maybe I wanted to be a cop. You know, the kind who solves crimes, not directs traffic. The reality's a little different, isn't it?"

"I guess. I was thinking, if they don't need me to help put that man behind bars, if I can't give them a description, I might know only what I read in the paper."

"If there's anything to read. That's what gets to me. Sorry, boss. Neither of us wants to hear that, do we? When are you going to start working with Mr. Steward?"

"Tonight," Mara told him and reached for the container of orange juice.

"I still wouldn't trust him any farther than you can throw him."

"Why not?"

"Because maybe he was giving you a line of you-know-what last night."

Mara remembered a man looking out at the night and talking about the sounds of silence. "I'm going to verify what he told me. There's a Captain Bistron..."

"Good. Call him, today. I was just thinking, if he's really doing undercover work, he's going to drop out of sight one of these days, isn't he?"

That shouldn't bother her. Certainly it didn't. After all, Mara had more than enough to deal with. Like whether she was going to buy a gun and let Reed Steward show her how to use it. "I imagine he is," she said and joined Clint in front of the refrigerator. Clint was right. There was nothing to eat.

REED SPENT the lunch hour talking to the young man with dreams of racing for a living. Mara hadn't expected the two of them to have anything in common. Their shared laughter held her attention. Reed could laugh. She was glad there was that side to him. After a few minutes spent listening to Reed tell the novice racer that his one and only attempt at drag racing had resulted in needing a wrecker to get his car out of a muddy field, Mara walked into her office and dialed Captain Bistron's number. Yes, the captain told her, he had been informed that she might be calling. He'd leave it up to Reed to explain the particulars, but the man did have police clearance. He could be trusted.

Trusted. The simple word framed Mara's afternoon.

When class ended, Reed hung around. Clint, despite needing to go to the airport to pick up his parents, stalled. He wanted to be sure Mara had her evening plans firmed. She should have already reserved a motel room. She shouldn't leave things until the last minute. Finally Mara pushed Clint toward his car. "I can manage renting my own room," she told her employee and friend.

Mara shook her head in exasperation and then softened. "Say hi to your folks for me. Tell them Iowa gets too cold, and that warm winters are what the doctor ordered."

"I'll try." Clint reached out and patted Mara on top of her head. "Take care of yourself, boss."

Mara was still standing where he'd left her when Clint's car started kicking up dust. Clint would wring her neck if she so much as hinted that a big, handsome, crazy, independent man like him missed his parents, but she understood that he did. It wasn't easy for either of them not to have their families around.

"He's quite a kid."

Mara turned. Reed wore a cotton shirt with no T-shirt under it and faded jeans. The shirt, she suspected, had been chosen because comfort was important when a man spent a day folded into a sports car. The jeans were loose enough for comfort too, but close enough to define a man's legs, a man's body. You can trust him, the police captain had told her. She wasn't sure but her questions had nothing to do with simple physical safety. "He is," she responded softly to Reed. "It's like having one of my brothers around. Are you ready to go to work?"

"If you are."

"I am," Reed said. He'd come here to learn a skill, he reminded himself. He was determined to make the most of the trust and money his employers invested in him. Beyond that, he'd committed himself to vindicating Jack. That, he repeated, was all he had the time and energy for.

Unfortunately his teacher was a beautiful young woman, and he was having a devil of a time shaking himself free from that fact. He'd watched her closely today, just as he had last night when he was trying to talk her into buying a gun. Every step she took as she moved about her professional world spoke of a woman who belonged here. When she told him she had no intention of moving because she couldn't afford to and was getting her locks changed, when she said she didn't need more than that dog of hers, he'd found himself without enough arguments to try to change her mind. It *was* her life. He had no right intruding on it. He could just worry and care. It was a delicate balance.

"I've been thinking about your needs," Mara said. "The kinds of situations you might come up against. Speed is going to be a major issue, isn't it?"

"It could be." Reed led the way to the Jag. Mara's weight barely registered on the asphalt, and yet he sensed her every step. Despite himself, he couldn't shake the image of her beauty and grace being slashed away by some animal who lived in alleys. An emotion which mirrored what he'd felt when he heard about Jack's accident rocked through him.

"THERE ARE LIMITATIONS here," Mara told her student an hour later as they quenched their thirst in her kitchen. He'd done well. He'd been able to handle every situation she'd presented him with. She'd sensed his tension, but he'd dealt with it and concentrated on what had to be done. She admired him for that. "If we could get out on a freeway, go through some city streets . . ."

"Maybe tomorrow."

Mara nodded as if that piece of information was the most important thing she'd heard today. She'd been unbelievably aware of his presence, his whatever-it-was he possessed, while they were in the same confined space. But, she told herself, she couldn't possibly be as aware of him now as she'd been when they were deep in concentration.

She was wrong. Reed was asking her something. He was lifting his damp shirt from his chest to fan himself and expecting an answer. If she touched him, she would feel the heat of summer, and life. "I'm sorry," she stammered, fighting the thought. "What did you say?"

"That I'd like to take you somewhere for dinner. A thank you for the overtime."

Lobo needed to be fed and his water changed. Mara felt clammy and needed almost desperately to get out of her hot jeans. And she still had to find a place to spend the night. Most of all she needed distance from the impact Reed had on her. She struggled with her feelings. "You don't have to do that."

"*Have to* wasn't part of the question. Unless you don't feel comfortable."

Could he read her mind? "That isn't it."

"Isn't it?"

"No. Reed, I called that captain today."

He nodded. "I wondered if you would."

"I understand more now."

"Do you?" Reed asked. "Bistron knows what I'm doing. But the *why*— Look, why don't I tend to your dog while you finish up. Anyplace you pick is fine, as long as it's airconditioned."

Mara had no idea which restaurant she would suggest. That didn't matter. What did matter was accepting that Reed wasn't rushing to end their time together, and she was following his lead. "You'd better let me take care of Lobo," was all she said.

When they got into the Jag, Reed hit the Seek button on the stereo and wrapped his fingers over the floor shift. Mara looked behind her, watching her mobile home shrinking, drawing away. She'd debated insisting that they take her car but she'd found sitting in his car was something she needed to do if she was going to stop feeling so trapped and helpless. The Jag hummed, a quiet backdrop for the music surrounding them. After a minute Mara leaned back and let go of other emotions, feeling somehow younger and more free at the same time.

Over the past few days she'd forgotten what freedom felt like. With a powerful engine under her and this uneasy, challenging presence beside her, Mara didn't have to think about fear or the end of the week when she wouldn't see Reed again. There was only movement.

And Reed Steward.

Still, she wasn't entirely comfortable sitting next to him. She was too aware of him for that. And although there was no making sense of the emotion, Mara needed the awareness.

"Does it feel good to have the day behind you?"

Mara concentrated on the question, or rather on the voice asking the question. "Does it show?"

"Yes. Are you relaxing?"

Relaxation was not what she was experiencing. "Sometimes life has a way of piling up," she offered.

"Yeah. It does."

"But music..." Mara closed her eyes. "Music and motion. When I'm in a car, I feel cut off from everything else. As if I'm somehow getting back to basics."

"Basics?"

"Myself," Mara tried. "Maybe I'm getting back to myself. I love to drive. That's what I was doing that night. Convincing myself I needed to go to the store. There was this energy in me, and I thought going for a drive might be a way of dealing with it."

"It's good you're able to talk about that. Maybe it will help make things easier for you."

"Maybe," Mara whispered, glad he wanted that for her. "I hope so. I want back my routine. Boring, comfortable routine."

"I hardly see your life as boring. Anyone with that kind of energy in her..."

Mara glanced over, acknowledged his easy smile and gave him one in return. "You haven't seen energy until you've watched my father and brothers drive."

For a moment Reed was quiet. Then he said, "What is it they say about certain cars? That they're an extension of a man's masculinity."

"Is that what this car is? An extension of your masculinity?"

"It isn't mine. The bureau leased it. Still, when I'm in it, I sense power. It's as if no one can touch me as long as I'm here."

Mara was unnerved to hear Reed speak openly about something that dovetailed so well with her own feelings, yet there was something about where they were and what they were doing that made the words right. They had the windows down. Air that smelled of everything and nothing whipped around her. "I wonder why we think of cars in masculine terms? The power I suppose. But speed touches certain nerves in me, too. I think women need that as much as men do."

"I hadn't thought about that."

"You haven't? Your mother never—"

"My mother isn't one for sharing her thoughts, Mara. I'm not sure she has much understanding of them, herself."

Mara's heart contracted in concern. He sounded hurt and confused. It was only by running her fingers along the Jag's leather upholstery that she was able to keep her hands off Reed. He wasn't a child; she couldn't pat him on the shoulder and undo the past. "You really believe that?"

"I do."

"I'm sorry."

"Don't be," Reed said with his eyes on the road and his mind now on nothing except her presence next to him. He regretted that their commitments would interfere with getting to know each other. If he were completely free to do such things, he'd find a deserted freeway, punch down on the gas, turn up the sound on the stereo and let the Jag absorb them both.

Maybe sound and speed would wash away the world.

He wanted to touch her. To learn what she felt like in his arms, to risk letting her reach more of him than she already had. He wanted to taste her and somehow reach inside her, until there was nothing she kept from him. They were already reaching out; he could feel it happening.

But he didn't know enough about how that was done. And for what purpose? He'd already committed himself to accomplishing something that would take all his time, all his energy. Something only he could and should be doing. So he would buy Mara Curtis dinner, then he'd go back to the hotel he needed to be seen in.

He wouldn't do anything crazy like tell her why he didn't want to talk about his mother, or risk letting her get close enough to ask.

MARA SUGGESTED a family-owned restaurant known for its salads. She'd only been there once, she told Reed, but Clint was more than a little interested in one of the waitresses there and praised it highly. The cool, clean restaurant was busy, but the tables were set far apart. Reed felt removed from everyone except Mara. They ordered, and then Mara leaned back, the gesture incredibly graceful. She looked somehow both wary and peaceful. Reed didn't know what to do with her silence. For too long he didn't know how to end it. Finally he said, "You haven't heard from the police today? There's nothing new?"

"Not that I know of." Mara sipped on her water. She touched her tongue to her top lip, trapping a bead of moisture. The gesture slammed into Reed.

"Good." No. That wasn't enough. Reed wanted Mara to have a lifetime filled with such simple pleasures as cool water flavored by a slice of lemon. He couldn't promise her that. No one could. But there was something he could give her. "I mentioned a gun."

"I know." Mara blinked. Her mouth parted. Reed gripped his glass to keep his fingers off those soft lips.

"For protection," Reed went on. "I came to you because increasing my driving skills is my insurance policy. I think you need the same kind of thing."

"Maybe I do."

"Mara." Reed leaned forward and lowered his voice. "I'm suggesting you buy one and get a permit. There are a couple of handguns I can recommend you look at. Then we can work on making you feel comfortable with it."

"Yes." She didn't look at him. "Yes."

What was she trying to say? The possibilities scared him. "Has he tried to get in touch with you?"

Mara blinked. She leaned forward, then back again, becoming somehow smaller and more fragile. "Do you think I'd be this calm if he had?" Even her question sounded fragile. "Detective Kline said it's rare for someone like that to come after one of their victims. There's always—how did he put it—new challenges out there."

"Kline's telling you to forget it happened?"

"No." She drew out the word. "Of course not. But I will not put my life on hold, waiting for something that isn't going to happen. That's not my way."

"Maybe." Her fingers were in constant motion, testing the tablecloth, tracing the edge of the table. He wanted to still the movement, wanted to close his own fingers over hers. "I'm glad you're staying with Clint."

Mara stared at him, unblinking. "I won't be anymore."

"Why not?"

Reed thought he detected a slight stiffening to her body, a certain vulnerability in her eyes, but when she spoke there was no hint of that emotion. "Clint has his own life to live," she told him. "I can't go on imposing."

"What are you going to do?"

Mara fell silent as the waitress brought walnut-topped Waldorf salads. She speared an apple slice and stared at it. "I'll be staying at a motel. But not for long. Just—"

"Have you talked to your family about this?"

"That's a little hard to do, isn't it? They're out of the country. Reed, my family's crazy. But no matter what else they are, they aren't cowards. They expect the same strength from me.... I expect it of myself." She sighed and reached for the salt shaker, fingering it. "Now that my locks have been changed— I'll be getting my car back soon. Maybe they found fingerprints. Maybe they'll be able to pick him up."

"If his prints are on record."

After a moment Mara nodded. "If his prints are on record."

Reed concentrated on eating, not tasting, just eating. He was relieved when Mara followed suit. She had erected a barricade between them. Its strength mocked him, forcing him to face his ineptness. He recognized the emotional distance between them; he just had no idea how to deal with it. When her silence became more than he could handle, Reed floundered around, finally finding a way to make her speak. Where was her family these days? he asked. What kind of cars were they racing now? How had Mark Curtis become a professional driver?

Mara spoke of a man in love with speed, a woman who shared that love and two sons who'd been born with that same passion flowing through them. "My brothers have some not-too-flattering things to say about why I'm not following in their footsteps. I tell them I'm the one who's using her brains. Starting a business wasn't easy, but I love what I'm doing."

"You're fortunate," Reed said. He didn't care what she was saying, just that emotion and life were back in her voice. "Not everyone gets to do something they enjoy."

"Do you? Do you like what you're doing?"

"It's what I do best."

"And that's why you're doing this—because you're good at it?"

Mara was right. It wasn't enough of an explanation. "I'm talking about commitment. Maybe that's what it all boils down to."

"You protect the interest of insurance companies because it's something you believe needs doing?"

"Not the companies, Mara. I'm talking about people with problems they can't handle on their own."

"And, no matter what the risk, you're going to stick with it. Why?"

Why? It was an incredibly hard question, but Reed needed to try to answer. "My father was career military," he started. "I didn't understand what he did, only that a lot of it was classified. His job was and still is his life. I think I have some of that in me."

"His job is his life?"

"Maybe that's an unfortunate choice of words."

"And maybe it's being honest."

"Yeah," Reed whispered. "Maybe it is." He focused on Mara's hands, now engaged in erasing moisture from the outside of her water glass. How could he be anything but honest around a woman with hands like that? "His choice of careers was hard on my mother."

"In what way?"

Another hard question, one he wouldn't be backed into. "A lot of reasons. The moving around."

"She had you."

"Did she?" Reed asked. This wasn't what he wanted to talk about. If he was going to change the subject, he would have to stop meeting Mara's eyes, stop thinking about her hands. But not yet. "My mother has emotional problems." Reed put down his fork and then picked it up again. "I'm sure the psychiatrists she's seen have done some good, but—"

"I'm sorry." Mara's voice was a soft promise of gentle understanding. "It must have been hard on you."

"It was what I knew."

Mara pushed away her bowl, then went back to holding on to her glass. She blinked; still, Reed saw the moisture in her eyes. "We can't choose our circumstances when we're children, can we?" she said. "It's only when we grow up that we take charge of our lives. Or at least try to. Do you have any brothers or sisters?"

"No. I was an only child."

"Maybe it was better that way."

"Maybe."

Did he have any idea how much of himself he was giving away? Mara wondered. An only child raised by a father who wasn't there for his wife or son, and a mother so locked up in herself that there wasn't enough of her to give to her child. Mara wanted to gift Reed with something he'd never had. To be the one to fill the holes in his life. "I was thinking," she said around her need. "So much of what we are is conditioned by our upbringing."

"You probably wouldn't have your business if it wasn't for what you learned from your parents."

He was right, but that wasn't what she wanted this conversation to be about. "Have you talked to your parents? Let them know how you feel? I don't know. Maybe family counseling . . ."

"It's a little late for that, Mara."

This was a man she'd once thought she never wanted to see again? "Maybe," she said softly. "But if there's unfinished business..."

"There isn't. What is, is. What are you doing here? In San Diego, I mean."

He was trying to change the subject. She let him. She explained that she'd chosen the city as the site for her business because she liked the climate, and her name had opened doors with the highway patrol, one of her most reliable clients. "The life-style agrees with me," she finished. "What do you think of Southern California?"

Reed hadn't been around long enough to have formed much of an opinion, but he had sensed a laid-back quality, a more relaxed air than he'd seen in most of the cities his work had taken him to. "I have a place in Sacramento," he told her. "The summers are awfully hot. People there take themselves so seriously. Maybe that's because it's the state capital."

"Why do you live there, then?"

"It seemed as good a place as any."

That was no reason for putting down roots to Mara's way of thinking. Or maybe the truth was, Reed, an army brat, still didn't have any roots. Didn't he want more of a sense of belonging?

"I've thought about moving," he was saying. "Only, I'm so seldom in one spot that it doesn't seem to matter enough to move."

"It was like that for us while I was growing up," Mara told him with her eyes on his strong hands, and her thoughts going no further than his words. She spoke without holding back. "Living out of suitcases. Half the time unable to remember which state, what country we were in. At least we had each other."

"And that made it right."

He touched her. Brushed his large, competent fingers over her knuckles. Mara didn't remember him reaching for her; she didn't remember being given time to prepare for the contact. Men and women touched. It was a natural evolution in relationships, nothing to instill fear in anyone.

But Mara couldn't stop the sudden stiffening of her body, the quick pulling free. She hated it; she just had no control over the instinct.

"I'm sorry. I shouldn't have—"

"No," Mara muttered. If only she could go back a few seconds, experience that reaching out over again, prepare for it. "It isn't anything you did. It's just…" It was too late. What she'd done was done. "I'll get over this. I just need a little more time."

"Is that all it'll take? Mara, I don't like the idea of you staying alone out there."

"You'd like it better if I turned tail and ran?"

"That's not it. There must be someone you can stay with. If Clint can't—"

"Don't," Mara warned. Reed's hands rested on the table a safe distance away. She didn't want them there. She wanted to feel his strength, his warmth. She needed to care and be cared for…just a little. But a little might become too much. "I'm the only one who can make these decisions."

"You're going along with what I said about a gun."

"That's different. Look, Reed, I appreciate your concern," Mara said, because what she wanted was too new, too potentially dangerous, to admit. "I mean, if this had happened to someone else, I'd probably be putting in my own two-cents' worth. But I didn't ask for advice. I don't want it."

"Want and need aren't always the same thing, Mara."

"What do you mean by that?"

"Maybe nothing. Are you done?"

Reed was right. They'd finished their meals, and since obviously neither of them was going to concede anything there was no longer any reason to continue the conversation. Still Mara wished he would say something, anything, as long as he didn't bring up the way she'd withdrawn from him. The only thing she came up with was an inane comment about the meal. She'd have to tell Clint she approved of his recommendation.

"The girl Clint likes, she wasn't there tonight, was she?" Reed asked as he was backing out of the parking lot.

"No. Why?"

"I'd like to have seen her. Maybe I'll get a chance to."

Mara shook her head. "I don't think so."

"Why not?"

Be honest, a small voice encouraged. "You'll only be around a few more days. You'll be off doing whatever needs doing."

Reed took his eyes off the road and stared at her. "I don't have a choice, Mara."

He didn't want what they had to be over any more than she did. Mara couldn't say how she felt about that. A little scared. Unnerved. Somehow more alive. "What do you mean, no choice?"

"The most important man in my life is involved. I made him a promise."

"And solving this case, that's what the promise is about?"

"It's a total commitment." Reed turned down the volume on the stereo. "That's the problem."

"Problem?"

Once again Reed looked at her. When he spoke, his tone skated under and around the sounds of a softly played guitar. "I need to know how this comes out for you."

Was the air-conditioning working? Surely the sudden heat she felt came from too-warm air. "Maybe it'll be in the paper."

"That's not the version I'm interested in, Mara. I need to know if you're safe."

Safe. He wanted that for her. "What happens if I want to know the same about you?"

"What?"

"Don't you understand?" Mara challenged. "You hired me, you've told me something about what you're going to be doing. I've never encountered anything like this before. It's...fascinating." How had the conversation taken this turn? She was trying to wedge herself into Reed Steward's life when it was none of her business. If he wanted to be kept apprised of the crime she was part of, she wouldn't stop him. But beyond that... All he'd done was touch her. Nothing else. Simply a touch, which she'd brought to an immediate end. "Reed. What you're doing is more than fascinating. The danger—it's natural that I'd be interested. Worried. Didn't that occur to you?"

"No," he told her. "It didn't. Not until now." As he thought about it, he realized that the idea was surprisingly comforting.

MARA HAD A MOTEL in mind, a new one a little over twenty minutes from her place. Despite her objections, after they'd gone back out to pick up her loaner car, Reed followed her into town. He waited while she paid for the room, and then walked with her to the second-story room. He stepped inside, looked into the bathroom and closet, checked the lock. "You'll be all right," he told her.

"I know I will," Mara said. She dropped her purse onto the floor. "Thank you, again, for dinner. And for the conversation."

Reed nodded. They were standing far enough apart that she didn't have to concern herself with whether he might touch her. He told her to get a good night's sleep and that he'd see her in the morning. Then he walked to the door and closed it behind him, and she was left with a restless and hungry wanting.

What that hunger was for, she wouldn't say.

After a moment, Mara turned the lock. Her hand lingered on the knob, absorbing the bit of warmth Reed had left there. Then she flipped on the TV, but paid no attention to what was on. Maybe she'd run downstairs for a copy of the evening paper. Maybe she'd wash her hair and climb into bed and pore through the real estate section, daydreaming about having enough money for a multiwindowed home overlooking the ocean. Maybe she'd tune in the small radio next to the bed and let music consume her. She remembered the station she and Reed had listened to.

The room smelled new. Lightly patterned, inexpensive drapes covered the window overlooking the parking lot. The peach bedspread picked up the colors in the still-life painting bolted to the wall.

Mara had been in a thousand rooms like this one. Only, this time her family wasn't here to share it with her.

She'd left behind what she'd slowly, lovingly turned into a home and was spending a night in an overpriced motel room complete with next-to-useless bars of soap because someone, maybe, knew where she lived and had a set of keys that no longer worked. She'd left Lobo out there, alone.

Reed Steward was facing the possibility that his commitment to a man might put his own life in jeopardy.

She was standing in a motel room she could scarcely afford because... Why?

Mara knew the answer to that. She'd been taken out of her world, and the backlash from that experience was still still controlling her.

What was wrong about one night at a motel? Clint and Reed both approved of what she was doing. Neither had made fun of her or asked when she was going to face her demon.

But being incapable of facing demons was why she had her own business instead of racing with the rest of the family.

She hadn't been proud of herself when she'd made her decision then. She felt the same way tonight, stuck in a room that reminded her of nights without end when there'd been no home base. When security had come from parents and brothers.

These days security was her home, her business, proof that she had made it on her own.

On her own. Not hiding out in a motel room.

AN HOUR LATER Mara sat inside her mobile home. She'd managed to convince the motel manager not to charge her for spending five minutes in his establishment. She hadn't questioned her need to park as close as possible to her front door and to have Lobo standing beside her, before she pulled out her new house keys. She'd fumbled with the stiff, new lock and weathered a moment of panic when confronted by the darkened rooms. But the switches and lamps all worked and now Lobo was locked in the house with her.

She wasn't sure she'd tell anyone what she'd done. Maybe not. After all, she didn't owe anyone an explanation, and she didn't want to have to answer their questions.

Especially not questions from Reed Steward.

Chapter Six

"There's no one else here," Reed said.

There was no denying Reed's logic. Mara had just gotten word that she could pick up her car but, because Clint and her secretary had both left with the students this afternoon, unless she took Reed up on his offer, she'd have to either pay an outrageous cab bill or ask a friend to take time out of his or her evening to drive her into town. "I just don't feel right about dragging you into my problems."

"There's no dragging involved. I offered. End of argument."

Reed, dressed in jeans and a cotton shirt that stretched over his shoulders, was sitting across from her in the living room, watching. His silent appraisal made Mara aware of her every move as she strapped on a pair of sandals. She should be so weary, after the wakeful hours spent listening to the sounds of her house, that she should be numb. But she wasn't. Or if she had been, awareness of Reed Steward had taken her beyond that.

Reed waited until she had both shoes on before he stood. Then he held out his hand to help her to her feet, a question in the way his gaze locked on hers. After a second, she placed her hand in his.

Touching him felt right. Right and at the same time wrong. "You're a stubborn man," she told him. There were callouses on his palm. His roughness surprised her. A man who made his living with his intellect shouldn't be so—so what? Physical?

"So I've been told." He squeezed her hand, then drew it close to his side until her knuckles slid over warm denim. She started, not as she had last night, but in reaction to the sudden electricity. Still, Mara didn't draw away.

"Why?" she managed.

"Why am I stubborn? I don't know. Does that bother you?"

If he wasn't a determined man, she wouldn't now have her hand cradled in his. Wouldn't be battling this thing without a name. "No," she told him and smiled, hoping the gesture would create a protective covering over what she felt. He smiled back, but his eyes were hooded, exuding sensuality and challenge. Or maybe she was reading something in their dark lights when there was nothing.

Mara drew her hand free and headed outside. She wasn't going to look at him again. She certainly wasn't going to let her thoughts of him go any further than they had.

EXCEPT FOR BEING CLEANER than she usually kept it, the Corvette didn't look different. The young man at the impound yard explained that he didn't often get to handle a hot car and had spent extra time cleaning and waxing it. "From what I heard, they didn't get any usable prints off it," he told Mara and Reed. "Bummer. At least he didn't wreck it. I hope you don't mind my waxing it. Maybe you use something special."

"Nothing special." Mara rubbed the keys between her fingers, trying to warm them, make them hers again. *He* had touched them. It bothered her that Detective Kline hadn't called to tell her about the unsuccessful search for prints.

Reed walked around the car as the attendant pointed out the Corvette's unblemished exterior and the leather upholstery. "What's the fastest you've taken this?" he asked Mara.

"A little over ninety. Not so fast, really."

Reed turned. "No. Not so fast."

It was time to get into the Corvette. Putting it off would solve nothing. Slowly Mara wrapped her fingers around the handle and opened the door. The interior hadn't held on to the man's smell. There were no indentations in the passenger's seat to remind her of his presence. The words they'd both spoken were gone. No one would ever know. Still—

Should she sell it?

"I have a suggestion." Reed stood close, much closer than Mara could handle objectively. "What if I follow you? We could grab something to take back to your place. There's enough daylight left that we can eat and then get me back out on the track."

She should remind him that he'd bought dinner last night, but Reed had a point. Going to get the Corvette had gotten in the way of what he was paying her for. Besides, this way she wouldn't have to drive home alone. Even if she didn't trust her reactions around him, he would be there.

Mara suggested a supermarket with a deli, and as Reed walked back to the Jag, she fastened her seatbelt and started the Corvette. She nodded at the lot boy and watched Reed pull out behind her. Mara turned on the radio, hunting unsuccessfully for the station she and Reed had listened to. The chopped sounds from stations, located and discarded, filled the air.

It took a little less than ten minutes to reach the supermarket. During that time, Mara concentrated on driving and making sure Reed was following. It was daylight. Traffic was all around. The air smelled, not of a lonely stretch of rock, but of exhaust fumes.

"This isn't where you were grabbed, is it?" Reed asked when they met in the grocery's parking lot. He ran his fingers over the Corvette's front bumper, frowning.

"No." This was daylight. The lot was filled with business people who'd stopped on their way home. Maybe, if Reed hadn't brought it up, she wouldn't be drawing comparisons. Maybe having him here wouldn't matter so much, and, despite the risk, she wouldn't be fighting the desire to place her hand in his again. "I haven't been back there."

"Are you going to?"

Mara slung the strap of the old purse she'd pulled out of her closet over her shoulder. She didn't look at Reed as they walked, side by side, into the bright store. "What does it matter?"

"Maybe it doesn't."

"I suppose it's something I should do." Mara waited while a woman with two school-aged children passed in front of her. "Like an exorcism."

"Only when you're ready."

Only when you're ready. "Thank you for saying that."

"I'm trying," he said softly.

"Trying? What?"

"To understand." Reed nodded, indicating that they were in the way of people needing a cart. "To help."

You are helping. In ways you might never know. "I appreciate that."

REED SUGGESTED barbecued ribs, a seafood salad, and sourdough bread. Mara approved. She'd never met sourdough bread she didn't like. Then, while Reed talked to a bakery clerk, Mara wandered through the produce section, finally choosing grapes and tangerines. She found Reed and showed him her selection, wanting his approval. They were waiting in the checkout line when Reed dashed back for strawberry ice cream and wine. "One of the drawbacks of being on an expense account," he explained. "Restaurant eating. Grocery stores are a kick."

Mara hadn't eaten ice cream since she'd left a carton splattered on asphalt. "You like grocery shopping?" she asked.

"You don't?"

"I avoid it for as long as possible. Believe me, the novelty wears off."

Reed slid around Mara, hip against hip, and started bagging groceries as the clerk rang them up. "Not if it's something you seldom do," he said and popped a grape into his mouth. "I could get carried away."

Mara touched her hand to the spot where he'd left his imprint. "You're a strange man."

"Not so strange." He pulled off another grape and, reaching over, offered it to her.

Mara leaned forward, taking his gift. She bit down on tangy sweetness and let juice trickle down her throat. No, she thought. Not strange. Distracting, yes. Dangerous, yes. But not strange.

WHEN THEY DROVE into Mara's yard, Lobo trotted over to the Corvette and thoroughly sniffed it before turning his attention to the Jag. They were unloading groceries when, with a sigh, the doberman flopped down in the shade of the mobile home. "Bored, aren't you?" Mara sympathized. "Nothing going on. And me gone so much. Don't worry. Things are going to get back to normal. Soon."

Mara led the way into the kitchen. She got out dishes and silverware while Reed poured the wine. She watched, marveling at the grace he made seem inherent in a task she'd always taken for granted. She'd started to put the ribs in the microwave to warm when Reed stopped her. "How about taking it easy for a few minutes?" he suggested. "Unless you're starving. Maybe we'll just talk tonight instead of trying to squeeze in a lesson."

"You're sure?"

"Sure. We'll do a double session tomorrow."

When Mara turned from the microwave, Reed touched his fingers lightly to her shoulder and led the way to the deck at the back of her place. He pulled two canvas lawn chairs together and sat in one of them. "I have this fascination with roses. I can't get over the colors they come in," he told her. "Their aroma. The different sizes. What it takes to make them grow."

"What it takes is the proper food at the proper time. And trimming them back ruthlessly." Mara loved the pocket of quiet she'd created out of sight of her clients. She'd had to erect a fence around the garden to keep the rabbits out and almost put herself in the poorhouse by making the mistake of going to the most complete nursery in the area, but the results pleased her. She was glad Reed had noticed.

Mara leaned back, kicked off her shoes and sipped the wine. Nothing touched her except the presence of the man next to her. "If you like roses that much, maybe you should grow them."

"No time."

"Because you're always on assignment?"

"Sometimes it seems that way. I can't get over your place," Reed told her. "You grew up with the freedom, the necessity to always be on the move. And yet here you are."

"Yes."

"Living by yourself. Running your own business. Why?"

"Why what?" Mara wasn't sure how, or if, she'd answer should the question turn out to be the one she anticipated.

"Why aren't you married?"

Mara blinked in surprise. "I guess it just hasn't happened," she said, voice faltering. "Getting the business off the ground has taken an incredible amount of work."

"It's off the ground."

He was right. "My brothers say there's probably no man alive who could put up with me."

"Do you believe that?"

Of course not. There had been men in Mara's life. A great passion when she was seventeen that had turned her world on end and passed in a flood of tears. A couple of times she'd found someone she thought might be the one. Dates. Enough casual dates that she was no longer interested in that. For a long time now there'd been no one's voice she wanted to hear, no one keeping her awake nights. She couldn't, of course, tell Reed that. "I don't go in for deep analysis," she said instead. "I don't believe in trying to come up with a profile of the right man, or right friend, or right employee, or right anything for me. When the connection is there, it's there.''

Reed chuckled, a deep, almost brooding sound. ''You have to be around someone for any kind of connection to work, Mara.''

Mara wanted to point out that he could be talking about himself, too, but he must know that. She leaned back, willing herself to relax and give up the effort of thinking. The sun was turning hot orange. She gazed at it, concentrating on the movement of hawks and wind. She thought about Reed sitting next to her, his space somehow infringing on hers, and her need for it to be like that.

When he left to do what was necessary, Mara would have nothing more than a memory of a strong, independent, self-reliant man. On those rare occasions when thoughts of him crossed her mind, she would wonder where he was, what he was doing with his life. Whether he was safe. Whether there was anyone to care about him. They would be casual questions. Casual. That's all.

She wouldn't tangle herself in what tonight hinted at.

''I thought I might get here before you did this morning,'' Reed was saying, his voice slow. ''You must have left the motel early.''

''I didn't stay,'' Mara said softly. She turned and looked at him, willing him to understand. ''I came back home.''

''You—what? You were here alone last night? You didn't tell anyone?''

''Don't.'' Mara stopped him. ''It was my call.''

She expected an argument. Instead Reed did nothing more than set down his wineglass. He shifted slightly, and the wind found a lock of hair to play with. Now Reed looked somehow off balance. Or maybe she was the one without equilibrium.

''I tried,'' she said. ''I sat down on the bed and thought about the luxury of washing my hair, reading the paper.'' *I thought about you.* ''But—''

"But you didn't stay. Why?"

"I'm trying to tell you. Please let me." She didn't owe him an explanation. Still, she didn't stop talking. "I come from gutsy stock, Reed. My father taught me a great deal about taking risks and facing life. He was almost killed five years ago. Still, he hasn't stopped racing. That— The man who kidnapped me— There are things, maybe there are things I'll never get back. But I'm going to fight."

"What do you mean, things you might never get back?"

"I don't know." That wasn't the truth. Mara knew she had lost a measure of courage, a certain sense of security. She'd seen a side of herself she didn't like. She understood vulnerability in a way she'd never dreamed possible. But how could she tell that to Reed—Reed with his courage and determination and dedication? "Friday night was hours and hours and hours ago," she told him instead. "I have new locks, my car back, a less-than-classy purse. Life goes on."

"Does it?"

"What do you mean?"

Reed retrieved his wineglass and pressed his fingers tightly around it. He spoke with his eyes on her and not on what he was doing. "You haven't given yourself much time. It's only been a few days, yet you're trying to act as if it never happened. You're taking risks...."

"If I am, that's my decision."

"If you're capable of making decisions. Don't," Reed warned when Mara tried to break in. "It's your turn to hear me out. I'm thinking about Jack. Maybe seeing some parallels. Someone tried to kill him. He changed."

"Where is he?"

"In the hospital."

"I'm not in a hospital, Reed. I'm not out of my environment," Mara told him. She stood, feeling somehow hemmed in by him. The roses Reed admired needed watering. If she remembered, she would cut a few buds and have them in the classroom tomorrow. "That's the difference," she went on, feeling her way word by word. "He's helpless.

I'm not. I—'' Reed didn't understand. She could see it in his quick blink, the constant worrying of his wineglass. ''Would you like more to drink?''

Slowly Reed set down his glass, his fingers sliding down the stem to steady it. Then he stood. The gesture was somehow both rapid and incredibly slow, incredibly controlled. ''No. Thank you. I called him this morning. He was still asleep. Chewed me out royally.''

''Still—'' Mara struggled to speak around what she was feeling and seeing. ''He must have been glad to hear from you.''

''He said I was acting like an old woman.'' Reed leaned over the railing and brought a rose to his nose. He inhaled, his features softening. ''I ordered some flowers for his room. Some kind . . . I don't remember what they're called. It should have been roses.''

''But not from a florist,'' Mara told him as if that was the most important piece of information she would ever pass on to another human being. Why were his movements so fascinating? ''They lose their aroma if they're refrigerated.''

''I'll remember that. Maybe—''

''Maybe what?''

''Would you mind if I took him some of yours?''

Mara nodded. ''I think that's a wonderful idea.''

''He'll give me a hard time, tell me he'd rather have a six-pack. But he'll like them,'' Reed said. Then he stretched his hand toward her. There was no questioning the message. No questioning her response. She had to take a half step to reach him, but she did it.

So that's what his hand felt like. Warm. So incredibly warm when she needed that. Big. Strong. She wished she could give him the same in return, but he would have to accept her cool, slender fingers.

''We shouldn't have stayed out here. You're chilled,'' he said.

What would it feel like if he put his arm around her shoulder and put an end to everything except warmth? He didn't. Thank heavens, he didn't. "I wanted you to see my garden," she managed. "I love anything that grows."

"I know. I've seen your house."

He'd read what of her heart and soul she'd put into her home. This moment of large, capable fingers wrapped around small, rapidly warming ones was about a great deal more than one of them guiding the other inside. He wanted to go back within her walls. And she was welcoming him, closing out the world and the things left unresolved between them. She wanted him to see soft pillows and smoky blue couches and pictures of her family.

He wanted to take her roses to his friend. A man like that, one who understood the sound of silence, might understand that she couldn't handle more than a few seconds of contact. He might even understand that those seconds would stay with her for a long time.

"I wasn't sure," Reed told her with his hand still wrapped around her fingers. "Maybe you don't want this. You didn't the other night."

"That was— It's all right."

Mara waited for Reed to say more, but he didn't, and she couldn't think of anything herself. He'd taken the lead by reaching out for her. Now she charted her own direction by pulling away and walking, silent and aware, into her kitchen. So much of her was revealed here: a love of light and space and efficiency. He would see. He would know.

Reed worked beside her with the ease of a man used to taking care of himself. Mara functioned automatically, telling herself that, despite his nearness, she felt nothing. She wouldn't be seeing him again, and nothing was all she should feel. She was still telling herself that when they were ready to eat.

But he wasn't saying anything, wasn't taking her away from the nothing that wasn't *nothing* at all. Finally, when all she wanted was for him to walk out of her house so she could breathe without taking part of him into her, he leaned forward.

"This isn't working," he said.

"What isn't?"

"What we're doing or not doing."

Was she that transparent? "I don't know what you're talking about."

"Don't you? Mara, if I ask you a question, will you give me an honest answer?"

"I don't know."

Reed brought himself even closer. Infringing on her space, when she both wanted and didn't want that. "I deserved that. Look, I don't want this to be the last time."

He didn't want... "Your job."

"Yeah. My job. Something I have to do. A commitment that has nothing to do with what the bureau's paying me. You understand that, don't you?"

"Yes."

"If I'm going to bring those men to justice, it has to be a total commitment. It isn't something I can walk away from. But there might be times... I want to know how you're doing."

"I don't need a keeper."

"We're not talking about a keeper, Mara. Though there's still the possibility that man might come back."

That man? Was this what Reed was talking about? "I don't need to be told that," she said, trying not to look at him.

"Don't you, Mara? If I thought I could get away with it, I'd haul you out of here."

As if she'd let him! Without her home, and without belief in her own strength, she was nothing. "Call me," Mara countered. She felt stronger than she had a moment ago. Sadder, yes. Disappointed, yes, because she'd wanted to hear that this was about the two of them and not her attacker. But at least Reed was back to acting by the rules that had been set between them, and she could handle that.

"Drop by if you can. I'll tell you nothing has happened, that I'm busy with a new group of students, and I finally found time to do some repairs on my loaner."

"I hope that's exactly what I'll hear. But I still want you to be able to get in touch with me."

"Oh."

"Mara..." The word trailed off, and Mara felt herself following it into nothing. Reed straightened. "I chose that particular hotel because Jack believes that's where some of the members of this ring stay when they come to San Diego. I'm using another name. But you can reach me there if you ask for Lane Reaves."

"I don't understand. You're undercover—I guess that's the right word—but you want me to get in touch with you? Isn't that a risk? Won't—"

"Let me worry about that, Mara." This time when he reached for her, there was no hesitation in the gesture. He knew he was taking. And she seemed to be willing to allow him to do exactly that. His fingers were cool, now almost as cool as hers.

He didn't want things to end between them. There hadn't been a beginning yet, not really. If she was wise, she wouldn't see him beyond tonight. That way she wouldn't begin to care. Or if it was already too late for that, at least she wouldn't care more than she did. But they were holding hands again. Simply and not so simply holding hands. Her fingers, and more, absorbed his reality.

She held on because she needed something of him to keep close, and safe, and real within her.

Reed stayed for another hour. They ate. They even managed to find safe and simple things to talk about. For most of that time they sat in the living room while Mara concentrated on the effort it took for Reed to remain still. He wasn't, she learned, a man who knew what to do with his body when it was at rest. He needed movement. In that respect he was a great deal like her father, her brothers. Like her. When it came time for him to leave, she watched him check the locks on her doors and windows, and then she followed him outside. "You'll have Lobo inside?" he asked.

"Yes."

"Good."

"Nothing's going to happen to me. Believe me—" His look stopped her. His eyes were so dark, his jaw clenched. Not asking herself why, Mara slid her arm around his waist and held on. Simply held on. "I'm sorry. I didn't mean to make light of your concern."

"If you want to go to a motel, I'll pay for it."

Where was this awareness of him coming from? Why did she feel this need to go on touching, when his hands were hanging by his sides and he'd stopped looking down at her? His body was rigid now, as if he was the one who didn't want contact between them. Still, until he moved to open the car door, Mara didn't know how to let go. "I stayed here last night," Mara whispered. "Nothing happened. Reed, please—"

"Yeah. I know. You don't want anyone telling you that you can't handle this."

"No. I don't," Mara said firmly.

Still, she didn't go back inside until she no longer heard the sound of Reed's car.

Chapter Seven

Somehow, maybe because she could hear the reassuring sound of Lobo snoring nearby, Mara managed to fall asleep. She didn't know what time it was when his growling woke her.

Mara's first thought was that the alarm had sounded and Lobo was trying to get her to shut it off. But when she realized he wasn't in the room, she forced herself out of bed to look for him. Lobo stood on his hind legs, bracing himself on the kitchen sink while he tried to look out the window. "Lobo," Mara whispered. The word came out as a half squeak. "Lobo. Be quiet. It's rabbits."

The growling continued. She knew she should turn on the light. Grab a flashlight and look outside. No. There was no way she could talk herself into stepping beyond the safety of her locked house.

"What is it? What's out there?" Mara asked the dog. Lobo gave her a quick glance before returning to his study of the night. His ears were pricked forward, his lean and strong body carrying the message of tension. For the better part of a minute he was motionless, growling.

It could be rabbits. They'd disturbed his nights before.

Mara started when Lobo dropped down onto all fours. She watched as he walked through the doorway leading from the kitchen to the small dining room and stopped with his nose pressed to the crack of the rear door. His deep breathing grated on her even more than his growling had.

Mara reached for the phone and dialed 911. No, she told the woman who answered, she wasn't sure anyone was out there. But she'd been abducted a few days ago and her abductor hadn't been caught. He knew who she was, where she lived. Would someone please...

Of course. The woman explained, slowly and patiently, that a patrol car would be dispatched as soon as possible. In the meantime Mara was to remain inside and stay on the line. "Try to calm down," she said. "It's natural for you to be jumpy. I'm sure they aren't going to find anything."

Mara hung on, speaking of nothing in particular, taking reassurance from the presence of the woman on the other end of the line.

Lobo was pacing. "What do you smell?" she asked him. "Rabbits? Is it rabbits?"

Lobo had no answer for her. Although he remained tense and wary for another five minutes, he wasn't clawing to get outside. It was as if he wasn't sure what had disturbed his sleep and was disgusted because his nose and ears weren't providing him with answers. At length he padded back into the bedroom and settled on the carpet with a disgruntled groan. Mara waited, calculating the minutes it would take the police to get out here. That time passed.

Lobo jumped back up when the patrol car arrived. Mara told the 911 operator that the police were there and hung up the phone. She waited until the police rang her doorbell and then, with her fingers wrapped around Lobo's collar, opened the door. "I thought— I didn't think it would take this long," she managed.

"I'm sorry. But you're pretty far off the beaten track," the heavyset rumpled policeman explained. "Would you like us to come in and check the house?"

"No. No. That won't be necessary. It's just that— I didn't hear anything. I don't know what bothered my dog. Maybe rabbits."

"Rabbits. There's a lot of them out here, aren't there?"

The policeman looked as if he hadn't slept in days. Mara muttered, "I'm sorry for disturbing you," and stepped back from the door. The officer's partner hadn't come onto the porch. He was heading toward the garage, his powerful flashlight cutting a lighted arc through the night.

Five minutes later they were gone. Mara concentrated on the sound of their car as long as she could hear it. "No one," she told Lobo. "False alarm."

She should go back to bed. If she was going to go on with her life, she had to stop jumping at every sound. Only a coward—

Reed had told her to call him. "I don't care when it is. If there's a problem, I want you to call."

Yes. Reed. He would—

Mara didn't give herself time to question what she was doing. Instead she picked up the scrap of paper he'd left near the phone and dialed the number of the hotel. Four rings later an elderly man answered. What was the name she was supposed to ask for? And if that nonexistent man came on the line, what would she say?

Lobo heard rabbits. It scared me. I needed to hear your voice. Mara muttered her second "I'm sorry" of the night and hung up without asking for Lane Reaves. She felt almost as cold as she had that hot afternoon five years ago when her father's car had burst into flames.

She'd cried that day. Cried and then pulled the scream inward so no one would know. She could do that again.

Shivering, Mara crawled back into bed. She tried to concentrate on the soothing sound of Lobo's breathing and the seemingly impossible task of quieting her own, but in the vast silence between Lobo's gentle sounds, she listened to the night. Listened . . . for what, she didn't know.

MARA WAS UP and showered before daylight. She killed another half hour by reading the paper and then stalled even longer by preparing an elaborate omelette that she wound up sharing with Lobo. Finally, when it was fully light, she walked outside with the animal. Lobo went straight for the back yard, sniffing at the mesh fencing around the flower garden. Was there more than idle curiosity to his actions? It seemed as if he was giving the fencing an intense scrutiny, but she'd never paid close attention to the way Lobo surveyed his territory.

"You're making an old woman of me," she said, following up her honesty with a laugh that had to be worked at.

Lobo woofed softly and lifted his head. Then he dropped his muzzle back down to sniff the ground.

"Tell me." It was more plea than order. "Tell me if you smell something."

Once again the dog woofed, the sound a little labored because his nose was pressed against the earth. And then, as it had last night, the growl rumbled through him.

CLINT'S PARENTS came to work with him in the morning. Because he was concerned that his father not overdo, Clint was unable to give his usual energy to his work. He asked Mara how she was doing, but she didn't think he was listening to her and told him little. Reed attended the morning session but had to leave in the afternoon. As arranged, he came back later, first for a private lesson and then to take her into town to help her purchase a revolver. He wasn't sure when he'd have time to show her how to use it. Until then she agreed to put it away. Mara had no problem with that. Holding the gun in the store had unnerved her.

"I can't stay," he told Mara when he brought her home, and she asked if he wanted to come inside. "I want to see Jack and then . . ."

"Then what?"

"There's someone I'm trying to connect with. It might mean spending the evening in the hotel bar."

"It doesn't sound as if that's something you want to do."

"It isn't," he said as she stood next to the Jag and watched him adjust the rearview mirror. "I'll call as soon as I can. I don't like leaving you like this."

A small ache settled deep inside at the thought that Reed had to leave her but Mara merely held up two fingers. To her relief, they were steady. "I've been here two nights now and nothing's happened."

Was that true? Mara wondered, when she was alone once again. Was she right in saying nothing to either Reed or Clint about last night? Lobo had barked. She'd had the police out. They hadn't found anything, and in the daylight her fears lacked substance.

Maybe, if she could keep her mind off Reed, she'd be able to concentrate on what else she was feeling.

The next morning Mara's acreage was gray, as if caught somewhere between night and day. It was Reed's fault. "I don't know when I'll be able to see you," he'd said when he called as she was getting ready for bed. "Things are happening." Another automobile had been stolen and, maybe, he'd made contact with one of those responsible. "I've got to work on gaining this man's trust. Make him think we have something in common. I wish..."

"Don't. It's your job. I understand."

She did. Didn't she?

Mara could make out the outline of the Corvette. It was a silent, hulking beast shrouded in too much dark. But it was only a car, a car surrounded by a predawn world. She could slip into a robe, put a key in the ignition and sit behind the wheel. There wasn't a thing in the world to prevent her from driving it.

Lobo was delighted to be released from the confines of four walls. After a quick tour of his turf, the doberman joined his mistress as she walked over to the sports car. "No," she whispered when he started to move away. "Wait. This will just take a minute."

Before she could open the door, Lobo stepped up to the sleek vehicle and began sniffing the back bumper. The dog breathed rapidly as he drew air deep into his lungs.

"What's wrong?" Mara asked. "Do you smell something?"

Lobo growled.

That was the only sign Mara needed. She had better things to do than drive a car around the training oval while still in her nightgown. She would get ready for the day and go to work. And she would ask her secretary to call her if Reed called.

"SORRY. Nothing from him," Diane explained when Mara came into the office during her lunch break. "Too bad. If I was a little younger—all right, a lot younger. I'm glad to see you're interested in someone. I saw his car. He's rich, is he?"

"I guess," Mara said absently.

"There's nothing wrong with a rich man. Oh, I have some good news for you. Someone found your purse."

"My purse? Where?"

"I asked, but the man was vague. He sounded pretty old."

"Oh. Does he want me to pick it up?" Why was she asking this? There was no way Mara wanted what her attacker had pawed through. "I don't suppose there's any money in it."

"I'm afraid not. But he did say the credit cards and your driver's license were in it. I guess that's how he tracked you down. He was kind of nosy."

Mara leaned against Diane's desk. A man had found her purse. A man. "What do you mean, nosy?"

"Well, maybe nosy isn't the right word. He went on about how people are so careless these days, how no one takes responsibility for their possessions. He sounded a little put out, like he had better things to do than try to get your purse back to you. You know, he reminded me of my father. I thought he was going to give me a lecture about how young people today haven't lived through the Depression and can't possibly understand what it means to lose everything."

Mara had met Diane's father. Her description of his lecture fit with what she knew about the man. The anxiety that gripped her evaporated, and she shared an understanding laugh with her secretary. "I'd probably feel the same way if I'd been alive when half the country was out of work. I can't believe my credit cards are still in it. Maybe the man who grabbed me guessed I'd have them canceled and that's why he didn't take them. If only he'd gotten in touch with me before I'd gone to all the trouble of having them reissued. The guy who called isn't going to mail the purse, is he? I don't want some old man going to that expense."

"No." Diane looked down at her notepad. "He said—this is kinda weird—he said to tell you he goes to this ice-cream parlor on Market and 5th every afternoon. He's going to leave it there and you can pick it up the next time you're in the neighborhood."

"An ice-cream parlor? He said . . . that?"

"Hey." Diane grabbed Mara's hand. "Are you all right? You didn't swallow something the wrong way, did you?"

Ice cream. Diane was still staring at her, but Mara couldn't think about trying to explain. "No. I don't believe— No. The number for the Harbor Island Police Department. What is it?"

"Just a minute." Diane grabbed the telephone book while Mara pulled the phone close. Mara almost came unglued, waiting for Diane to give her the number. But finally she made the necessary connection.

She wound up having to talk to two other people before getting hold of Detective Kline. She locked eyes with Diane but didn't really see her. An old man? Maybe *he'd* disguised his voice.

Detective Kline wasn't so sure. "Let one of our units check it out, Miss Curtis," he offered when Mara finished her disjointed explanation. "Yes. I understand. You had ice cream with you when you were attacked. You think it isn't coincidence.''

"I know it isn't," Mara protested. "He's playing a sick game. If he thinks I'm going to walk into that place... He'd just laugh at me and then he'd..." Mara had been going to say the man would follow her home, but she couldn't. Not with Diane listening and an experienced detective telling her not to jump to conclusions. "All right," she forced herself to say. "I'll wait until you call. If my purse is there...I don't care if I ever get it back."

For the next three hours Mara went through the motions of trying to teach while she waited for Diane to tell her the police had called back. Finally Diane poked her head in the classroom and gave the thumbs-up sign.

"It was there," Detective Kline explained. "There wasn't anything when my men went by the first time, but we got a call from the manager a little while ago. Someone had left a purse on one of the tables."

Mara slumped into Diane's empty chair. "They don't know who? An old man. Did anyone see an old man?"

"I'm sorry. School's been out about an hour. The place has been pretty busy. There are senior apartments nearby. They get a lot of repeat customers, some of them are in there every day."

"What are you saying?"

"I'm saying we don't know anything. It could be some public-minded citizen. That's what I'm inclined to believe. An old man who didn't want to get any more involved than he has."

Mara's head throbbed. She had been aware of the growing headache all afternoon, but there was so much pain now that it was hard for her to talk, or think. "But an ice-cream parlor."

"It could have been McDonald's."

"Or a police station. Why didn't he take it to the police?"

"Like I said, he probably thought he would have to answer a lot of questions. This was a place you could find, one
that wasn't out of his way."

But why had he left it on one of the tables? Hadn't Diane
said the man was going to turn it over to one of the employ-
ees? Even with the throbbing in her temple, Mara realized
that further argument would serve no purpose. Detective
Kline with his years of training was telling her not to let her
imagination get away from her. Maybe he believed what he
was saying, and maybe he was trying to keep her from becoming too alarmed about something neither of them had
an answer for. Mara concentrated while the detective item-
ized what was in the purse. He offered to keep it in his office until she could come for it.

"I appreciate it. I just wish I understood."

"I know. At least you got everything except your cash
back. You're pretty lucky."

Yes. Lucky.

IT WASN'T UNTIL after seven that night that Mara got around
to fixing something for dinner. She was sitting down with a
tuna fish salad when the phone rang. Although she told
herself it would be Reed, she had to force herself to pick up
the receiver. The connection was bad. For a moment she
wasn't sure who was on the other end of the line. Then she
heard, "You're home. Do you have a few minutes?"

Reed. "Yes," she told him with her eyes on the curtained
window and her mind wrestling with the question of what,
if anything, she would tell him. "Where are you?"

"At the hotel. I've got company coming in a few minutes. But I've been doing some checking. There's a target
range we can use."

Mara gripped the phone, trying to bridge the distance.
"When?"

"Tomorrow evening if you can make it."

They'd be together tomorrow. She couldn't tell him how
important that was; she couldn't admit it to herself. "I'll be

there," she told him. "But you don't have to do this. If you don't have the time—"

"I'm making the time. Damn. He's here. Look, let me give you some directions."

Mara nodded and picked up a pen so she could jot down what he was telling her. Reed didn't know how much time he would have, but made it clear that teaching her was a priority. "Wear old clothes," he told her and then hung up.

The sound of Reed's voice carried Mara through the next hour. Maybe she should fix something so they could eat together. But maybe he had to meet someone later and her effort would be wasted. If only she could call him back and get the answer to that question. But she couldn't. He was with a man, maybe one of those who'd tried to kill Jack.

This wasn't the way it was supposed to be between two people getting to know each other. He should come here for a home-cooked meal and conversation. They'd talk about how to make a garden grow and the purity of desert sunsets and some of the places they'd both lived. She'd ask him what she believed could be done to protect the environment, and he'd be interested in her political views. She'd ask him if he knew that his eyes darkened whenever his thoughts turned serious. He'd tell her he could gauge her moods by the warmth in her fingers.

But Reed wasn't here. The night settled around Mara until she had no choice but to bring Lobo inside. When she stepped out to call him in, the porch light cut only a thin slice through the night. Beyond that was a world of black, capable of concealing a man—a man who dropped off a purse at an ice-cream parlor because, for him, it was an obscene joke.

Maybe.

Chapter Eight

Heat rose from the parking lot in waves and put its stamp on the stretch of dirt and weeds and browning grass that made up the Inland target range. Mara parked her loaner car between a camper and a small pickup and reached for the packages in the front seat. One was a cooler containing fried chicken, sliced tomatoes, rye bread and cream cheese. The other was the box containing the gun. Reed wasn't there yet.

Mara watched the men and women grouped around dirt berms and weathered wooder seats. Everyone's attention was focused on the distant bull's-eye targets. At first the random, staccato sound of gunfire jolted her, but Mara stood her ground. She was determined that learning how to load and shoot a weapon would be something she'd handle well.

It had to be: Reed would see.

A half hour ago Mara had held out her hand and Detective Kline had placed her purse in it. After thanking him, she'd carried it to her car and tossed it inside. Before she'd gone more than a half dozen blocks, she'd stopped. After pulling out her credit cards, driver's license and an envelope containing the latest batch of pictures from her family, Mara had dropped the forty-dollar purse into a roadside trash container.

He'd seen the pictures of her brothers pretending to strangle each other. How dare he!

Reed's Jag pulled into the dusty parking lot. Mara turned, every thought stripped from her except the simple awareness of how long it had been since she'd seen Reed Steward.

He was a shadow moving among the shadows cast by cars and trucks and campers. He wore a T-shirt proclaiming his loyalty to the Los Angeles Angels and jeans that had long known his body. There was a small rip in the side of his right tennis shoe. He was alive and well.

"Did you have to wait long?" he asked when he was close enough to be heard over the constant, discordant sound of discharging firearms.

"No. Not long." She felt like a girl finally on a date with the boy she'd been dreaming about for months—tongue-tied and uncertain.

"I hope not. If I'm ever going to get around this city, I'm going to have to learn more about the side streets," Reed told her, his voice clearer and more vital than it had been over the phone. He smiled. "How was your day?"

Tense. Disconcerting. At this moment, worth everything that had come before. "Okay. What about yours?"

"Strange. It's a little like being Alice in Wonderland."

"What do you mean?"

"It's hard to explain," Reed said. He resettled his weight, but didn't come closer. "You brought something to eat. Great. Did you bring the bullets?"

They were going to talk about bullets? He was going to stand there, with five feet separating them, and talk about bullets? "I didn't know if you'd be hungry," she told him.

"I haven't eaten since breakfast."

"Oh. Why?"

"Lots of reasons. Lots of things to do. Weird people." As the word trailed off, he moved toward her with silent grace. "You look wonderful."

Mara felt anything but wonderful, but he was saying that, and looking down at her, and for the moment she believed him. For the moment there was nothing for her except their being together.

His eyes, the shifting of his body toward her told her one thing. If she wanted it, he would kiss her, here, in the middle of a parking lot. Openly. Honestly. For the first time. Did she want that? Was she ready for their relationship to take that step?

The answer lay in her erratic breathing, the way her heartbeat caught and then regained its tempo, her awareness of him. Knowing nothing and yet at the same time knowing everything, Mara moved into him. The last thing she saw before the world blurred was his smile, clean and uncomplicated.

His mouth, the touch it seemed she'd waited years for, felt both firm and soft; his arms felt sure around her.

Challenge waited in his embrace. The challenge was stronger than she could possibly feel comfortable with. Still, Mara didn't attempt to draw back. Instead she felt herself drifting into him. The line that marked where she ended and he began blurred. She should be alarmed. Just now she needed to stand on her own. And yet, being in his arms gave her certain essential answers, and the molding of her mouth against his made her feel strong. For a few minutes Mara was no one except a woman who'd come to meet a man. Without knowing she was going to do it, she slid her arms around him and held on. She felt bone and muscle sheathed by flesh. As long as she held on, as long as she pressed her mouth to his, this moment might last forever.

A pickup pulled into a stall behind them, its oversized tires grinding over gravel. Mara tensed and waited for the sound to end. When it did, Reed spoke. "You've been all right?" he asked.

"Yes."

Groaning, Reed leaned back, his breathing ragged. He no longer smiled, and Mara found gut-level honesty in his eyes. "I saw Jack again. When I think of what he went through—and you . . . It's an insane world sometimes."

Was that why he'd kissed her? Because it was an insane world?

"Sometimes."

"But you are all right?"

The opening was there. She could tell him about her purse and what she'd done with it. She might, if she was any good at thinking, tell him about calling 911. But if she was going to do that, he would first have to let her go. "You had a meeting with some man," she managed.

"Yeah."

"And?"

He dragged his hands downward, over her shoulder blades, past her waist, sliding momentarily around the swell of her hips. "It's too soon to tell," he said while she concentrated on breathing. "That's part of why I saw Jack. Some things I need to verify."

"Oh" was all she could say.

"I'm getting a clearer idea of what happened, some ideas about who's responsible for trying to kill him."

Kill. The world intruded again. "Someone really tried?"

"There's no doubt, Mara."

"No doubt. Just like that."

"What do you want me to say?"

Mara didn't know. It was all she could do to keep up with her roller coastering emotions and remind herself he was no longer touching her and it was time to bring her body and thoughts back under control. She remained silent while Reed unpacked the gun. He handled it as comfortably as she did any garden tool. Still, she wasn't repulsed. She now understood that a firearm was part of him. When he held the unloaded weapon up to his eye and sighted down its length, Mara spoke. "Tell me about Jack."

"I did."

"Not enough. I want to know why you're doing this for him."

"Because?"

"Because I do. Isn't that enough?"

As far as the bureau and Captain Bistron were concerned, this was just another assignment for Reed. More dangerous than any other which had the desk jockeys nervous. But Mara was the one demanding explanations that would never find their way into his written report. He could turn the conversation around to why they were here. He could reach for her again and risk his ability to concentrate at all, or... "I owe him everything. Without him— I told you about my parents, about my father not being there. Mom's problems."

"Yes."

"Jack straightened me out."

"Do you owe him your life?"

"I'm not going to make the mistakes Jack did."

"Don't be so arrogant, Reed."

Was that what Mara thought? "I'm not. Jack deserves to know how much he means to me."

"I wish I did." She was whispering.

Reed believed her, enough that he let the gun dangle from his fingers and turned to face her. He should be concerned with getting her over to an unoccupied berm and making her feel comfortable with her weapon. That should take precedence over everything. But the setting sun lent rose and orange hues to her hair, and compared to that putting a gun in her hand seemed unimportant. Maybe it was the sunset; maybe it was her whisper. He had to turn something of himself over to her. "Mara, if it wasn't for Jack I don't know what I'd be doing with my life. Probably nothing."

"Don't sell yourself short."

"I'm not. I'm simply being honest. My father was never there. Mom had all she could do to deal with herself. I did what a lot of kids do. I took the freedom that was given me and messed up."

"You aren't messed up now."

"I was when Jack got hold of me," he said with the gun still in his hand. If he put it down, he could reach out and bring Mara into him. He knew better than to do that. "I wasn't going to school anymore. There didn't seem to be any reason. By the time I turned seventeen, I had five speeding tickets and hadn't paid the fines.''

Mara slid a few inches closer, tipping her head upward. She frowned, her eyes somber. He noted that. "Did your parents know?" she asked.

"Dad was gone. As usual. My mother didn't want to hear that her son had problems. I think she wanted to believe I was fine. Maybe that's how she convinced herself she was doing something right. I don't know." The gun seemed heavy in his hand. "I'm not a psychiatrist. I don't think I ever understood my mother."

"That's sad."

Reed slumped onto a weathered bench, hoping she couldn't see the sudden loss of his strength. He felt heat on the back of his neck and the weight of the pistol. After a moment, Mara sat down beside him. Breathing hard and deep, he concentrated on what needed to be said. "Her problems intimidated me, Mara. I think maybe Mom wanted me to be what her husband wasn't. Only, I didn't know how to fill that role. The more she tried to lean, the more I backed off."

"Why?"

"Why? Because I didn't know how to prop her up. I got arrested," Reed went on. Suddenly he wanted only to get this over with and onto the business that had brought them here. "For trying to elude a police officer. I'd been drinking, but not enough that they could add that to the charges."

"Why were you trying to get away?"

"Those speeding tickets. I knew if they caught me, they'd take away my license."

"And tell your mother."

"Maybe."

"Maybe? Let me ask you something. What bothered you more? Your father's reaction, or your mother's?"

Reed straightened and tried to focus on a tall, skinny young man carrying a rifle over to the range. "Mom," he told her because he had no choice, not if they were ever going to be more than they were to each other at this moment, if he wasn't going to simply hand her the pistol and walk out of her life.

"Because you didn't want to hurt her."

"She was so fragile. I resented the pedestal she tried to put me on. I wanted my father to be what she needed, what she wanted. It took me a long time to realize he couldn't be those things. That no one could fill up the emptiness in her."

"Reed, did you ever think that maybe you set yourself up to fail your mother's expectations? Not to hurt her, but because that would relieve you of a certain burden?"

When he had called Mara and asked her to meet him here, it had simply been because he'd wanted to see her. If he'd known it was going to turn out this way... "Maybe. Why do people do that?" he asked, the question spoken so low he wasn't sure she could hear over the sound of nearby gunfire. It didn't matter. The question was for himself, not her. "Jack was the cop who arrested me. He called my mother. When she came to the station, and after he saw Mom's reaction, I think he understood."

"What was it? He took you under his wing."

"Forced me there is more like it. I fought that man tooth and nail. Hanging out with a cop was not cool. But—"

She'd taken his hand. Reed looked down at what she'd done, marveling at the strength in those long, soft, slender fingers. An unbelievable amount of emotional baggage was rolling out of him this evening. Was it because he was living in a world that might blow up in his face, and had visited a man who'd already felt the explosion? Or was there something about Mara Curtis that made confession necessary?

He didn't know. Damn it, he didn't know.

"Your parents? Where are they?"

"Divorced." Mara rubbed the back of his hand, distracting him. He wanted to pull away. He wanted to spend the rest of the night feeling her soft and unsettling impact.

"It was my father's idea. I don't think Mom would have done anything to disturb the status quo, no matter how bad it got. He's remarried. I've never met the woman."

"And your mother?"

"She lives with her sister. She works for an auto dealership, in their office. Filling in the blanks on contracts, balancing books. There isn't much pressure and the salesmen spoil her."

"A safe job."

"Yeah. A safe job," Reed repeated. "Work. Going to garage sales on weekends. Watching TV. And telling people about her son the investigator."

"She's proud of you, is she?" Mara asked, still touching, still making him aware of very little except her.

"I guess. She doesn't really understand what I do, and I'm not going to tell her."

"Why not?"

"Why? She'd worry."

Mara's fingers stopped. She tried to will them to begin moving again, but it was too much of an effort. Reed believed it was sometimes necessary to keep certain things from people to protect them. How would he feel if, weeks from now, she told him about having the police out to her place and throwing away a perfectly good purse? She should tell him now. Lay herself open as he'd done. "You said Jack might retire," she said instead. "What's he going to do then?"

"I don't think he knows."

And if you lose Jack, it'll just be you. "You'll miss working with him."

"He might change his mind."

"I don't think so, Reed."

"You don't know him."

"No. I don't."

They were supposed to be joining those who were concentrating on cardboard targets. She had no right taking up his time this way, not when he obviously didn't want to face the possibility she'd posed, and it was none of her business. Mara released Reed's hand and reached for the pistol. He shoved himself to his feet and explained that when they reached the range they'd have to wear earplugs, and conversation would be all but impossible. He demonstrated how to hold the weapon in both hands. His orders were brisk and impersonal, and she wondered if, like her, he hadn't been able to leave the memory of their conversation behind.

Mara might never be capable of working past her fear, but an hour later she'd gone through a box of bullets and could consistently hit the target. Her wrist ached and her sight was blurry from staring, but she didn't mind. She'd done what was, for her, necessary.

After repacking the gun, Reed leaned close and spoke into her ear. "Mara. I can't stay long."

She stared. "Long enough to eat?"

"Yeah. I think I'd better. There might be some serious drinking later."

They walked back to Mara's car, and Reed put the pistol away while she got out the dinner things. To the left of the parking lot was a small grassy area shielded by a half dozen trees. They sat cross-legged on the well-maintained lawn, and Mara poured ice tea. "Who?" she asked.

"Who what?"

"Who are you going to do this drinking with?"

"Those characters from Alice in Wonderland. Some so intelligent it scares me. Others who can't think their way out of a paper bag."

Mara plucked a grass blade and with her fingernail slit it in two. "What scares you about them?" she forced herself to ask.

"The places their minds take them. If there's a chance they can make money from it, they'll explore any possibility. No matter how bizarre or dangerous."

"I don't understand."

Reed's reply was interrupted by the loud arrival of a couple of boys who immediately dropped to their knees and started wrestling on the grass. For a minute Reed and Mara ate in silence, watching, listening to other people's laughter. Mara wasn't sure Reed was going to answer her, or if she wanted to hear any more.

"I'm not sure I understand, either," he finally said. "But I have to try. I feel better about you now. Just knowing you can handle that pistol...."

Mara didn't want to talk about weapons or men with dangerous intellects. If she and Reed were normal, everyday people, they'd be laughing at the boys' antics. But there wasn't any laughter in her.

It was getting dark and he had to leave. He hadn't said when or if they'd see each other again.

"I guess we're done," Reed said.

"I guess we are. Thanks again."

Reed stood first. Mara scrambled to her feet and held the box she'd carried the meal in close to her as a buffer between them. Turning her back on Reed, she walked toward the parking lot. She felt him behind her. Did he want to kiss her goodbye?

"Where's your Corvette?"

Mara opened the door to the loaner car, dropped her burden in the back seat and stepped back from the car. Reed was standing too close. "Home. I felt like taking this one."

"Did you?"

"Yes. Just because you're suspicious of those men is no reason to question everything anyone does."

"You aren't anyone, Mara." Reed placed his hands on her shoulders and turned her toward him. He thought she might pull away. He wouldn't blame her if she did; but she didn't. He breathed in what aromas were left of her day in the sun, felt the shaky lifting of his own chest. He watched her do the same. With that breath, Reed pushed aside the unease that had come from seeing her in the wrong car. She looked up at him, not smiling. Not drawing away. After a moment she flicked her tongue over her upper lip and left her lips slightly parted.

Reed accepted her invitation.

Her lips were soft. He found the trace of moisture left behind by her tongue and drew it into him. Somehow they'd come together slightly off balance so that his lips closed over her upper lip. Sucking a little, he drew that in, too. He felt her quiver.

"Reed..." The word was a feather floating over and around him. What, he wanted to say... What...

Again. "Reed."

Like a man reaching for the sunset, Reed touched his tongue lightly to her lips, taunting and teasing.

Mara unnerved him. This woman with her haunting whisper was beyond his understanding. Beyond his control. And yet the only thing Reed wanted in life was to explore the emotions she roused in him.

Her share of the kiss had begun gently, but now he felt her reaching out. Her fingers dug into the back of his neck, not painfully, not something he could dismiss. She arched her body toward him. The raw embrace lasted only a moment, but it was long enough for his body to respond.

He caught her to him, molding them together once again. He heard her deep and quick breath, felt her begin to tremble. Then, when he'd begun to damn their surroundings, she drew away like a wild creature who has remembered the need for caution.

Reed didn't try to go after her, didn't attempt to draw her back again. He let her go. He could hear himself breathing hard. It was the sound of a man dancing a dangerous dance.

"I... have to go," he made himself say.

"Go?"

She blinked, bright eyes capturing the reds and rusts of the dying day. Reed felt the weight of her absence in his arms. He needed to reach out again. Needed a great deal more than the little he'd taken of her. Otherwise, how could he get through the night? "But I'll call. Whenever I can."

Reed's promise comforted Mara on her way home. The support of his words lasted until she came around the final turn and her headlights picked up the silhouette of a dark car parked in front of her mobile home. For a moment not enough registered. She'd been thinking of Reed standing, simply standing, while she drove away from him. But Lobo was crouched beside the door of that dark and unfamiliar car. Mara slowed, her heart beating a tempo that froze her where she was until she saw the domed light on top of the other vehicle. Still, Mara didn't trust her first look. She waited until she was close enough to make out the uniformed man sitting inside and then willed her heart to return to its usual pace. She pulled up next to the car, cut the engine and slowly got out. She spoke soothingly to Lobo, easing him under her control. Lobo continued to growl.

If this was about her parents. . . .

If it was about her kidnapper. . . .

At least she knew it wasn't about Reed. She'd just left him.

A beefy policeman with a receding hairline got out. "I'm glad you're here," he said. "That dog of yours wasn't going to let me move."

Mara kept her hand on Lobo's head. "I don't like to chain him up."

"That's probably a good idea. I figured if I wanted to keep my leg, I'd better stay where I was. I didn't know how I was going to leave you a note."

"A note? What about?"

"Maybe nothing." The man came closer but not so close that Lobo would be forced to take action to protect his mistress. "I came by a couple of hours ago. Then—well, for once things were kinda slow, so I came back again. The first time your dog simply looked at me with this 'I dare you' look. But when I showed up this time he came running over, growling and showing his fangs."

"He did?" That was unusual. Trying to judge Lobo's mood, Mara kept her hand on his head.

"How long have you been gone?"

"A couple of hours," Mara said while her heart slipped through a beat.

"Would you mind if I looked around?"

Mara would have minded if the policeman didn't. While he went back to his car for his flashlight, Mara took Lobo over to his seldom-used doghouse and filled his bowl with fresh water. Lobo drank deeply and then raised his head, his eyes glittering.

The policeman didn't find anything around the grounds or in the house. Because of the amount of traffic in and out of her property, it was impossible to tell whether any of the tracks on the gravel drive were fresh. "I don't know. Maybe some kids wandered out here and he chased them off."

"Maybe. Will you be back tonight?"

"I'm planning on it."

Mara waited outside until the patrol car could no longer be heard. Then she picked up the gun and forced herself to carry it into the house. She was grateful the policeman had left some lights on, but that didn't stop her from hitting two more switches until every room was lit. After taking the gun into the bedroom, she turned on the radio and then, although there was nothing worth watching on TV, she turned that on as well.

If a face appeared in the window, what would she do? Mara asked when the image refused to fade. Less than two weeks ago a certain face had propelled her into hell. That monster had turned everything she believed about herself into a mockery. He'd made her—

Had, Mara reminded herself. Past tense.

She was free, and if he came back here, she had her pistol. She now knew how to use it.

Was she really capable of violence?

Without questioning what she was doing, Mara walked to the front door and opened it. "Lobo. Come here boy," she called.

But later, even with the dog snoring comfortably at the foot of her bed, Mara was aware of each passing hour.

THERE WERE ALREADY three students in the classroom the next morning when Reed called. "What's this about a search of your place last night?" he asked as soon as she came on the line.

"What? Where are you?"

"At the police station. They were there when you got home? Damn it, I knew I should have followed you."

"You couldn't," Mara shot back. "You had to go drinking, remember."

"Yeah. I remember. What happened?"

Mara gave him a thumbnail sketch of the incident, downplaying it as much as possible. She told him nothing of the emotions she'd had to weather overnight and the constant battle she was fighting to force herself to remain here. "Lobo might have been chasing rabbits."

"Rabbits? Come on Mara, don't give me that."

"All right. Look, I don't know why he was upset. Maybe the police did something to disturb him."

"And maybe someone was there who shouldn't have been."

Maybe. Mara turned so she could look outside. It was an incredibly beautiful day, not too hot, just enough of a breeze. She should want that...not flight. "Lobo isn't used to having people come by when I'm gone." She was talking to a man who'd spent last night with dangerous men. What would he have in common with a woman who panicked because someone left her purse in an ice-cream parlor? "I get hikers sometimes this time of the year, kids wandering around."

"Yeah? Damn it Mara, he knows where you live."

She was surrounded by people. Today was an ordinary workday, and she wasn't a character in a horror movie. Reed hadn't mentioned her call to 911 the other night. Maybe he didn't know. "What are you doing there? Who told you about last night?"

"I had to use the department's computer. Last night's log was there." From where he stood in Captain Bistron's office, Reed could see the reception room. It was here that he'd first seen Mara Curtis and felt the need to reach beyond himself. Now he wanted almost nothing except to be with her, keeping her safe. But she was a grown woman, Mark Curtis's daughter. She didn't need a keeper. "Mara? I want some time with you. Away from all this."

"Time? Away?"

"I've been asking around. If you want, I can get the keys to a place on the beach for the weekend. A rental the captain knows about. I think I can get away."

"This weekend?"

"That isn't enough notice?"

Mara took a breath. "That's not it. It's just, I didn't— I had no idea you were going to suggest that."

"Neither did I. Will you come? We could walk along the beach, barbecue hot dogs for dinner. Talk. We'd each have our own bedroom. Clint can look after Lobo, can't he?"

Silence spread over and around Mara and took her away from the surroundings that suddenly felt both alien and stifling to her. He wanted to be with her. Despite everything they'd said to each other, and more important, what hadn't been said, he didn't want things to end. If she said yes now, he would know he was much more to her than someone she'd taught how to keep from getting run off a road.

"Mara?"

Separate bedrooms. He wasn't going to pressure her. All he was offering was conversation . . . and a weekend away from waiting for shadows to move. "Yes," she said with her eyes closed, remembering the challenge of his body. Remembering her own need. "I'll come."

Chapter Nine

It was dark by the time Reed and Mara reached the two-bedroom cabin at Pacific Beach. The exterior wood had been bleached by years and weather, easing the building's impact on its surroundings. The high-ceilinged living room opened onto a large, yet private, deck overlooking the ocean. There were two shelves full of books, a fireplace, an old-fashioned kitchen and a wheezing refrigerator. Best of all there was no TV.

Mara breathed the tang of salt air and lifted her head so the breeze from an open window touched her cheeks. For a moment she did nothing more than acknowledge where she was and what had brought her here. Then, feeling the energy rolling up unseen from the ocean, she spoke. "You really were able to get away? This isn't— If this is going to cause trouble for you . . ."

"Everyone thinks I'm headed to Chicago."

Feeling both bold and shy, Mara closed the distance separating them. He'd broken free. That alien and frightening world he lived in these days couldn't claim him in this cool and quiet place. He was here for her; she didn't know what to do with him, but he was here. Reed held out his hands, and she placed hers in them.

"No regrets?" he asked.

"Please don't ask me any questions. It's just, I'm not sure whether this is right."

"It is," he said. "You need it. I hope you can relax here."

"How could I do anything else? Look at this place. It's perfect." Mara tightened her fingers around his, making him, if it was possible, even more real than he already was. "Clint's watching Lobo. There's nothing I need to think about until Monday morning."

"Good."

Suddenly Mara was frightened. Not of Reed, but herself. It might help if she could convince herself that any woman facing a weekend with a man would feel a certain amount of trepidation. But she didn't know what other women did or felt at times like this. She didn't know what, if anything, she was expected to say.

Despite the cost, Mara drew away from Reed and moved unsteadily to the deck. The moonlight was barely strong enough to allow her to make out the tips of the waves, but sound filled in what her eyes missed. This wasn't the desert, and yet the physical impact was the same. Nature dominated. Man was nothing more than a visitor.

Reed came and stood behind her, resting his hands on her shoulders. She could have leaned against him—a great deal of her wanted to—but she held herself erect. Mara breathed deeply, feeling salt air settle through her lungs. She was aware of nothing except the sound of the surf, and Reed's touch. Most of all Reed's touch.

"What are you thinking?"

"I don't know," she told him. "It feels so different here."

"Are you nervous?"

Mara could have given him a quick denial, but both of them deserved more than that. "No," she began slowly. They hadn't touched during the drive over. She hadn't trusted herself to reach for him. But that was before, when they were listening to the stereo and talking about the weather and the incredible sense of isolation that was part of any middle of the night storm. When they were learning that they both loved spring mornings and hot afternoons and Sunday football games. Now, gathering what she'd learned about him into her, Mara leaned against Reed's chest. His arms tightened around her shoulders, and the back of her neck tingled where his breath touched it. He made her feel strong. He made her weak. "But—"

"But what?"

"I don't know."

"What don't you know?"

"What we're doing."

"Mara, we'll go at your pace. Listen to me, will you?" Reed turned her around. The gesture was a question and, possibly, an answer. "When I asked if you wanted to spend the weekend at the ocean with me, it was because this was the only way I could ensure that we would be together, without interruptions. Do you know what I'm saying?"

"I think so."

"I hope you do." Reed leaned forward and brought his mouth close and yet not close enough to hers. "I'm not sure I've really stopped thinking about you since that night in the police station." For a moment he was silent. "But what you're feeling, thinking, experiencing . . . unless you tell me what's going on inside you, I can't put myself in your place. Knowing what's happening inside someone, that's not something I'm good at. I wish I could make everything right for you. I wish I could reach out and haul that man in and throw him behind bars, but I can't."

"Oh Reed. I'm not asking you to live my life for me. Just as I can't take over yours."

"Mine?"

Mara shook her head. She blinked but didn't drop her eyes. If she faltered now, she might never get started again. "Do you have any idea what I'm talking about? Let someone else do it. There must be detectives, or the FBI, or someone, who can do it. You don't have to be the one taking those risks."

"Jack . . ."

"Yeah." The word tasted bitter. "I know. Jack. I just hope he's worth this."

"He is, Mara. He'd like to meet you."

Mara leaned back, but not enough that he couldn't go on touching her. "You told him about me?"

"When I brought him the roses."

Jack knew about her. Reed had told him. "The roses. Did he like them?"

"He was surprised, but yes, he liked them."

After days of feeling cold, Mara was suddenly aware of heat flowing loose and easy through her. She felt like a leaf twisting in a swift current, a child clinging to the metal bar holding her in a roller coaster seat. Like a child she shivered in fear. Like a child, she could barely wait for the ride to begin. "What did you tell Jack about me?"

"That I've met someone."

Someone. She was someone to Reed. Still, Mara resisted, briefly, when Reed drew her into him and touched his mouth to hers. She didn't want to care any more than she already did for this man who was so filled with dangerous and incomprehensible courage.

Did she?

The battle surged, then died. Shutting out everything, Mara gave in to the need to absorb the warmth of him, to run her fingers past buttons and fabric to strength and heat. In gratitude for the quiet oasis he'd given her, she touched her mouth to his throat. When he sighed, she arched toward him, feeling him along her length. Her daring courage shocked her, yet felt right. He'd put his own urgent task on hold to be with her. He'd told Jack about her.

When she drew away, seeking his eyes, he pulled her back to him. Their kiss began gently as if they'd never done this before, then deepened. When he asked, she parted her lips and let him in. He probed at her mouth, his hands hard and strong on her back. Mara slid her hands up to his neck. She held on, feeling the roller coaster gain momentum.

"Mara?"

"Yes?" she made herself say.

"Do you know what you're doing?" he asked with a forefinger now at the base of her throat, his mouth close to the vein at the side of her neck. Through his finger she felt his pounding heart. "What either of us is doing?"

Yes. "No."

"We should..." Now his breath feathered downward, warm and moist, touching at cleavage. "We should have talked about this. Made some rules."

Mara shivered and tossed back her head. She remained silent until his fingers took over the journey already mapped by his breath. "Yes. We should have."

But maybe it was too late for rules. He kissed her throat, the side of her neck, ran his tongue over her ear while she shivered, while she moved her fingers to his waist. They hadn't turned a light on in the living room. Night spun a shadowed web over her, the ocean a soft backdrop for emotions that weren't soft at all, that might be no easier to control than the tide.

Then, as everything except wanting was in danger of being stripped away, Mara pulled back, breathing deeply. Still wanting. Hearing the other message.

This exploration was laced with incredible danger. She was raw and fragile, her thinking skewed. In another minute, maybe in only a few seconds she might not be able to stop. And taking any more steps before she understood herself, and him, was unthinkable.

"Reed?" How had she remembered to speak? "I think..."

"You think..." His voice was as harsh as hers.

"We don't know each other well enough."

"You really believe that?" he asked, his hands now settled over her collarbone.

"You don't?"

"What I know," he said with his mouth too close to hers, "is that I want to understand you in a way I've never understood anyone else. But I'll do it at your pace. Tell me what you want, what you need."

He was handing her that awesome responsibility? "What we need is to unpack."

Holding hands, they walked out to the Corvette and pulled their belongings out of what storage space the sports car had. Reed had driven because he wanted to see how her car handled. Now, with his hand draped over her shoulder, he told her he preferred her Corvette to his Jag but wasn't sure why. Maybe it had to do with the motor sounds. Maybe it was simply because this was her car.

Mara explained that she'd been able to buy it for less than market price because the former owner had picked up too many speeding tickets and his insurance was being canceled. "I don't know if buying it was a wise move. I swear every cop in the county does a double take when he sees it." She didn't tell him how easy it had been to slide into the vehicle when he was the driver, and how difficult it was when she was the one sitting, alone, in it.

They went back inside. Reed dropped his overnight bag on his bed and followed Mara into the heavily paneled room where she'd chosen to sleep. Her belongings were folded into a duffle bag that had begun service when the Curtises all but lived in motel rooms. She pointed at a frayed strap. "I should retire this sad, old thing. It's just that every time I see it, it brings back memories."

Reed lowered himself onto the side of the bed. He watched as Mara unzipped the bag and began unpacking her clothes. She had another pair of jeans, a sleek one-piece bathing suit, shorts. A nightshirt. "No dresses? What if we decide to go out to dinner?"

"Dressing up is not my idea of a vacation."

Reed flopped back on the bed, just missing Mara's clothing. "What is your idea of a vacation?" he asked with his eyes closed and his hands under the back of his head.

The gesture stretched the fabric over Reed's chest. Mara could see the outline of his ribs, the breadth of his shoulders. His nipples pressed against taut cotton. His jeans rode low on his hips. Between his hipbones there was a firm stretch that tested her self control. She stood over him as his body drew her to him, and pressed her nails into her palms. "I don't know. I've been so many places."

"You don't have any burning desire to go anywhere?"

"I love the feeling of being settled somewhere. Of having—" *Having a sense of security? That wasn't hers these days.*

"Settled," Reed repeated. "Not having to look for new banks, no more disconnecting and connecting utilities."

"Getting to know people. Planting roses." Mara shook out a shirt, wishing it was silk because even polished cotton felt too rough at this moment. "Have you kept Jack up-to-date on what you're doing, how things are going?" she asked, trying to care without worrying.

"I've tried, but he doesn't ask many questions." Reed opened his eyes; they weren't quite focused. Mara felt as if she'd been rubbed with sandpaper. "I talked to his doctor about that, about his depression."

Mara turned away, pretending to be concerned with hanging up her clothes. "Are you sure it's depression?"

"It has to be." Reed spoke forcefully. "He wouldn't just give up like that. Not Jack."

"Maybe you don't know him as well as you thought you did."

Reed pushed himself into a sitting position and then, so quickly that it startled her, he stood. "No. I know Jack. He's one person I do know. Look, I hate admitting this, but I was up until four a.m."

"Doing what?"

"Business. Telling lies and listening to lies. Mara, I've got to hit the sack. We'll have tomorrow for..."

She'd said something to upset him, something about Jack. "Of course," Mara muttered and reached for him. The only thing she could touch was his arm. "It's exhausting, isn't it? Having to weigh everything you say." His arm under her fingers was taut. Was he thinking about that damnable commitment of his? Even tonight was he unable to shake himself free?

"I guess," Reed whispered.

Then give it up. Walk away from it. "Maybe you're the one who needs this weekend."

"Maybe. Mara? Tomorrow we could walk along the beach. Talk. Maybe we'll go swimming."

"Maybe," Mara said and dropped her hand, spreading her feet in preparation for turning away.

No. She couldn't let him go this way. Not if they weren't going to wake up strangers.

Uneasy, Mara stood on tiptoe and ran her hands over Reed's shoulders. For a moment he simply stared down at her, a puzzled look on his face, his fingers flexing and relaxing, flexing and relaxing. Then, slowly, the dark faded from his eyes. She no longer touched muscle laced with tension. "I love this place," she whispered then. "Thank you for bringing me here."

"Thank you for coming."

MARA WAS the first one up. She tiptoed around the kitchen familiarizing herself with it. She debated showering and dressing but was afraid the sound of running water, a wall away from where Reed slept, would wake him. She slid her bare feet across the floor, while the breeze from the open window over the sink cooled her legs, trying to remember if she'd actually slept or simply spent the night wrapped around the echo of Reed's final words.

Mara had poured herself a cup of coffee and was sipping it, trying to rouse her brain, when she realized she wasn't alone. For a moment she did no more than hold on to her cup and tell herself she would go through the day without touching Reed, without undoing everything she'd spent the night fortifying herself against. Walk along the beach, he'd suggested. Talk. Swim. That was enough to build a day on.

Then Reed touched her back. "One of my greatest fantasies," he whispered, his voice husky with sleep. "Waking up to find a woman fixing me coffee."

Gathering what was left of her resolve, Mara stepped out of his reach. Concentrating on what she was doing, she picked up a cup and waved it at him. "It's instant."

"Instant." Reed watched while she spooned out crystals and added hot water. "Instant always smells better than it tastes."

He'd pulled on jeans but hadn't bothered with a shirt. Mara stood barefoot in the middle of the enormous kitchen a foot away from his sleep-warmed body. Now, feeling Reed's presence, she knew why she hadn't slept. "Eggs? Are eggs all right?"

"Anything. Can I help?"

"You could mix up some orange juice."

He presented her with a little boy's smile. "Orange juice it is. You look wonderful. I had to tell you that. You look wonderful."

Under the weight of his compliment, Mara dropped her eyes. They should talk about the tide, about how to regulate the gas range. He shouldn't be taking up space she needed for herself. Still, when he moved to the refrigerator, she felt the small loss.

It was too chilly to eat on the deck. When breakfast was ready, Mara and Reed took their plates into the living room with its sliding glass door and sat on opposite sides of the couch while they watched distant seagulls playing in the wind. When they were done, Reed refilled their coffee cups, this time settling himself a few inches closer. Mara asked if he knew who owned the cabin, but afterward she couldn't remember what he told her. He still hadn't put on a shirt. He needed a shave.

And he hadn't touched her again.

After doing the breakfast dishes together, Reed brought up his earlier suggestion that they explore their surroundings. In an effort to keep the moment light, Mara pulled a coin out of her purse and flipped it to see who would get the first shower. She won.

She was standing on the deck running her fingers through her hair to dry it when Reed, smelling of soap and shampoo and clean cotton, joined her. Wordlessly, he took her hairbrush and began brushing the back of her head. Mara started to lean toward him, then caught her balance. His scent, his dangerous scent, was already inside her.

"A walk?" she began unsteadily. "Before other people show up."

The brush moved toward her crown. Reed's fingers blazed the way, once again sanding her flesh into sensitivity. "I love your hair."

"I need to have it cut."

"The sun's on it. It looks as if there's gold in it."

Gold in her dark hair. Mara pulled the brush out of Reed's hands, knowing she wasn't strong enough to meet his eyes, and stumbled into the first thing that came to mind. "I wish we had the beach to ourselves," she told him. "Can't we chase everyone away? Claim squatters' rights."

"They'd just come back, Mara."

"Yes. I guess they would."

He reached out to do nothing more than curve a strand of hair over her ear, and she couldn't think. "If I could," he whispered, "if it were possible for me to do such things, we'd have the world to ourselves."

Oh God! Tears stung Mara's eyes. Her arms felt both leaden and lighter than air. This was a solitary man, one who had devoted himself to only one other human, and now he was telling her he wanted to give her the world. "We can pretend," she whispered. If she turned, if she so much as moved, they would wind up in each other's arms, and she would make love to this stranger.

Yet she wanted. Despite all reason, she wanted.

But the need to know how he'd come to this place in his life, and whether there was room for her in it, was stronger. "You can't," she told him and walked into the house.

He didn't immediately follow.

MARA'S EMOTIONS were easier to handle once they'd put on tennis shoes and were wandering along the beach. Except for an older foursome who told Mara and Reed they were there from Kansas for the summer, the clean stretch of sand was deserted. While Mara studied the sand-flecked suds left behind by retreating waves, Reed asked the vacationers detailed questions about their homes. By the time they parted company, groups of teenagers had begun to show up. She'd been right. Reed couldn't keep the world away.

It didn't take Mara long to realize that a separate universe from any she'd ever been part of existed on the beaches of Southern California. Girls in bathing suits so brief she had no idea how the fabric did its job were being ogled by muscular young men. Boom boxes blasted out everything from hard rock to rap. The scent of suntan oil filled the air.

"Don't any of them work?" Reed asked as, hand in hand, they skirted a large group in the process of setting up a volleyball net.

"It's the weekend," Mara reminded him.

"People don't get tans like that if they don't live in the sun."

Mara had to agree. She felt out of place, herself, in her shorts and loose top, but she wasn't about to dress in two square inches of fabric just to blend in. She didn't want strange men staring at her. If Reed wasn't with her, she wasn't sure she would have stayed on the beach at all.

"My college roommate went to Fort Lauderdale three years in a row," Reed told her. "I always figured spring vacation was a good time to make some money. Now I'm sorry I didn't go with him."

"Are you?"

"Yeah. I am. We weren't that close, but I think we would have had a good time."

"If you could, would you go back?" A beach ball bounced off her foot. Mara picked up the ball and tossed it to a grinning blonde with a tan so dark that his sleek black suit blended into the background. The blonde ran his eyes down her, then nodded. Mara tensed and avoided eye contact. "Would you want to live your teen years over?" she asked.

"They weren't my best. Would you?"

Mara watched a trio of girls being chased by musclemen. The girls didn't put out much effort and were soon hauled, squealing, into the ocean. Because Reed was close, the hard contact didn't make her shiver. "No. I don't think so. The emotional ups and downs that go with being a teenager... I can't help thinking about the young people who don't fit into this scene. The majority. Maybe they don't have the right bodies or the freedom or money. Do they feel as if they're missing something important?"

"I don't know." Reed squeezed Mara's hand and smiled down at her. His touch was casual, nothing more than a way to keep them together in the growing crowd. Still, Mara felt rich for the contact. This weekend had been planned so they could become friends. It was happening.

A moment later Reed led her toward an ice-cream stand. "Maybe they do," he continued. "It's hard to judge something we don't have. To imagine a different life. To be objective, even critical about something that looks perfect from the outside."

This was a man who claimed to know not enough about the forces ruling his parents? "Yes it is," she said before stepping up to the stand. In a clear voice, she placed her order.

Over chocolate cones, Reed elaborated on his belief that, although these sun-kissed young people enjoyed a freedom most people never experienced, in the long haul it was those who were working at fast-food restaurants and construction sites who would be better prepared for life. Mara agreed.

They sat cross-legged on the sand watching a volleyball game in which the only point seemed to be the amount of body contact allowed. Mara lingered over the rich taste of her ice cream before tossing the cone to a stalking seagull.

"I haven't spent much time trying to analyze life," she said, deeply appreciative of her ability to once again enjoy the food she'd associated with her attack, and knowing who was responsible for the change. "Discussing philosophy isn't something the Curtis family does."

"Action, not contemplation?"

"Something like that."

Because noisy children had discovered the ice-cream stand, Mara and Reed got up and wandered away from the attraction. They walked aimlessly for a long while, while Mara tried to hold on to sights and sounds. But Reed had his arm over her shoulder, and her arm was around his waist, and she couldn't think.

The beach stretched for miles. After emptying her tennis shoes of sand several times, Mara gave up and walked barefoot with her shoes dangling from her free hand. A few minutes later Reed did the same, leaning on her while he struggled with a lace.

Reed helped a man drag a large piece of driftwood to his car. Mara kept an eye on a toddler while the mother nursed a baby. They talked and sometimes they were silent. Eventually they turned around and started back toward the beach house. They passed expensive homes, speculating about what kind of people lived in them and occasionally trying to picture themselves as the ones surrounded by luxury.

Mara knew she didn't need luxury; she had Reed's hand.

The house's interior was now too warm. While Reed opened windows, Mara made iced tea, and they went onto the patio to watch more seagulls and discuss the vital issue of what they would eat for lunch. Reed maintained they needed to go to a grocery store. Mara, grateful to have something mundane to talk about, contended that they had enough on hand and anyone with an ounce of imagination could come up with a decent meal. The teasing made her feel a little, but not enough, like a long-married woman.

"Tomato soup and crackers is not going to keep me alive," Reed grumbled a half hour later. "Do you have any idea how much sodium is in canned soup?"

"You're eating it."

"I'm eating but I refuse to enjoy it."

Once their meal was out of the way, Mara gave in. An expedition to the grocery store was, like it or not, in order if they were going to eat in tonight. Maybe, Reed offered, they could go to a restaurant. He didn't look enthusiastic about it, and Mara told him that it wasn't necessary. She knew he ate more meals in public than in private. She wouldn't subject him to yet another restaurant. Besides, they hadn't come to the ocean to sample the skill of some chef.

THE FIRST STORE they walked into was outrageously expensive. Even though it meant putting more mileage on the Corvette, Mara refused to patronize it.

"I have no idea how you managed to live in southern California for as long as you have," Reed teased a half hour later. Although a stop at a gas station would have cleared up the mystery, at the moment, neither of them had the slightest idea where they were. Somehow they'd managed to leave the beach road and were weaving through Pacific Beach's residential streets.

Mara didn't care. The Corvette was humming, its sounds as familiar as before the attack. Reed sat beside her, easing the car through quiet streets. He kept his hand wrapped over the gearshift, muscles contracting as he slipped through gears. When a teenager driving a black pickup with massive tires pulled alongside, Reed looked over at it, then nodded. His fingers tightened around the steering wheel, and he straighted his spine. For a moment Mara thought he might answer the challenge being issued by the truck's revving engine. She would have. With Reed's nearness driving her mood, she needed sudden, dangerous speed. Instead, after a moment, Reed shrugged. Still, a boyish smile touched his lips. Watching him, Mara felt young. Together they'd race the wind.

He turned his smile on her, and she became interested in something far different from a simple race.

Reed was responsible.

Mara nodded as they passed through a neighborhood of Spanish-style houses. The yards were tiny but the houses large and clean and expensive looking. Swimming pools and garage door openers were the norm. "Would you like to live in one of these?" she asked, surprised that her voice sounded normal.

"Whatever for?"

"Wouldn't you rather have a home than an apartment?"

"Maybe. But not one of these cookie cutter things." Reed turned down a narrow street and slowed to avoid a cat that darted in front of him. "When and if I buy my own place, it's going to be in the country. Maybe I'll farm. Grub in the earth."

Reed, a farmer? "There isn't any acreage left," she told him. "Not around here."

"Yes there is. You just have to be willing to pay for it."

He was looking at her, his eyes asking . . . what? "I don't see you as a farmer," she said.

"Don't you?"

"You'd have to put down roots, Reed." Mara kept her tone light.

"Yeah." The word took a long time. "I've never done that, have I? Never tried. Mara, do you do this much? Wander around. Look?"

He'd changed the subject. "No. Not much," she told him.

"Because you're happy where you live?"

"Because . . . maybe because I've never seen the purpose. Never taken the time." Today she had the time. And the reason was sitting beside her. "I think, if I had a choice, maybe I wouldn't be living in this part of the state. I love the climate, and it's a good place for the business. But . . ."

"But what?"

"Maybe I'm just feeling restless these days. I'd like to show you the Sierra Nevadas, the wine country. The pace is different there. Slower. There are seasons. And colors so vivid it makes me want to cry." Had she really said that? Felt that? Reed was responsible; he made her feel so much.

Once again he gifted her with a smile. "I'd like to do that."

Ahead of them a young boy waited for the Corvette to pass so he could cross the street. Mara turned, watching the boy gather himself and explode into action. He ran as if propelled by the joy of life. Mara hadn't touched Reed since they got back in the car. Now she placed her hand over his. And tapped his energy when she was already exploding with her own. "Maybe we can," she told him. "Head north. Follow one-lane roads through rolling hills."

Under her fingers Reed rotated his hand, pressing palm to palm. "When this is over for me. We'll do it then."

We.

Groceries weren't important. Wandering aimlessly through neighborhoods neither of them knew existed before today no longer diverted her. Mara pointed at the first grocery they came to. She grabbed a basket and began tossing items into it. Eat? She couldn't imagine ever needing food again. The store wasn't large enough to contain her. There were too many people. Too many lights. Too much noise when she needed to hear only Reed's heart.

The world narrowed, fading away as they left the parking lot. Once again Reed spread his fingers over the black gearshift, and Mara fought to keep her hand off his. He looked over at her, not smiling. Not speaking.

It was just as well. She seemed to have forgotten how to speak.

After the groceries had been put away, Mara slipped out of her shoes and stood in the doorway to her room, waiting for Reed to come out of his. They should have raced that black pickup. She would suggest an ocean swim instead. Would she tire before they reached Hawaii?

Feeling both nerveless and nerve filled, Mara walked into the living room and sat on the couch closest to the patio. A half second later she got up and slid the door open. The ocean breeze touched her temples but cooled nothing. She breathed, deep, not deep enough.

If she didn't do something, she would explode.

Reed walked into the room. His bare feet made the faintest sound as he stepped around the couch and stood before her. She stared at his feet, his ankles. He'd changed into shorts. Softly curving brown hair caressed his calves and thighs. A single, faded scar trailed around the outside of his right knee. Mara opened her mouth; for too long nothing came out. "How did that happen?" she whispered.

"Bicycle accident," Reed said and sat down. His thigh, his naked thigh touched hers. Mara held her breath. It seemed that he was doing the same.

Slowly Reed ran his forefinger over the thin, white line. "I was looking at the stereo system here," he told her. "Maybe you'd like to hear it."

"Later."

"Have you looked at the books? Maybe there's one you'd like to read."

"Maybe."

Again Reed held his breath. "Are you all right?"

"All right?"

"You're quiet."

"I—I guess I didn't sleep very well last night," she said, although that wasn't it at all. "A strange bed."

"Yeah." Before she could stop him, Reed turned her away from him and began rubbing her neck, not as she ministered to her father when old injuries bothered him, but with fingers that tapped into something deep inside her, something struggling to be set free.

She had to think, about anything. "You slept all right?" she asked.

"Well enough."

"Good."

Reed worked his fingers lower, pressing his thumbs against her shoulder blades. Mara concentrated on breathing. She was tired. That was it. Exhaustion had depleted her defenses. If she'd slept last night, she wouldn't be so aware of his knee nudging the base of her spine.

Reed spoke with his mouth so close to her temple that every word sent a shiver through her. "I love it here," he told her. "Maybe I belong on the edge of the ocean."

Fighting for strength, Mara nodded at a couple of joggers kicking up sand in the distance. "Even if you don't have the beach to yourself?"

"There won't be anyone on my beach. No one I don't want there," Reed said as he touched his lips to the back of her neck.

Mara started. She told herself to relax but wasn't sure that was possible. All he'd done was begin to work the tension out of her body. She should be grateful for that. She was. Only...

"Mara? What's wrong?"

You. You're what's wrong, and what's right, with me. "I'm just tired."

"Lean against me," he whispered, his breath taking over where his lips had been. "Try to sleep."

Sleep? With Reed touching her? "I don't know if I can."

"You can if you listen to your body. You've been walking for hours, breathing in salt air, fighting the wind. Give your muscles the opportunity to unwind."

"How do you know that's what they need?"

"I've been walking over the same sand, breathing in the same air. And I probably got more sleep than you did. You're just lucky I decided to give you a neck rub instead of the other way around."

"You'd do that?" Mara asked teasingly. To her surprise, she felt her body begin to grow slack. "You'd make me do all the work?"

"If I thought I could get away with it." Reed's voice slowed. Either that, or the whole world had shifted down to first gear. "No. Not really," he said, his breath touching her. "This is something I want to do for you. Something you need." He ran his thumbs over the top of her spinal column, the sensation somehow spreading throughout her body.

"I could— This is something I could grow very accustomed to."

"Good. You deserve to be pampered." Reed rotated his thumbs outward, erasing tension as he went. "And I deserve to be the one doing it for you."

"Deserve? That's how you..."

"Yes," Reed went on when she couldn't think of what she'd been going to say. "That's the way I see it."

Chapter Ten

An hour later Reed was still sitting while Mara, asleep, nestled against him. He'd been aware of a warm breeze and salt air and distant, indistinguishable sounds, but those were in the background.

Mara represented reality. And an incredibly hard battle.

Reed touched his lips to her temple, then slid away from her. The cabin came equipped with a telephone, but he had no intention of making contact with the outside world. If he thought Jack could help him deal with wanting to make love to Mara and knowing they weren't ready for that, he would have called his old friend. But this wasn't something Jack or anyone else could help him with.

After tucking a pillow under Mara's head, Reed stepped onto the deck so he could watch the sun set. The distant sound of voices reached him, but this stretch of beach was almost deserted. The hot colors cast by the setting sun reminded him of the evening he'd taught her to use a gun, and made him pensive.

She was an incredible woman.

Mara, brave and competent and utterly unlike the woman who'd raised him, had taken steps to put her attack behind her.

She'd moved back into her home. That act itself served as his yardstick. She trusted her surroundings. Surely he could do the same. But there was still a criminal on the loose.

Every time he thought about her—which seemed to be all the time—Reed slammed up against that reality. True, Mara had learned how to use a gun and now kept it close to her. She *had* drawn back the first time he'd touched her. But for her, that was yesterday.

He was the one who'd jumped to the worst possible conclusion when he'd heard that the police had come across an agitated watchdog. He'd called her, demanding what? He'd wound up bringing her here for the weekend, and then risking this fragile thing they'd begun by letting his physical need for her threaten to take over.

He should go for a cold swim. A long one.

"Reed? I'm sorry. I didn't know I was going to pass out like that."

Without turning from the fading day, Reed reached back for her hand. She came willingly and stood next to him. "That's all right," he said, thinking that he should be halfway to Hawaii instead of holding her hand. "I was watching. Thinking."

"About what?"

"You," he said and faced her.

"What kind of thoughts?"

"Complicated ones."

"What do you mean?"

"If I knew, they wouldn't be complicated." He had to stop talking like this. Otherwise, everything might pour out of him. "Are you hungry?"

Mara leaned her head against his shoulder, her sleep-warmed body reminding him yet again of why he'd left her on the couch. "After all that tomato soup? Maybe a little later. Did you want to do anything?"

It was a loaded question, one Reed had no intention of touching. "Do you think there are any islands for sale?" He pretended to scan the horizon. "The idea of living where I could see the ocean no matter where I turned..."

Mara's laugh was a breeze touching nerves already too alive. "You keep changing your mind," she chided him. "You don't know where you want to settle, do you?"

No. That's the hell of it. "I'm keeping my options open," he told her. "One of us would have to become a pilot. Otherwise we wouldn't have any way to get to the island."

"We? I don't remember my name being on the deed."

When she shifted her weight and brought her leg too close to his, Reed decided it was time he changed the subject. It would be dark in a few minutes. He suggested they either start dinner or go down to the beach. Mara wanted to walk.

They didn't go far this time. Muted sounds still came from others out there somewhere, but within a few minutes of stepping into the surf, they were surrounded by enough shadows that the sounds didn't matter. Mara held Reed's hand and buried her bare feet in the sand. She felt foam bubbling around her ankles. She couldn't remember the last time she'd wanted it to be night.

Reed had wanted to spend the weekend with her. Despite his commitment to a man named Jack, he'd planned this time for them. He'd said it was so they could get to know each other, and she'd agreed. Only, friendship didn't have enough to do with why she needed to be out here with him, the ocean chilling her legs. Hopefully chilling more than that. "This island of yours? You promise no typhoons?"

"Absolutely." Reed drew her further into the water until it boiled around their thighs. "And no property taxes. That's the way it is with islands."

"I get to be the pilot. I've always wanted to fly."

"Have you? If you fly the way you drive—"

"You've never seen me drive, not really."

Reed gave her a not quite lazy, not quite teasing look. "I've been thinking about that. You know what I've concluded? You aren't racing with your family because you're too much of a menace. You've probably been banned from every track in the country."

"What do you know? You're the one with the speeding tickets."

"Probably because you bribe cops."

"What?" Mara jerked on Reed's hand, turning him toward her. She loved the glint of amusement in his eyes. "How dare you!"

"What's the matter?" he taunted. "Can't you handle the truth?"

Teeth bared in mock rage, Mara leaned into Reed as if to push him into the ocean. When he resisted, she catapulted herself at him. Reed staggered and gave way. He landed first, hips and shoulders digging into wet sand. As she collapsed on top of him, Mara felt cold water and flesh, hard bones and firm muscle beneath her. A wave washed over them; sand rubbed at her skin. "How dare you!" she repeated. "I happen to be the greatest driver in the world."

"The greatest? Don't make me laugh." Reed waited until the wave retreated and then surged to his feet. Before Mara could do more than scramble to her knees, he planted his hands on her shoulders, holding her down so that the next wave covered her to her neck. "Mediocre, maybe. No better than marginal."

"What? Let me up!" Mara scrambled out from under Reed's grip, but before she found her footing, another wave caught her. This time she floated; her legs trailing against his.

As the wave began to retreat, Reed reached down and grabbed her around the waist. He was off balance. If she wanted to try, she might be able to upend him again and defuse the charged moment.

Instead, with her hair streaming into her eyes, Mara reached for him.

Fire. Water and sand had become fire. In a moment, a breath, a heartbeat, everything became electric. The flames were fanned by Reed's breath. Reed's touch. The heat settled so deep inside her that Mara could only guess at its core. As long as she remained in his arms, she would be on fire.

No part of her wanted anything different.

Mara leaned forward to taste the salt on Reed's chest. His groan spurred her on. Now she stood with her legs spread against the waves and touched her tongue first to one nipple and then the other. He pulled her close, imprisoning her. For an instant Mara acknowledged fear.

But this wasn't an angry man with a grating voice. Reed held her. Reed with a courage she was determined to match and a commitment that made every day, every moment they spent together precious.

The waves continued to play with her ankles, legs and hips, separating her from the world. Mara shut her mind and heart to everything except the promise in Reed's kiss. The challenge in his touch.

Reed pushed aside fabric and touched the swell of her breasts with cool, wet fingers. The slight friction caused by sand-dusted flesh made Mara forget the surging water. "If you don't want this," he whispered, "tell me."

"I want."

"You're sure? Last night—"

Mara wrapped her arms around Reed and drew him to her, savoring the taste of salty lips. She shivered, regretting what she'd done. He could still hold her and warm her, but her breasts were no longer accessible to him. "I can't believe we're here," she whispered. "That we're actually—"

"I wish it didn't have to be this way."

"It's all right. Reed, it's all right."

"I hope." She felt the quick warmth of his breath on her face and stood on tiptoe, savoring him. Standing in the cool, foaming surf she could be reckless and bold. She could part her lips and allow him access. She could—

He still held her against his strength. His legs, like hers, were parted against the pull of the ocean. Mara absorbed the powerful give and take, but where the sea gave up and her need for Reed took over she couldn't say. She felt an ageless rhythm and knew it came from within her.

She wanted to stand here forever, holding, swaying, being tempted by dark wetness. Ignoring the cold.

"Not here," Reed whispered. "We can't stay here."

Mara might have argued except that he was right. He'd known she needed to be with him this weekend, that she had needed her own room last night. Now he'd known that it was time to leave the water and return to the cabin. "Someone might see?"

"You're going to freeze. Take my hand."

He expected her to walk. How could she do that when she felt as if she was both capable of flying and just learning to crawl? Still, Mara stumbled after Reed as he led her out of the water. Now the breeze on her wet, naked legs and arms made a chilling impact. Her numb toes dug into the path that led up to the house.

"I didn't plan that. What happened in the water, I don't know if it was right," Reed told her as they stood on the patio and slapped at the sand that clung to them.

Mara found her voice. "I don't, either."

"Are you sorry?"

Mara had no way of answering him. It hadn't been said. Neither of them had spoken the words. And yet she knew he was thinking about exchanging their separate bedrooms for one. She had only to feel him next to her to think the same thing. Making love with Reed would be an act of supreme trust. To share her body with him meant giving up her independence and, even more important, her privacy.

The consequences both thrilled and terrified her.

"I don't know," she told him. "I'm scared."

Reed eased her inside and shut the door behind them. "Of me?"

"Maybe I'm afraid of me." Saying the words took a great deal out of her. Mara slid onto the couch and let her head fall back. She was still aroused and that made thinking nearly impossible. She spoke slowly, feeling her way. "I wanted to be with you. When you told me about this place, all I could think was that we'd be together. But, Reed, I didn't want any pressure to—''

Reed touched her shoulder, roughened fingertips catching against damp, cool, sensitive flesh. She jumped and tried not to let it show. ''Do you feel as if I'm pressuring you?'' he asked.

''I don't know.'' No. That wasn't enough of an answer. She had to speak; he had to hear. ''I don't feel that kind of pressure. If I said no, you'd respect that. And if I said yes...''

''But?''

Did she really want to tell him this? Could she not? ''Reed, there's something... You're part of my life, and yet you're not. No. Don't shake your head. You know I'm right. What you're doing—if something happened to you, it might be days, weeks before I found out. There's so much you can't share with me.'' *So much I haven't shared with you.*

''What do you want me to say?''

Mara whispered. ''Nothing. Reed, you believe in what you're doing. I think I understand why. I'm trying to. If I asked you not to do it, it would be like asking my father to give up his love affair with speed. I'd never do that.''

''But—''

''But I'm not sure I'm ready to be part of what little you can share.''

Reed looked as if she'd slapped him. ''This isn't enough?''

''No. It isn't,'' she told him, wondering at her wisdom, or if there was anything wise about what she was saying. ''If we became lovers...anything like that, and then... Don't you see?''

''Maybe.''

For a long time Reed did nothing except hold her. Slowly she stopped shivering. She told herself she couldn't possibly want him as much as she did. It was a dream. When he finally spoke, Mara held on to his every word. "You're strong," he said. "Stronger than I wish you were."

No, I'm not. Don't call me that. "Reed, I don't know what I'm saying. What I feel around you. What we're doing now, this weekend, I need it."

"But you're saying maybe this is as far as it should go?"

Mara tried to take a calming breath. It came out a shudder. "Yes. That's what I'm saying."

They didn't leave the beach house until late on Sunday. They spent hours walking, talking, looking through a newspaper for unoccupied islands and million-dollar beach homes, sharing dreams, being together. To the outside world, they knew they must look like friends, but Mara knew they were more than that. Friends didn't sit together on the same couch talking about islands and scarred knees while energy hummed and arced between them.

Mara remembered little of the drive home except that Reed didn't turn on the car stereo and spoke only when she did, which was seldom. As soon as he dropped her off, he would head back to the city. That alien world of his would reclaim him. She couldn't follow him. She didn't know when she'd see him again. Or, if she would.

"I wish there was another way," he told her after he'd checked her house and garage and asked her to show him that the gun was within reach on her nightstand.

"There isn't."

"No. I don't suppose there is." Sighing, Reed cupped Mara's shoulders, holding her against him. "Thank you. For... instant coffee and tomato soup. Mara, you can call me. Remember that. You can call."

"What if you aren't there?"

"If I'm not— Look, no matter what, I'll stay in touch."

In touch? She knew she should tell him she didn't want to see him again, that her own life was all she could handle. Only a crazy woman would let herself care about a man who had to watch his every step, weigh each word. Who disappeared into an Alice in Wonderland world.

"I'll leave the answering machine on. Be careful." *Don't get yourself killed.* "Please."

"I will."

Silent, Reed dipped his head, asking permission. The "crazy woman" she'd become met him halfway.

A minute later she stood at the door to her home and watched Reed drive away. Then Mara stepped back, called Lobo to her, and locked the door, closing the two of them inside.

When she could no longer hear Reed's car, she snapped on the TV. Maybe Reed would be turning on the car stereo, like her, needing to escape the silence of thoughts. But he wouldn't cry. Oh no, Reed wouldn't cry.

MARA WOKE before the alarm went off, the tension that had driven her from racetracks dominating her. The feeling lasted until the shower took her away from the night. She and Reed would be together again as soon as he could arrange it. He'd promised. In the meantime she would be strong.

The vow lasted until Clint showed up for work. He looked at her more frequently than usual but said nothing until the lunch break. "You're looking calm," he said. "A lot calmer than I thought you would."

"Calm?"

"You read Sunday's paper didn't you?"

The newspaper had been the last thing on Mara's mind. "What did I miss?"

Clint looked like a man who'd just opened Pandora's box. "There was another attack."

Mara took a deep breath. "It's a big city, Clint. There are attacks all the time."

"Not to women leaving grocery stores." Clint took her arm, forcing Mara to face him. "Believe me, I tried to tell myself the same thing. But I called that detective. He said it sounds like the same man."

"It does?" Her voice sounded thin. "Why didn't Kline call me? He could have left a message."

"Haven't you heard? The victim is always the last to know. How was your weekend?"

The weekend seemed a hundred years ago. "What else did Kline say?"

"Not much. The woman was grabbed early Sunday morning. She's a nurse. She'd just gotten off work and was doing her shopping at one of those places that stays open twenty-four hours."

"Is she—" Mara stared up at Clint. She couldn't form the words.

Clint ran his hands over Mara's shoulder. The touch felt nothing like Reed's, but it helped. It reminded her she wasn't alone. "She's alive. She wasn't as lucky as you."

Lucky? "She's—"

"She's in the hospital."

"Oh." Mara felt both concern and compassion for the other woman. Those emotions fought for time with an inescapable fact: her attacker was still shattering people's lives.

"Are you going to be all right?" Clint asked. "You don't look so good."

No. I'm not all right. "Do you— Maybe I should visit her. See if there's something I can do."

"I asked Kline. I guess they've got some rape counseling people at the hospital. I'm sure they're talking to her."

Mara almost laughed, but she knew if she let the sound begin, it might turn into something ugly. Of course she didn't want to be in a hospital, facing the aftermath of having been raped, but if she had been, there would have been a support group for her, too. She might even have found someone to tell certain things to. "That's good," she said distractedly. "Clint? Thanks for telling me."

"Don't thank me. It's the last thing I wanted to do."

SOMEHOW MARA got through the rest of the day, but the thought of what the other woman had endured was never far from her mind. She thought about calling Reed at the hotel, but stopped herself. He had his own agenda to deal with. This was something she had to handle. As soon as she could, she went through the newspaper until she found the article. It said that the woman had been taken to a downtown hospital. Mara called Detective Kline and got the woman's name. She called the hospital. Yes, Rennie Chambers was a patient, and yes, she could have visitors.

Mara climbed into the Corvette and started toward the city. She'd covered a mile before she realized which car she was driving. It was too late to go back and change vehicles. Besides, if she did, she would be admitting defeat. Still, she slowed.

Rennie Chambers's husband was with her. Hesitantly, Mara introduced herself. "I should have come sooner," she stammered. "Maybe it won't make any difference, but I wanted to let you know. You aren't the first."

Frank Chambers indicated the other chair in the room. "He got you, too?"

Mara sank into the uncomfortable seat. "I managed to escape before... Maybe it wasn't the same man, but... I guess..." She ran her fingers through her hair. She hadn't remembered to comb it. "I thought maybe you needed someone to talk to."

Rennie's right hand was in a cast. With her left hand she gripped her husband. "I think I've told my story a thousand times," she said in a hoarse voice. "I can't seem to stop. I feel sick every time I go over that horrible— A social worker came to see me. She said it was normal to act and feel the way I do. I guess the more I talk, the sooner I'll be able to put it behind me."

Mara wanted to tell Rennie that she hadn't been able to put her attack behind her, but they weren't the same people, and the circumstances were different. Yes, Rennie had been raped, but Rennie had a supportive husband and the hospital social worker and people from the rape crisis center coming to see her.

There wasn't anyone for Mara.

Mara stayed for the better part of an hour. She was able to talk about most of the details of her own abduction. She even hinted at the aftershock she was experiencing. The couple expressed outrage toward the rapist and their determination to do whatever they could to bring him to justice. Rennie had tried to remember details, but except for build, her description of the man didn't match the ones given by the earlier victims. Frank Chambers pointed out that Detective Kline had mentioned he suspected the rapist was deliberately altering his appearance.

"I keep thinking about that," Frank said. "He knows what he's doing."

Mara remembered little of what they talked about after that. Rennie was going to be released in the morning. Her sister was taking time off work to watch the Chamberses' two children while their mother recuperated, and Frank's parents had flown in this morning. Because Frank never left his wife's side, Mara hadn't felt free to ask Rennie if her attacker had forced certain words from her.

"YOU'VE NEVER HEARD the word *fear*, have you?" Mara asked Lobo once she had brought him inside the mobile home and locked the doors and windows. "There isn't anything you don't think you can handle."

She checked her answering machine. There weren't any messages from Reed. Had he forgotten her already?

Of course not. He'd given her his weekend, let her know he wanted to make love to her. If he ever found a deserted island, she'd be the one to fly him there.

Call me, he'd told her. She could do that. They'd talk about— No. She would not run to him seeking courage. She would not!

With the help of a glass of warm milk and thoughts of a man and a woman tumbling together in the surf, Mara fell asleep. She woke in the middle of the night, a thought hammering through her. Was it possible...had that animal come looking for her first, and when he hadn't been able to find her, gone after another victim?

Mara slipped out of bed. She pushed aside the curtains and looked out at the night. She could see the garden Reed had admired, the rose bushes he'd culled to take to Jack when he told the older man that he'd met someone. The moon was as bright as it had been on the coast, but this time there was no promise in its silvered light. There were only shadows.

Was that a movement? No. Of course not.

Mara continued to stare at the base of the tree her father had planted soon after she'd bought the property. The tree had grown quickly, but the trunk wasn't broad enough to hide anyone.

There. The trunk looked misshapen, as if someone was standing behind it. Mara shut off a moan. No! It wasn't anything.

A movement? Had her eyes caught a movement? Thoroughly frightened now, Mara dropped the curtain and hurried from the bedroom. It wasn't until she tore a fingernail trying to lock an already locked kitchen window that she stopped herself.

This was insane! She'd spent an hour talking to Rennie Chambers; her imagination was in high gear. Despite what she told herself earlier, and although she knew she might waken him, she would call Reed. Talking to him would calm her nerves. Then she would climb into bed and go back to sleep.

Only, Reed wasn't at the hotel. And what she wanted to tell him wasn't something she could share with the woman at the switchboard.

MARA HAD JUST let Lobo out and was heading toward the shower when she heard a car approaching. For a moment her middle-of-the-night thoughts ruled her, but this was morning. Sane, rational morning.

And Reed was driving the car.

Mara stood at the door, waiting for him. She hadn't lost him after all. He hadn't been lost to the night, to whatever it was that claimed him these days. Now all she had to do was keep him from learning that she'd spent the night half believing she'd never see him again. "What are you doing here?" she asked.

He jammed his hands into his back pockets and then pulled them out. "Seeing you."

"But—"

Ignoring her disheveled hair and the short gown clinging to her body, Reed stepped forward and took her in his arms. There'd been no way he could contact her last night. None, damn it. He wouldn't blame her if she gave up on him.

But she let herself be held, and if she kissed him now, he could stop asking himself if she had regretted their weekend. Regretted ever meeting him. Her soft response supplied the necessary answer. Still, Reed held back. "Kline told me there was another supermarket abduction," he said.

"I know."

Reed ran his hand roughly up and down Mara's back, warming her through her nightshirt. If he wasn't careful she would sense his fear, and he had to be calm for her. He had to let her think—what? "You know?"

Still holding on to him, Mara explained that Clint had made the connection. "I went to see the victim, Reed. He broke her wrist and she has a concussion."

"Was that wise? Going to see her, I mean?"

"Wise? I'm glad I did. I think it helped her."

"Her?"

"Yes, of course. Why do you think I went?"

"I don't know. I just didn't expect it. I hope she's going to be all right. Mara, you're shivering."

"Am I?" Her body tightened. When she took her next breath, the trembling stopped. "I was on my way to the shower, Reed. It's cold standing around in a nightshirt."

Wondering if the cool morning air explained everything, Reed steered her toward the bathroom. Then he went into the kitchen to make breakfast. He'd found a cantaloupe and was cutting into it when he realized it had to be almost eighty degrees in the trailer. He unlocked a window and pushed it open. For a moment he stood leaning over the sink, one hand on the window, the other holding the cantaloupe.

Forget Jack. Forget the insane assignment. Stay here.

But he couldn't.

"You didn't tell me," Mara said when she returned. She wore jeans and one of her cotton shirts. She'd put on a little makeup. For him? "What were you doing seeing the detective?"

Reed went back to looking for bowls to put the cantaloupe in. She was standing across the room, at the entrance to the kitchen, yet he could smell her shampoo and a hint of perfume. "Touching base. Getting some more information from the computer. Kline was there." Reed didn't add that he'd sought the detective out because he'd wanted to be told that Mara's abductor had left the state.

"What kind of information, Reed? Those people you're dealing with, how many times have they been arrested?"

"They haven't. At least not most of them. But I'm not here to talk about them." There was nothing left for him to do at the counter. "You're all right? Damn it, Mara. He knows where you live."

Mara shrugged. She'd washed her hair, but hadn't combed it yet. It lay close to her head, making her look young and small and in need of being held. Every nerve in him ached with the need to go to her and do exactly that, but she wasn't closing the space now separating them. He had to respect that. "We've gone through this before, Reed."

Reed started to hand her a cup of coffee. He wanted to pretend they were nothing more than lovers sharing a few moments together. But they weren't lovers. And what had brought him here... Shaken, Reed set down her cup and held out his hand. For a moment she simply stared at him. Then, her steps slow, she came into the light. Wordlessly, Reed folded her into his arms. He kissed her, or rather they kissed. The embrace lasted a long time and nearly stripped Reed of everything except wanting her. "When I heard—" he managed.

"I'm sorry you had to."

Sorry? The word stung. "Tell me something. If I hadn't found out, would you have mentioned it?"

"I don't know. I tried to call you last night. You weren't in."

"You don't know? Why not? Because I'm not important enough to tell."

"Stop it." Mara pulled away and reached for her cup with a trembling hand. A little coffee slopped out, and she set it back down. "You have to know the answer to that."

"Do I? Look, I'm sorry." He picked up a washrag and wiped the counter. This was insane. He sounded like a jealous lover. If he wasn't careful, he'd push her away. "I had no business saying that. It's just that when I heard..."

"I understand," she said softly, gifting him with one of her rare and beautiful smiles. "I felt the same way when Clint told me. But, what happened to that woman happened. My being shocked, either of us being shocked, isn't going to change that."

He's still around. That's the issue. He's still around. "No. I guess it isn't. Look, all I could find was some bread and melon. Do you want more than toast?"

"Toast is fine." This time when Mara picked up her cup, there was no mishap. Her smile didn't quite evolve into something he could take with him, but at least they were talking to each other. He knew better than to press.

He also knew better than to take her in his arms again before he'd gotten himself back under control.

There wasn't time for anything except a shared meal before Reed had to leave. Because she asked, he explained that he was going to be shown a man's private automobile collection today. The owner, who might be one of the ring's financial backers, had a monumental ego. It was Reed's job to feed that ego and thus gain the man's confidence. He shook his head. "I don't understand people like that. If it were me, I'd be keeping a low profile."

"That's the problem. You aren't a crook."

"That's what makes this so hard, trying to second guess..." Reed trailed off. He didn't want to talk about the blowhard he'd be spending the day with. He wanted—that was the problem—he didn't dare put a name to what he needed.

MARA WONDERED if she'd suddenly become the most popular woman in town. Not only did Clint hang around after work asking about her visit with the rape victim, but his parents called and admitted that Clint had told them what she'd been going through. She'd just hung up after accepting an invitation to join them for dinner the following night when the phone rang again.

The connection from Paris wasn't good, but Mara didn't care. Rachael Curtis could hardly contain herself. She'd entered a cross-country motorcross race and actually finished ahead of several younger women. Her shoulders felt as if she'd been beaten, but Mara was the only one she'd admit that to. Life was as hectic as ever, but Rachael needed to touch base with her daughter.

Mark Curtis came on the line. "Your mother knows no modesty," he said laughing. "You know, Paris is a fascinating place. All the history..."

"You've been to Paris before," Mara reminded him.

"I know. I just never get tired of it. I'm bringing back a dress for you. A Paris original. I forget the name of the designer, but he must be famous. His clothes cost a bundle."

"What am I going to do with a dress that fancy?"

"Wear it to your high school reunion."

Mara laughed. She wanted to know about her brothers. Had either of them gotten their heads out from under a car hood long enough to notice that there were such things as members of the opposite sex? Where did Mara think they were? Mark asked. Although several French women had been giving out less than subtle signals, her brothers were dating a couple of female members of a rival pit crew.

"How are things going in your neck of the woods?" her father asked through the static. "Anything exciting?"

"Exciting in reference to what?" Mara sidestepped. "I saw you on ESPN the other night. Cars do have brakes, you know."

"So I've heard. There's no chance you can join us? I miss my number-one fan."

"Dad."

"I know. You've got better things to do than watch an old man, who doesn't know enough to retire, make a fool of himself. Oh. I might have drummed up some business for you. Some folks on vacation, who learned we were from San Diego, took us out for dinner. Their son's insurance is going through the roof. If he takes the course, I want a finder's fee."

Again Mara laughed. She asked how her brothers' cars were holding up and brought her father up-to-date on a new advertising angle she was trying. Then her mother came back on the line. "Men," Rachael snorted. "They think the world revolves around work. Honey, you thought there might be a chance Clint could hold down the fort while you flew over here. There's really no way you can get away?"

"I don't— Mom, things have gotten kind of complicated."

"Complicated?"

She couldn't tell her mother about being abducted, while a continent and an ocean separated them. "Maybe that's not the right word," she tried. "I, well, I've met someone."

"A man?"

"Yes." Mara sighed. "A man."

"At last! Are you going to tell me about him?"

Where would she start? "I'll write," Mara promised. "I haven't known him long. I don't know where, if anywhere, this is headed."

"But you feel good when you're around him."

Oh yes. She felt good. And more confused than she had in her entire life. "He was a student," she explained. "We spent last weekend together, just, you know, getting to know each other. Nothing happened."

"Did I ask? Honey, I'm delighted. Do try to take it slow, though. Find out everything you can about him before you fall in love. Otherwise you might wind up in as big a mess as I am with your father. Believe me, love makes a person lose every bit of sense they ever had. Don't forget that."

"I won't," Mara assured her mother.

After the phone call was over, Mara spent some time going over the latest stack of applications, but she couldn't concentrate. She'd told her mother about Reed. Not enough, of course, because nothing made sense when it came to how she felt about him. But something. Maybe more than Reed had told Jack about her.

Because doing anything that called for her brain seemed a lost cause right now, Mara got out the vacuum and cleaned a carpet that really didn't need it. Then, still restless, she dusted. It was moving her family's trophies that stopped her. In a few days her mother's latest plaque would arrive. What would that bring the grand total to? Every member of the Curtis family had more than enough proof of their skill and courage and recklessness. Everyone but her.

She was the one who couldn't stop screaming when her father's car burst into flames five years ago. It was she who slept with her dog in the room and her windows locked, and who'd tried to call Reed in the middle of the night when there wasn't a thing he could have done.

Although it would soon be dark, Mara stepped outside, slid into the Corvette and eased it onto the track. She turned on the headlights and stared out the window. If her family didn't understand why she no longer watched them race, at least they respected her feelings enough to remain silent.

But, did she respect herself?

Would Reed?

The speedometer needle inched forward as she pressed down on the accelerator. Almost out of reach of the headlights, Mara caught the movement of a rabbit hopping off the track. She would show the rabbit that, unlike him, she didn't run. The Corvette responded, taking the course as if the car had been born to it. If the grease slicks hadn't still been on the track, Mara might have brought the vehicle up to racing speed. Still, it helped to be doing this much, and she convinced herself that she was the only one inside the small space. After circling five times, Mara felt ready for the next challenge, almost.

Because she didn't want to have to contend with traffic, she waited until close to midnight before heading toward the freeway her abductor had left the Corvette on. She didn't want to be here. She wanted to be home, waiting to hear from Reed. Writing her mother about him.

But there'd been another man. A man with a knife.

Eighty-five miles an hour, a fraction of what her family took for granted. Mara whizzed past a couple of trucks, not taking her hands off the steering wheel when they waved at her. The left-hand lane had been recently resurfaced and the Corvette moved easily over it, engine humming. Mara breathed in night air and pushed down the gas pedal. The Corvette responded. Ninety. Ninety-five. The world became haze. Signs whipped past almost before she was aware of their existence. The median strip was a blur. A little more pressure.

So Reed wanted to see her family compete, did he? If he was here tonight, if he saw her control, he would tell her she belonged with them.

Or would he?

Something distracted her. When she took her eyes off the road, it was for less than half a second. But that was all it took to break her concentration.

Mara wasn't alone after all. She could sense a man beside her. A man with a knife. A laughing, animal-man.

The Corvette slowed.

Chapter Eleven

On Saturday Clint suggested they attend a unique car show together. The idea of viewing automobiles her father had raced against was appealing, but what tipped the scales was Clint's unnecessary reminder that her alternative was to spend the day rattling around a too-silent house. Waiting. Wondering when Reed would call, where he was, what he was doing, if he was all right. Making herself half crazy.

Mara was walking out with the keys to the loaner when she forced herself to look at the Corvette. "No. Damn it. You can't rob me of everything," she hissed. Despite the firm words, it took an act of courage to walk over to her car and slip inside. Before leaving the driveway, Mara spun the radio dial until she found a talk show. She drove slowly and concentrated on that.

That and Reed.

Clint was pacing when Mara pulled up at his apartment complex. He jumped into the passenger's seat. Thanks to Clint's chatter about having convinced his parents to spend the day with a realtor, she was able to hold back the image of the man who preceded him in the passenger's seat, and halfway convince herself that tying herself into knots about Reed's safety changed nothing.

The huge showroom was filled to capacity with displays of cars that had raced at places most of the people present had never seen. Mara and Clint wandered from one auto to another, commenting on features that meant nothing to the majority of spectators. For her, each car triggered a response. A blue Maserati had been driven by a highly competitive man who'd put such unreasonable demands on his sponsors that he finally lost all of them. The red Ferrari with the crumpled rear fender? Its driver was a close family friend. Although she intended her stories to be for Clint, it wasn't long before they picked up an interested audience. Parents wanted Mara to tell their eager-eyed sons about the hard work and sacrifice behind the glamor of racing. She met a man her father's age who had worked on several professional pit crews, and although Clint became a little restless, Mara was reluctant to put an end to the conversation.

"You know what I've been thinking," Mara told Clint when they had a minute alone. "So much money went into the development of these cars. Then, bam, they became obsolete. Race drivers owe so much to their sponsors."

"They wouldn't have sponsors if they didn't have the guts to get out on a track," Clint reminded her. "It's a mutually dependent relationship."

Mara started to answer but stopped when Clint pointed.

Reed was here. Alive. Safe, for now.

For a moment Mara did nothing but stare, absorbing that essential fact. She wanted to give Clint a casual nod so he wouldn't guess what she'd been going through, but she felt too light-headed with relief for that. Still, was the man weaving his way through the crowds really someone she knew?

Reed wore a white turtleneck that clung to him, accenting his body's strong lines. A gold chain circled his throat. He'd combed his hair in a rakish style Mara had never seen that changed him in a way that disturbed her. He set his lips in a hard line as his eyes remained boldly focused on the man he was talking to.

Clint whispered, "What do you think he's doing here?"

"I don't know." Mara gripped Clint's forearm. "We can't let anyone know we recognize him."

"Do you want to leave?"

Mara hadn't seen all the cars on display, but that wasn't why she shook her head. Even if she knew better than to acknowledge his presence, she needed to be near Reed, to have proof that he really had been, and still was, part of her life. That the insane world he lived in hadn't swallowed him.

The next car Clint dragged her to, an older Aston Martin, momentarily held Mara's attention. The driver was on hand to give out autographs and answer questions. Although he'd never raced against her father, Mara and the lean man found people and races in common to talk about. Carrying on a conversation helped. If she was going to keep her turmoil to herself, she had to act normal, whatever that was.

Mara knew when Reed joined them; her nerve endings transmitted that essential information. Finally, keeping the search casual, she turned to take in the bystanders. For a half second their gazes locked; there was time for only the briefest message. *I missed you,* Mara transmitted.

I missed you, she read in return.

Mara hadn't paid attention to the large, flashily dressed man with Reed before. What she saw now chilled her. His eyes were even colder than Reed's.

The beefy man nodded. "You sound as if you know what you're talking about," he said. "Not one of those damn groupies, are you?"

"It depends on what your definition of a groupie is," Mara said, her tones clipped. She didn't dare take her eyes off the man to assess Reed's reaction.

"You figure it out. You know, I lay money on Indy every year, but I wouldn't remember the name of last year's winner unless I had backed him." The man poked an elbow at Reed. "My friend here, he knows racers. Photographic memory. You remember this lady's old man, Lane?"

"Lane" nodded. His cool and assessing eyes remained on the man who'd poked him. "Mark Curtis was a pioneer," he said. "Tried some things that hadn't been tried before. Most of them panned out. I admire a man like that."

"A man with guts. Yeah. You'd like that all right." The big man took a step closer to Mara. His mix of cologne and sweat clogged her nostrils. "Join us for a drink. I've always been interested in what it's like down in the trenches. You know, the behind-the-scenes scoop. Can a driver really fix a race?"

Despite the impulse to tell the man to shut up, Mara simply shook her head. This man was part of the underworld Reed had infiltrated. He wanted nothing more than to goad her. "I've always made a point of not talking shop with outsiders," she said.

"Outsider?" The man's cold laugh grated on her nerves. "I'm hardly that. What's the matter? You afraid you're going to give away trade secrets? Maybe you should be."

Mara fought down a shudder. Before she could think of anything to say, Clint wrapped his arm around her and drew her close. "Does that invitation for a drink include me?" he asked.

The big man gave Clint a telling glare. "What are you, her bodyguard?"

"Hardly. The lady and I are getting married."

Not missing a beat, Mara slipped her arm around Clint's waist and looked up at him, adoration shining in her eyes. "Next month, no matter what my father says. We don't need his money."

Reed shrugged and started to turn away. "We don't need this, Zack."

"Says who? I'd like to match wits with this one. It sounds like she'll stand up to anyone."

"And I'm supposed to care? Look, if you want to play games, do it without me."

It was Zack's turn to shrug. "Don't get all bent out of shape." He grunted as Mara and Clint moved off. "The lady had her hackles up. I just wanted to see if it was more than bluff.''

Reed's cold laugh was the last sound Mara heard until Clint touched her. ''You all right?''

No. She wasn't. ''I've... never seen him act like that.''

''That wasn't Reed. Wow! I hardly recognized him.''

''Do you—'' Mara tried again. ''Do you think he's all right?''

''All right? That man knows exactly what he's doing.''

Mara needed to believe Clint. If she didn't, she'd rush after Reed and haul him away from that evil-looking man. ''He does, doesn't he?''

''I know I'd hire him if I needed something dangerous done. I wonder what I'd have to do to get into that line of work?''

Mara didn't bother trying to answer the question. Mindful of the fact that Zack might still be watching, she turned back to the race car driver she'd been talking to. She couldn't look at Reed again, couldn't touch him, couldn't talk to him. She had to become what Reed needed her to be.

Another hour passed. By then Mara and Clint had seen everything, including the fact that Reed and Zack were no longer at the show. ''We could grab a bite before you take me home,'' Clint suggested. ''I know this fantastic hot-dog stand. Dutch?''

''Hot dogs?'' Mara tried joking. ''Do you know what your mother would say if she heard you?''

''What my mother doesn't know isn't going to hurt any of us.'' Clint glanced at his watch. ''If Dad's strength is holding up, I don't imagine they're done looking at places yet. I could starve waiting for them.''

Shaking her head, Mara led the way through the crowded parking lot to her Corvette. She wasn't sure her stomach was in any shape for hot dogs, but neither was she in any hurry to return to the silence of her home.

"Do you really think your folks are serious about looking at places?" she asked as she reached for her key. "They'd be able to—"

An ice-cream cone, or rather what was left of it, was running off the Corvette's hood. For a mind-numbing half minute, Mara simply stared at frothy pink liquid surrounding small bits of strawberry.

"Damn." Clint swept the mess off the hood with the back of his hand. It plopped onto the pavement, the soggy cone splitting apart. "Kids!"

"Kids?"

"Yeah. Someone didn't like their ice cream so they thought it would be a joke to plant it on your car. Look—" Clint pulled a handkerchief out of his back pocket and began rubbing at what remained. "I think we'd better get this washed. It could damage the paint."

"The paint?" Think! Why couldn't she think? "Yes," Mara went on when Clint turned to her. "I don't want . . . that."

"Are you all right? You look like you just met up with you-know-who. The guy who attacked you."

Desperate, Mara sucked in a lungful of night air. *Please,* she thought. *Please don't remind me of that.*

Only, it was too late.

IT WAS ALMOST midnight on Sunday before Reed managed to break away again. He left the Jag at the hotel and put in an order under an assumed name to have a rental left in the parking lot. He made a show of telling the hotel staff he had some long-distance calls to make and didn't want to be disturbed. Then, when he was sure there was no one in the hall, Reed slipped out. He kept to the shadows until he reached the rental. A minute later he was pulling out of the lot, sure that, if Zack was having him watched, the tail would think he was still in his room.

Mara obviously didn't need him showing up trying to play White Knight. She'd made that clear at the car show. It didn't matter. He needed to see her. Oh God, how he needed to see her!

Although Lobo was already growling, Reed rang the doorbell. He heard Mara's soft footsteps, but she didn't open the door. "Who is it?" she asked.

"Mara." He held on to her name, making it real. "It's me."

"Reed." He heard the lock give and then she stood in front of him with the living room light behind her and her eyes huge. Reed breathed. Yes. It was her, reaching for him. For a moment he simply held on, fingers to fingers, breathing in her light perfume. The scent swirled through him, confusing him. Then Reed, unable to bear the emptiness any longer, drew her close. Her soft yet strong curves nestled against him. He felt her body's heat and for the first time in days felt warm. She trembled.

"Mara?" Emotion rolled out of him. "Is something wrong?"

"Wrong? It's late, Reed. I didn't expect you."

"Do you want me to leave?"

"Leave? Oh no. I—I didn't mean that."

He should have stayed where he needed to be. There was risk in coming here. But seeing her, hearing her, taking her into his arms, right now was what Reed longed for in his life.

She looked up at him, her eyes shimmering in the overhead light. He pressed his fingers and palms gently against the side of her neck. Her pulse beat ever so gently, ever so faintly. She'd parted her lips slightly, and he could no more ignore that than he could give up breathing. Asking, he covered her mouth with his. Their kiss began delicately, almost shyly. Then, slowly, wonderfully, things changed. Hours, days, weeks of wanting her ruled him. He tasted her, darting his tongue between her soft lips, gaining entrance.

She let him in. That was the greatest wonder of all. Despite everything he'd put her through yesterday, she welcomed him.

In the distance a coyote howled faintly. Reed's thoughts caught on the lonely sound. That had been him today, a solitary coyote waiting for night. Waiting to hold this woman in his arms. To know she wanted him here.

To no longer be alone.

Mara sighed. He felt the whisper of sound as it vibrated against and into him. His heart quickened, and he held her even tighter. Their lips remained locked together in silent awareness. Silent need. She wore perfume, or dusting powder, or something, that reminded him of roses. Her roses.

How could he think of roses? Mara rested her weight on her toes, the gesture increasing the contact between them. Reed held her tight against him. She wore her nightshirt. It moved freely under his hands, teasing and tantalizing him. It would take so little to strip her. Instead Reed simply held her, listening to her heart beat.

He had no right to ask her to become his lover. All he deserved, all he could ask for was this simple and yet incredibly complex embrace.

A long minute later Mara sighed again. She, or maybe it was he, was shaking. "Lobo started barking," she whispered, her breath grazing his throat. "I didn't think you'd— I'm glad it was you."

"Lobo? What's he doing inside?"

"What?"

"I thought you might be keeping him outside. So he could warn you."

"He did. He heard you." Still trembling, Mara reached for him again, putting an end to her words. She was heat in his arms; Reed wanted nothing in life except this moment. To admit, if only to himself, that he had been waiting a lifetime to be wanted and needed by someone.

"Were you asleep?" he asked.

"No. I don't think so."

"You don't think? What do you mean?"

She drew back, maybe a half inch. Maybe a mile. "Reed? Where is the Jag?"

"The Jag?" Reed forced himself to concentrate. "It's a long story." Because he didn't trust his strength any more than he trusted his emotions, Reed led the way into the living room, closed the door behind him and sat them both on the couch. After days of holding himself in check, of mistrusting every move, every word, after weighing everything he said, the need to be himself almost overwhelmed him. "You don't want to hear it."

"Yes I do." Her body, soft and strong, distracted his. "Everything."

Did she have any idea what she was doing to him? How hard she would make the leaving? "You smell wonderful. What is it?"

"Rose-scented talc," Mara whispered. "My mother gave me some last year. I forgot I had it until . . ."

Reed took her hands and rested them on his thigh. His muscles contracted at the contact. "Until when?"

"After I got back home from seeing you with Zack. I went out to water my flowers and then, I was thinking of you."

She'd been thinking of him. "I love it," he told her. *I love you,* echoed through him for the first time.

The unbidden words served as Reed's warning. He still felt the impact of Mara's fingers resting on his thigh; there was no way he could fortify himself against that.

But he still didn't understand enough of what Mara was doing to him. Until he did, he had to protect his vulnerable core. He had to shield himself against caring too much, against exposing more. He could do that, couldn't he? After all, he'd spent his adult life protecting himself from the painful lessons of his childhood. "I can't stay long," he forced himself to say. "I wish I could, but . . . Maybe I just should have called." Her hands still heated the taut flesh and muscle beneath his jeans. "I wanted to tell you, I was damn proud of the way you acted. You didn't give a thing away." That wasn't what he wanted to say. But the other? The other terrified him.

"Neither did you," she said with her eyes on his. "Reed? You were so cold. So distant."

"Was I? When I'm working undercover I become a chameleon. What my contact needs, that's what I become. Zack is a cold man. He doesn't give a damn about anything except himself."

"No. He doesn't."

"You didn't bat an eye. There's no way anyone would have guessed we'd ever met."

Mara's sigh was so low Reed almost didn't hear it. "Clint helped," she whispered. "I told myself that if I wasn't careful I might put you in danger. That was possible, wasn't it?"

"Yes."

Reed's voice was so matter-of-fact. Danger acknowledged and then dismissed. Yet Mara didn't expect anything different from him. She'd felt the heat of his reaction to their embrace, their kiss, her hand on him. She shared that same heat. But then she'd felt him draw back, and she wasn't going to let him know how much the loss hurt. "Where's your car?"

"At the hotel. I didn't want anyone to know I was coming out here."

"Didn't you?"

"I think you know why."

"Yes," Mara made herself say. "I think I do. You're sure you weren't seen? That you'll be all right?"

"There's no way I can be sure of that. But I took precautions."

Mara didn't want to hear about precautions. Or danger. She didn't want anything except the unsettling challenge of touching him. "I hope so, Reed. When I think..."

She couldn't stop with that. Somehow she would match Reed's raw courage and, maybe, absorb from him what she needed to deal with her own life. Reed dealt daily with violent men. She'd spent hours feeling raw and wounded because someone had left an ice-cream cone on her car.

"Zack." She forced out the name. "Before, I had no image, no way of knowing. Why can't he be five foot five with skinny shoulders and a paunch?"

"The Zacks of the world don't come that way."

"No. I don't guess they do." Mara rocked to her feet. She tried to turn away, but remembered Reed had noticed her talc. He knew she'd worn it because it reminded her of something they'd shared. "I'm glad you're here," she said. "Even if you can only stay a few minutes, I'm glad you came."

"Are you?"

"Did you think I wouldn't be?"

"I don't know what I thought, Mara. When I saw you at the show, I realized I had no business drawing you into what I'm doing. Endangering you."

"No." Mara swayed, caught herself. He couldn't be saying goodbye. He couldn't! "Reed?" She struggled for the right words. "You aren't drawing me into anything. What happened was coincidence. It isn't going to happen again."

"Isn't it?"

Mara's throat contracted. She pictured him walking out her door, closing it behind him. Driving away. Fear and an incredible sense of loss nearly engulfed her. Mindless of what she might expose, Mara reached out and drew his hand to her throat, her breast. "You can't protect me from life," she whispered. "I don't want to be protected. I never have."

"But deliberately..."

Mara shook her head. It pounded from the effort of not crying. "Reed? Don't block me out. Please."

"Block you out?" Reed's hand over her heart stiffened. "Is that what you think I'm doing?"

"I—I don't know what you're doing." She dropped her eyes and shut them, squeezing tightly against her tears. "I don't know anything about you." *Anything except that I'm lost without you.*

Reed drew her into him, inch by precious inch, taking away the cold and stopping her tears. Her eyes remained closed, but she could feel his breath on her temple, his strong arm around her shoulders. Mara felt safe and protected. Whether she wanted to feel that way wasn't important. She was in his arms. He hadn't walked out the door.

"You said you don't know anything about me," he whispered. "You really believe that?"

Mara nodded.

"I'm sorry. Oh, Mara. I'm sorry."

Had she touched something deep inside him? Did she have that kind of power? "I don't want it to be like that," she whispered back.

"You don't?"

"No, Reed. Oh God, no. Last weekend was wonderful. You knew that I needed to get away. That I needed...other things."

"What things?" Reed asked. He stroked her hair, his fingers gliding along her temple, around her ear, down the nape of her neck. "Tell me about those things."

"Things," Mara repeated. How she wanted to lay herself open to him, to put an end to reserve!

"Say it, please. I have to know. Before anything else, I have to know."

With her head buried against Reed's chest, and the beating of his heart soothing away her headache, Mara listened to her own heart. For them, there was only tonight. "What I said when we were at the coast? About not knowing you well enough? It isn't like that anymore."

"Are you sure?"

Mara sighed. It came out sounding too much like a moan. "I'm not sure of anything." Oh Lord, should she say this? Could she not? "I watched you with Zack. I didn't know the man you'd become. I didn't like that person. Who are you, Reed? I want to know the real you. I want to feel you against me and know that the man with me isn't the one Zack called Lane."

"What do you want me to say?"

"Nothing. This isn't about words."

"Then—" his hand feathered down her cheek and throat "—what is it about?"

"You want me to say it?" That wasn't enough. She had to give him an honest answer. Give herself one. "Reed, I want you here. With me."

"Making love?"

"Yes." *Yes.*

"Yes?" Reed's hand stopped in mid-caress. "You're telling me yes? Oh, Mara."

Mara. He made her name a song, a promise. Then, with his hand once again tracing the outline of her cheek, her jaw, he whispered, "Don't you think you should let Lobo out?"

"Lobo? If you think so."

"I'm not sure what I think, Mara. When I'm around you, I don't know myself at all."

Shaken by what he'd just revealed, Mara slipped free and walked to the door. She stood as Lobo pushed past her. It was a beautiful night, warm, cloudless. The air on her arms and legs was part of the spell. When Reed remained silent and still, Mara gathered her courage and turned around.

He was beautiful. This man, whose eyes had been all but dead on Saturday, was beautiful. There was strength in his arms and questions in his eyes and promises in his smile and, for a moment, something of a boy in the man. *Who are you? Why are you here?*

The answer wouldn't be found in words. There was another way, the only way that mattered. It called for closing the door and walking back to him. Looking up and into his eyes. Asking questions. Being afraid. Wanting as she'd never wanted before. For a moment Reed waited with his hands by his sides, frightening her.

Maybe this wasn't what he wanted after all.

Without knowing she was going to do it, Mara reached out and touched. He touched in return. His hands found her shoulders, and she came to him. The sleek velvet of his throat when she brushed her lips over him took her beyond doubt and questions, into a world lit by emotion. Her question died unspoken.

"Mara?" Once again his whispering of her name flowed through her. "You understand, don't you? Tonight. Until I've done what I promised, that's all we have. Tonight."

Mara forced herself not to shudder. "Don't. I won't talk about that."

"Not talking won't change things."

"I know," Mara said in a voice both strong and weak. "But we can pretend."

Reed ran his hands down her thighs, caught the hem of her nightshirt and brought it slowly up. "This isn't pretend, Mara. Tell me. Tell me this is what you want," he whispered with his hands brushing against her hips. "I have to know. You have to tell me what's right."

"This—" She pressed her hands against his, flattening his fingers against her naked flesh. "This is what I want."

A moment later the lightweight gown dropped to the carpet. "You are so incredibly beautiful."

Beautiful. Mara had been told she was committed and intelligent and gutsy and half-crazy, but never beautiful. She'd never needed to be told that, but the word came from Reed, and it was precious.

Mara felt no shame about standing naked before him. He touched her with warm and roughened fingertips, every touch erasing fear and questions, replacing those emotions with wonder. With feeling. She had, she could believe, been created for him.

A touch? A single night? No. It was much more than that.

Mara remembered placing her hand in Reed's, but not the effort of making her legs work. She didn't know when he'd turned off the light or how he'd guided her into the bedroom, or whether, maybe, she'd been the one to lead him there. An hour ago she'd had nothing except this house and her dog and a thousand self doubts. But now Reed had pulled back the covers on her bed and was looking at her, saying nothing, waiting for her.

Yes. Oh yes.

"No doubts? I won't push—"

"Reed? Please."

Mara's quiet plea echoed, fading, evaporating. Then Reed touched the swell of her breast, dispelling all but her need for him. It seemed unbelievable that this was the first time she'd trusted Reed with her body this way. After the impact he'd had on her life, her senses, her thoughts, her every emotion, they should be more to each other.

But they had to begin somewhere. Here. Tonight.

"I don't know what you want," Reed told her when the last of his clothes had been discarded. "Tell me what's right for you."

"You," Mara managed. "The rest—"

Reed covered her mouth with his and shut off the words she couldn't finish anyway. Although she trembled and gripped his back with fingers that dug into his flesh, he treated her as if she was a work of art. His fingers and palms moved over her, touching lightly where she needed a whisper, pressing to reach below the surface when she needed that.

They were still standing. Mara felt she could have stood forever with his body moving so lightly, so wonderfully against hers. But her body longed for more. Feeling for the bed, she sank onto it and brought Reed down with her. He settled with her. He was here. Here.

She touched him tongue to tongue, quick pressure, quick surrender. He tried to slide off her, but she gripped his shoulders and held him close, wondering at her brazen courage. Once again he brushed her breasts, igniting her passions until her nipples puckered and hardened. She shifted restlessly under his touch as waves of wanting rocked her.

But tapping into herself wasn't enough. Tonight, the only night they might have, was for both of them. With that commitment guiding her, Mara roamed with her hands and toes and legs and tongue over him, wondering at planes and valleys, flesh and muscle. Life.

Her thumb found a small lump near his right hipbone. She explored the tiny mass, her fingers tracing its contours, trying to imagine what it was.

"War wound," Reed whispered.

"An injury?" She rested her palm over it. His stomach tightened. "Who did this to you?"

"I did, Mara." He shuddered and drew her hand away. He settled her hand over his ribs and shuddered again. "When I wrecked my bike. I'm not like you, perfect. I have flaws."

"Oh Reed. I have flaws, too," she whispered, sliding her hand downward again to settle it over his scar.

"I can't find any," he said, his hands moving, moving. "Your waist. It feels so sleek, so smooth." His fingers dipped lower. "The way your stomach disappears when you draw in a breath. The way—" he touched her breasts again "—the way your body tells me what you're feeling. That's what makes you perfect."

Perfect. Mara wanted to embrace the word, to believe she could be that for Reed. But he held her nipple between thumb and forefinger, held it so he could draw his moistened tongue over it, and she couldn't think.

She felt the strange roughness of her sheet, air sliding over her breasts and belly, the slow glide of Reed's leg as he covered hers with his own. Feeling as if she might explode from the symphony of sensations, Mara reached out blindly and found Reed's shoulders. Reed's powerful, competent shoulders. She felt as if she'd grabbed hold of a waterfall-slickened boulder, but this rock had life pulsing through it. And she'd tapped into that life.

Using Reed as her guide, Mara touched her tongue first to the small hollow of his throat and then worked downward past lazily curling hairs, over the hard ridge of his breast. She found his nipple and took it gently into her mouth. Her teeth closed over him, a captor with a willing prisoner.

"Mara . . . Mara!"

She could wrest that emotion from him? Mara opened her eyes. In the dark she met his eyes. Then, unnerved by what he'd exposed in that gaze, Mara closed her own eyes again and let touch, taste, smell take over.

Reed took her into the waves, introduced her to powerful currents. Mara gave herself up to him, feeling a reckless freedom she'd never known herself capable of. She drew him into her, and renewed herself in him. Her body jumped, filled, exploding almost with him. She felt his sweat-slickened body, felt his movement, felt her response. Yes! He was there, matching her stride for stride, wave for wave. Yes!

Reed had satisfied her; hadn't he heard her abandoned cry, felt her shivers of release? For minutes, hours maybe there'd been nothing but him and her. Them. It wasn't just his sweat after all. His hard and urgent breathing. His release. They'd done that together. They.

That wonderful knowledge would take Mara into the morning.

Only, what she'd experienced during those moments when they clung together had been more than lovemaking. It might simply be that she'd broken loose from everything she'd ever believed about herself.

It might be no more complicated than the act of falling in love.

"I didn't know," Mara whispered. "When I heard the car driving up, I had no way of knowing."

"This wasn't why I came. Not the only reason," he whispered back. "I had to see you. Just see you."

"Yes. Yes. And then—" Mara touched her tongue to Reed's chest, tasting salt. "Then this happened."

"You're not sorry? There aren't any regrets?"

Maybe. In the morning. "Oh no, Reed." Then because morning stalked her, she had to ask, "You can't stay?"

"No. I wish . . ."

"I know," Mara finished. She should let him go. Putting off that moment would only make the leaving harder. But not yet. Not until she had something more to take her through days and nights when she wouldn't know where he was, if he was alive. She touched her tongue to his flesh one more time. She ran her toes over his calf, feeling hair and skin, muscle and bone. Then she began to cry, silent, secret tears.

There was nothing planned or calculated about her sigh. "Go. Now. Please," she begged.

"I'm sorry. I can't give you any promises. I don't know when I'll see you again."

"I know that. Reed, please just go now."

Hating his job, hating the bonds that tied him to Jack, most of all hating her fears for his safety, Mara watched Reed dress and start for the door. She wouldn't get out of bed to watch him go. It was the only way she could let him leave her tonight. But she couldn't remain silent. "Be careful. Please."

Reed turned around. He was backlit by a living room lamp. His eyes were even darker than they'd been when need for her had ruled him. He gripped the doorjamb, and his knuckles were white. He said nothing.

Mara heard the door close behind him. She slipped back under the sheets and pulled them tight around her. The heat Reed had stirred in her veins cooled, and she shivered. She didn't know if he'd seen her tears. She had no way of knowing whether he understood that a woman falling in love would cry at the loss of her lover.

That her need for him was that strong.

REED DIDN'T CALL the next day, and Mara felt herself slipping. She told herself it was just concern for Reed that made her jumpy. Some of that was the truth. How could it be otherwise when her sheets smelled of him, when his mem-

ory remained silhouetted in the doorway, when her heart
cried out for his return.

But it was more than that. The police were warning
women not to shop alone at night. A local TV station had
called to ask if she would be part of a program on serial
rapists. She had declined.

The program, which Mara tried not to watch, but did,
aired on the evening news. The focus was on the supermarket rapist, a man the police claimed to believe was driven by
a need for control.

Clint called as soon as the piece was over. Was she all
right? he asked. If she wanted him to come over he would.
Mara did want him to come, but told him no. Instead she
spent the next hour loading and unloading the pistol, feeling its weight, gaining strength from having it at hand. Remembering everything of what had been said and left unsaid
the evening Reed had taught her how to use it.

The next night she cooked dinner for Clint and his parents, and they stayed until bedtime. Mara changed from her
morning radio news station and avoided reading anything
more serious in the paper than the advice column. She threw
herself into her work by planning an ad she would place next
to the weekend car sales information.

And then Reed called. At first she couldn't concentrate on
anything as unimportant as what he was saying. She could
do nothing except breathe and fight tears of relief.

Suddenly his words came into focus. "I wish I didn't have
to say this, but Jack was right," he told her, his voice
stripped of emotion by the poor connection. "This case isn't
going to be easy. I met Zack's partner. The man wouldn't
trust his own mother."

No. "You have their names, don't you? Can't the police
arrest them?"

Reed explained that a good lawyer, which the ring members could afford, would find loopholes in the case he'd
built. "The case has to be airtight. I have to be able to doc-

ument what everyone's role in the ring is. I'm sorry. It's going to take time. I wanted you to know that."

Time. "Will I . . . You can't get away?"

"That's why I called, Mara. Zack and his partner are going to Reno in a couple of days. Some kind of meeting. They don't want me along."

Mara pressed her free hand to her throat. "What will you be doing?"

"How long would it take you to get to the beach place?"

"Reed?" She breathed his name. "You can get away? It's safe?"

"It's as safe as it's ever going to be until it's over."

"When?" Mara asked with her heart pounding.

"Friday night?"

Chapter Twelve

Two cars were parked in front of the cabin when Mara arrived. One was Reed's Jag, the other a nondescript Ford. Fighting back her disappointment at having to share Reed with anyone, Mara rang the doorbell. She recognized Captain Bistron when he opened the door. Reed stood behind him.

The police officer stuck out his hand and shook Mara's. "I'm glad to see you again. Things getting back to normal, are they? I was telling Reed. Except for, maybe, that one time, the patrols haven't seen anything to make them suspicious."

Mara nodded noncommittally. Unlike the Captain, Reed wasn't smiling. But he was coming toward her, and that was all that mattered. Reed was wearing canvas pants and a shirt he'd left partially unbuttoned and tucked into his pants, drawing her eyes to his waist, and lower. Mara had dressed carefully, a soft yellow blouse and white skirt. Both blouse and skirt had been bought for this weekend. "I don't understand," she said as Reed took her hand. He squeezed; she squeezed back but kept her voice neutral. "Are the two of you having a meeting?"

"A strategy planning session," Reed explained. "Bistron's spending the weekend on the coast himself. We figured if he came here we could talk without interruption. I'm sorry, but it shouldn't take long."

Mara nodded and then sat down. Despite her need to b
alone with Reed, it helped to have the captain in the cabin
This way she would listen and maybe learn something abou
the alien world that consumed Reed.

From what she gathered, Zack and his partner left fo
Reno to straighten out some problems with one of the mid
dle men. If Reed had accurate information, whoever wa
responsible for taking stolen cars into the Midwest had got
ten greedy.

"I'm hoping intimidation will do the trick," Reed ex
plained. "If they have to get rid of the guy, that means I'l
have to wait until someone has taken his place."

"Is there that much money in this...whatever it is?"

"There's a lot, Mara. A lot," Reed said and then ex
plained that most auto thefts were major headaches for th
police. The majority of stolen cars were sold as parts afte
the chop shops were done with them. If valuable autos lik
the ones involved in this ring weren't stripped, they wer
sold with altered ID numbers. If the autos didn't go throug
reputable auto dealers, the police or department of moto
vehicles might never be able to track them.

"This ring's got us both ways. Cut a car into pieces an
we'll never patch it together. Change the VIN and how ar
we going to trace it?" Captain Bistron explained. "Th
buyer who gets a great deal is going to keep his mouth shut
And the guy who sold it to him? He isn't going to admi
what he did."

Reed grunted. "Especially since he has a pretty good ide
what his life is worth if he rats."

"Enough," Captain Bistron groaned after they'd been a
the table for the better part of an hour. "You're right, Reed
We still don't have everything we need. I just needed to b
brought up-to-date. I know I don't have to say it, but b
careful."

Reed glanced over at Mara. With an effort she kept he
features expressionless. "I am," he said simply, then con

tinued, "Captain, the other thing you and I were talking about. Mara needs to hear about that."

"Yeah." Captain Bistron drew out the word. "You saw that TV bit about the supermarket rapist? For the record, the station got the bare minimum from us before they ran the piece."

"You don't approve?" Mara asked.

"I don't approve of the way they handled it. They're after sensationalism. It's a ratings game. To hear them talk, you'd think we'd doubled the force so we can get this scum. Unfortunately, it doesn't work that way."

Mara nodded. "What are you saying?"

"What I'm saying is, if this joker watched that program, maybe he's thinking there's too much heat. He could back off. There's a chance we'll never catch him now."

Never.

"THEY WON'T BE ABLE to keep the patrols coming by my place indefinitely, will they?" Mara said after the captain left. "If he isn't caught in a few days or weeks, if there's no proof he's been around, the police are going to back off."

Reed locked the cabin door and turned toward her. He looked wary and resigned. "I don't see as they have any choice. Mara, I'm sorry."

"Don't apologize," she told him. "I've never been convinced of the effectiveness of having the police drive by, anyway. He'd hear and hide before they got anywhere near him."

Reed stopped with his hand poised over the light switch. "What are you saying? You think he's been around?"

"Of course not." Despite her attempt to defuse his dark mood, her tone sounded stilted even to her. Mara wondered if Reed noticed. "I'm simply stating the obvious."

The light was off. He came toward her, not rushing, but not holding back, either. "You have the gun," he said into the dark.

"Yes."

"And Lobo. He's a good warning system."

"Reed," Mara said, "I got an hour's worth of advice from Clint's parents the other night. My secretary was almost as bad. I don't need any more."

"I'd like to believe that," Reed said, his hands settling warm and alive, on her shoulders. "I don't want this conversation any more than you do. I want to forget there's anything in the world except us being together. But, Mara, I'm surrounded by men without conscience, men who'll do anything if the price is right."

Abruptly, Mara pulled away and paced to the glass door leading to the deck. It was too dark to see the ocean, but she could hear its timeless rumble. The ocean couldn't share its strength with her. Neither could Reed. He was only human. She loved him and lived for these moments when they were together, but her strength and courage had come from within her.

Reed joined her, bringing with him the challenge she felt whenever he came close. "I understand how you feel," she told him. "The things you hear, what you've seen. But Reed, I'm not dealing with a man who thinks nothing of killing someone else."

"We don't know that."

"He isn't that brave," Mara protested. She wasn't sure whether the argument was for him or her. "He's an opportunist. A coward. That's what the TV program said."

"And they know?"

As Mara tensed in response to Reed's words, she could see he already regretted having brought the subject up.

"I'm sorry. That's not why I asked you to come here."

"It isn't?" Mara asked, knowing the answer.

"I wanted to see you. I like what you're wearing. It's lovely. You're lovely." A few seconds later, with his mouth inches from her ear, Reed whispered, "I thought the captain was never going to leave. You really are here."

"I'm really here." *And so are you.*

"And no one except Bistron knows where we are."

"Clint has a pretty good idea."

"Did he say anything?"

"He didn't have to," Mara admitted. "All he had to do was look at me."

For several minutes they simply stood, touching, while Mara cleared her mind of everything except awareness of Reed's presence. At length she looked up at him. There were a thousand promises in that look. Reed threaded his fingers through her hair, testing her self-control. For three, maybe four heartbeats they remained motionless with need arcing and Mara focusing on nothing except Reed's gentle strength. Then Reed lowered his head and covered her mouth with warmth and life. And she molded, melted into him.

For the next hours she would think about nothing except making love and the sound of the ocean.

BECAUSE SHE KNEW he wouldn't be able to give her an answer, Mara didn't ask Reed when he'd get in touch with her again. Instead she used their time together to memorize his embrace, his words, the solid lines of his body as he stood watching the ocean early the next morning. Then she got in her car and drove off without looking back.

She didn't cry during the drive home. She walked into her house and turned on the stereo to Reed's favorite station. Although there couldn't possibly be a message from him, she ran her answering machine. Several would-be students had left messages, but she couldn't be bothered to jot down names and phone numbers now. She hit the Save button, and carried her new blouse and skirt to the washer, and stood, watching it fill. When her clothes started sloshing, she closed her eyes and pressed her palms against them, denying her loneliness.

ON SUNDAY DETECTIVE Kline called. There'd been another attempted kidnapping. "It might not be our guy," he explained. "But I thought you should know. Apparently this girl's a member of her high school track team. When he pulled the knife she took off like a scared rabbit. Unfortunately her car wasn't so lucky."

With her hand clamped over her throat, Mara asked him to explain.

"She'd left it unlocked. Kids! They think they're invincible. Anyway, by the time she got to the police and they came back to the parking lot, her seats were ripped."

Mara swallowed. "How old is she?"

"Sixteen."

Mara didn't want to hear that. She asked the detective a few more questions about the investigation, but it was obvious that the police were frustrated. A man who didn't leave fingerprints, who was cunning enough to alter his appearance, and who was continuing his sick game despite public awareness, wouldn't be easily caught.

Mara weeded her flower garden, cleaned house and gave Lobo a bath, but those activities weren't enough to distract her. Her body remembered Reed; Reed who'd left her after their night of lovemaking because he had had no choice. She'd told him about getting her purse back but not about throwing it away. She'd said nothing about her reaction to finding ice cream smeared over her car, or why she'd sat alone afterward with his gun in her lap.

A little after ten on Monday morning, Mara was standing on the track with Clint and a half dozen new students when a police car came down the long drive. She moved, not toward the car and the uniformed man getting out of it, but closer to Clint.

If Clint hadn't taken her hand, Mara wasn't sure she could have faced the patrolman. What if something had happened to Reed? The patrolman's first words dispelled that worry.

The police had arrested a suspect. Would Mara come to the station to take a look at him?

"Now? He's in custody?"

"We picked him up last night. He was hanging around the supermarket where Mrs. Chambers was grabbed. But if we're going to make a case stick, we need a positive ID."

"I told the detective, I didn't get a good look at him."

"We'd appreciate your coming down, Ms. Curtis."

Mara took a deep breath, trying to make sense out of what she was feeling. Today the sky was touched with high, trailing clouds. There weren't any hawks out, but she remembered the night when she had had only the winged creature for company and then he'd flown away.

"What's wrong?" Clint asked.

"Nothing." The lie came too easily. "But what if it isn't the right man, or I can't help?"

"You'll never know if you keep standing here. Do you want me to go with you?"

Mara wanted to tell him yes, but their students were waiting. In a voice that belonged to a woman far braver than she believed herself to be, Mara assured Clint that she was capable of attending a lineup on her own. Still, when the policeman offered to drive her and see she got home afterward, she took him up on it. She was too distracted to drive safely. She gave Clint unnecessary instructions on how to conduct the afternoon lessons. Then, finally, her hands tight around her middle, Mara slid into the police car.

Detective Kline was waiting for her. Rennie Chambers was already there, her arm still in a cast, her husband seated next to her. Mara and Rennie exchanged nervous smiles as the detective explained the situation. The earlier victims had already seen the suspect but hadn't been able to help. The teenager's parents felt their daughter would be traumatized if asked to come to a police station.

Detective Kline was still hopeful that Rennie or Mara could help. The man in the lineup had made a female employee nervous when he started following her as she was getting ready to leave work. The young woman had decided not to risk going to her car. Instead she hurried back into the store. When she returned with the manager, the stranger was standing near her car. He started to run, but a patrolman, alerted by the manager, took off after him.

"Our suspect had been drinking. Not enough to make him legally drunk. Did either of you notice liquor on the breath of the man who attacked you?"

Mara remembered foul breath but not the smell of alcohol. Rennie was even less sure. "Look at me," the nurse said and held up her hands. "I'm shaking."

Mara was shaking, too, but she managed to hide that from everyone except herself.

"It's natural to be nervous," the detective said as he got to his feet. "You're getting close, maybe, to someone who hurt you. It's bound to bring back memories."

Memories. Thousands of them. Some she wouldn't put a name to. The others were waiting for Mara to join them, but for a moment she could only sit. Rennie had her husband with her. When she was done, Rennie would go home to her family who would help her regain the courage that monster had stripped from her. Mara was alone.

Then the detective opened his office door and Reed stepped in.

Mara stared. She started to speak, but nothing came out. *Reed.*

"Detective Kline told me about the lineup," Reed explained, gripping the doorjamb. His eyes were warm and caring. "I didn't want you to go through this alone."

Alone? How could she feel alone with Reed beside her? Mara stared at him, her mind a jumble of thoughts and emotions. Despite the magnetism between them, a single message emerged. He was an incredibly brave man. He'd come here to be with a woman he believed his equal. Somehow she had to convince him that he was right. "Thank you," she said calmly, getting to her feet. "How you manage to keep track of everything amazes me."

"I'm just glad I was able to make it."

"Well, it should be interesting," she said with a flippancy she didn't feel.

When he placed his arm around her shoulder as they left the office, she resisted the urge to lean against him. Instead she gave him a squeeze and forced a quick smile.

Rennie Chambers and Mara took seats in front of a darkened window. Frank Chambers and Reed stood behind them, silent. After giving the two women last-minute instructions, Detective Kline ordered the lights in the lineup room turned on.

Mara was vaguely aware that the men were all approximately the same height and build and casually dressed. Although she tried to concentrate, her muscles contracted. There, maybe, was the man who'd robbed her of so much!

"You turn me on. Say it. You turn me on."

Mara noticed that Rennie was holding her breath. She turned away from the six men. Frank Chambers had his hands on his wife's shoulders and he was whispering something to her.

"Party time."

When a shudder claimed her, Reed spanned Mara's shoulders with his own strong, warm fingers. "Take your time," he said. "There's no rush. Think carefully. Very carefully."

The words helped. Those in the lineup were on the opposite side of some kind of heavy glass wall. The men standing in front of her were unarmed, and if the one who'd abducted her so much as moved, Reed was there to come to her aid.

Detective Kline instructed the men to turn slowly. Despite the distraction of Reed's presence, Mara concentrated on their movement, looking for something familiar. If she could touch an arm or study fingers wrapped around a knife, that might help. Could she ask the men to speak?

"You turn me on. Say it. You turn me on."

Mara remembered fear. And she could still see and feel that intimidating knife. But sounds and gestures, mannerisms, those things were beyond her recall.

It had been night. The man had worn dark clothing. He'd stripped her of everything she'd spent years fighting to believe about herself. He'd degraded her.

With her palm pressed to the tiny scar at the base of her throat, Mara's mind caught on the act of driving, recalling a cold knife on her flesh, her body's solid impact on the ground and then the incredible freedom of being able to run. The utter necessity of running.

"I'm sorry. I'm sorry. He ordered me not to look at him."

"I wish—" Rennie filled in the silence. "He was bald. There aren't any bald men here."

"He might have shaved his head, Mrs. Chambers, or worn a skinhead wig. Think. Surely you recall something about his features."

Rennie swallowed. "He hit me and he hurt me."

"I know," Detective Kline said reassuringly. "I'm sorry. But what did he look like?"

"I don't know! God! I don't know. Please." Rennie stumbled to her feet and reached for her husband. From the safety of his arms, she managed a whisper. "Can I get out of here?"

ALTHOUGH SHE WAS STANDING in the sunlight outside the police station with Reed beside her, Mara felt sick. The detective's discouraged dismissal echoed in her ears. Once outside the room, she and Rennie had held on to each other, and in that moment, Mara understood that she wasn't the only one who'd been forced to say the unspeakable. But now Rennie was gone. Frank Chambers was guiding his wife toward their car.

Mara looked up at Reed, unable to read his expression. "I tried. I really tried," she muttered, her earlier flippancy a vague memory. How could she pull herself back together? "But the whole time I was with him all I could think about was the knife and having to do exactly as he said. I knew what was going to happen."

"Don't think about that," Reed said. "It's behind you now."

Mara clenched her fists and stared as Frank Chambers helped his wife into their car and leaned over to kiss her. "I was so sure he was going to kill me when he was done. Then I remember breathing in the night air and wanting to go on breathing. I ran. All I knew was—" Shaking off the tears building inside, Mara forced herself to relax her fingers. If she didn't stop babbling, Reed would see the holes that had been carved in her. Only, the words kept coming. "I had to go on living. I would do anything to stay alive."

"That's behind you," Reed repeated. "You're safe."

Mara stared down at her hands. Her nails had left sharp indentations in her palms. This unreasoning terror had to stop, now! "I know."

"I hope so."

Frank and Rennie Chambers were driving away. Rennie sat next to her husband, and he had his free arm around her shoulders. Rennie didn't have to hide her fear from her husband. But Mara couldn't bear to disappoint Reed. "What? Yes. Of course."

Reed took Mara's hand and began massaging the slight wounds she'd inflicted on herself. "Are you sure?"

"I'm mad," Mara lied. "I should be able to help more." She blinked. It didn't help the dry heat behind her eyes. "If...if only I'd looked at him."

"You did the best you could do. That's all any of us can do. Mara, are you going to be all right?"

"All right?" With an effort, Mara met Reed's eyes, nearly undone by the concern she found in them. "Of course I am. I just didn't know what to expect. I was a little unnerved, but...thank you for coming. I know how hard it was for you to find time."

"It's something I wanted to do for you." Reed touched a thumb to Mara's chin, tipping her head upward for a kiss. "Something I needed to do."

AFTER RETURNING to her students and allowing Clint to pull her aside so she could pass on what had, or rather what hadn't happened, Mara moved like a zombie through the afternoon session. She waited until she was alone before calling Detective Kline. She wanted to apologize, again, for the way the lineup had turned out. "Is he—did you have to let him go?"

"I'm afraid so. He frightened the girl at the supermarket, but he didn't commit a crime. We didn't have any choice."

"Oh." The word came out in a long breath. "Detective? Maybe I have no business asking this, but do you think he was the one?"

"Between you and me, I think it's a good thing that girl had the presence of mind to go back into the store. But whether he's the same man who abducted you, I'm not going to swear to it. Are you going to be alone tonight?"

Mara hadn't expected that question. It was still daylight, but suddenly she could sense the coming night. Maybe if she drew the curtains now, made sure the gun was loaded...
"Why?"

"Because you might feel some backlash from what you went through."

Where was Reed?

No matter how she tried to fill the evening, Mara couldn't put an end to that question. If only there was some way she could reach him. He'd left without telling her where he was going; she hadn't thought to ask. Now, with several hours between her and what she'd weathered, she'd had time to think through the emotions she'd kept from him, time to regret her decision.

Tonight with the blinds drawn and Lobo pacing in the living room and the gun a cold, heavy weight in her lap, Mara felt compelled to tell Reed everything.

He would accept that she wasn't the strong, resourceful woman she'd pretended to be, or he wouldn't. He could understand that the instinct for survival had allowed her to say things to her attacker that made her sick just to think about, or he wouldn't. She'd turn to him for understanding the way Rennie Chambers turned to her husband, and if Reed was a man worthy of her love, he would understand.

If he wasn't...

"Oh, Lobo," she told her dog when the large animal settled in front of the door, sighing restlessly. "I've tried so hard to convince him I'm something I'm not. What's so impossible about the truth?"

Lobo didn't have the answers. All he could do was cock his head when the telephone rang.

Mara snatched the receiver. "Reed?" she blurted without thinking. He'd told her he wouldn't be able to get in touch with her. Why had she called out his name?

Silence.

Mara frowned. "Hello? Hello. Is anyone there?"

More silence.

For almost a half minute, Mara stood with the phone pressed to her ear, listening. Then, with the hairs on the back of her neck rising, she hung up the receiver. "Wrong number," she told Lobo. She didn't know if she believed that.

The phone rang again five minutes later. This time Mara waited until after the third ring before reaching out with numb fingers and picking up the receiver. She listened to silence for a few seconds before saying anything. Once again no one answered.

It wasn't funny! If this was some kid's idea of a joke... Mara dismissed the thought. Maybe it wasn't a random call. A man had been forced to stand in a lineup. He, if he was her attacker, had a pretty good idea who would be on the other side of the glass. And now, tonight, the phone had rung twice.

Make that three times, Mara thought when once again the phone shattered the silence. This time she let the ringing continue until Lobo started to whine. She should have turned on her answering machine. Only, if she did that, the act would serve as further proof of her cowardice.

"Hello," Mara whispered.

Silence. Damnable silence.

"Don't do this!" No. She wouldn't lose control. "You're sick. I hope you know that. You are sick."

Silence.

"You're a coward. A stinking, shriveling coward." Emotion formed Mara's words; she had no control over what was coming out of her. She understood only that fury and fear were kin. "I don't know what you think you're trying to prove, but it isn't going to work. Do you hear me? If it was up to me, you'd spend the rest of your life in prison."

She could hear breathing.

The sound acted like a pin puncturing a balloon. The words Mara had just uttered echoed through her. She'd gone on the attack. Issued a challenge. If that animal wasn't a total coward, maybe he would accept the challenge.

Maybe he would come after her.

For too long after slamming down the receiver, Mara stared, her thoughts going nowhere and everywhere. Then, because she had to do something, she dialed Detective Kline's office. He wasn't there and the best that the man who answered could offer was to pass on Mara's information.

"Phone calls don't mean anything," the officer, who sounded barely out of his teens, explained. "I wouldn't let them get to you. But, yeah, we'll have a patrol come out your way."

"I'd appreciate that."

After the police patrol came and went, Mara spent the rest of the night on the couch, her legs curled up against her body, the phone off the hook, her ears tuned for the slightest sound or movement outside.

Lobo slept.

Chapter Thirteen

In the morning, Mara showered quickly, her ears tuned to any sound. Without being aware of what she was doing, she put on the same clothes she'd worn yesterday and passed on coffee because her nerves were already jangling.

What was Reed doing?

"Call," she whispered. "Please let me know you're safe."

The sound of Clint's car rumbling down the drive almost reduced her to tears. It felt so good to have someone around!

A moment later Mara was furious at herself as much as the stranger who'd turned her night into hell. This pale woman with hollowed-out eyes she saw in the mirror wasn't her. Somehow, somehow, she would get herself back!

"How are you doing?" Clint asked by way of greeting. "I'm sorry things turned out the way they did."

"I am too." Clint headed toward the kitchen and whatever he could rustle up for breakfast. That turned out to be Mara's salvation. If he'd said any more about the attack she might have told him about the phone calls and then had to listen to his anger and frustration, when her own emotions were all she could deal with right now. She trailed into the kitchen after him. "Don't you ever eat at home?" she asked as he opened the refrigerator.

"Sure I do. But I'm a growing boy. You didn't make any coffee."

"That's right. I didn't."

Clint turned. "And you're wearing what you had on yesterday."

Because she couldn't think of a thing to say to that, Mara simply shrugged. She left Clint to dismantle her kitchen while she went in search of shoes. She was sitting on her bed tying the laces when the phone rang. The sound undid everything she'd gained since last night.

"You want me to get it?" Clint yelled when it rang again.

"No." Her voice was higher pitched than she wanted it. If this was a repeat of last night, she'd turn the phone over to Clint. Maybe his deep tones would make an impact.

"You sound wonderful," Reed whispered almost before she was done saying hello.

Reed. The strength went out of her, and she sank down on the bed. "Where are you? Or maybe you can't tell me."

"I'm in Reno. I flew out on a private plane not long after seeing you, thanks to our friend Zack. But I should be back in San Diego later today."

He was out of the state. He hadn't been anywhere around when her phone rang last night. "Reno. That was fast. Are things . . . going all right?"

"Confusing. A little tense. I'm going to be alone tonight."

"Oh."

"Can I come out?"

Mara couldn't stand the idea of spending another evening at home, even with Reed here. The phone might ring. "No." Hating the quick way the word came out, she tried again. "It's been rather hectic. A lot of things piling up. Could—is there anywhere else we could meet?"

"Of course. Mara? Are you sure you're all right? You sound tense."

"No. No. I'm fine. I'm just glad you called."

"I needed to hear that," Reed said with a soft warmth that erased a great deal of what Mara had been through. "You could come to my hotel. If you want."

"Wouldn't that be a problem?"

"I honestly don't believe so, but that has to be your decision. You do understand that someone might see you with me, don't you? Someone who thinks they know who I am."

Mara understood what Reed was getting at. If she were spotted going into Reed's room, that person or persons would think she was connected with the persona he'd created. "If you say it's all right, I believe you. I just don't want to do anything that might make things more difficult for you."

Reed's voice was low. "There haven't been any women in here. I've taken a couple out because it's expected, but none of them have been in my room. You believe that, don't you?"

"Yes."

"Mara, I wouldn't have you come here if I thought there was any danger. The reason I brought this up is that the people I've been dealing with are bound to wonder whether I have any private life. Seeing a woman come into my room..."

"Reed," Mara interrupted. "You don't have to explain. The thought that I might be able to help, well, it's the least I can do. After all, you must know how much it meant to me to have you there at the lineup."

THE DAY JERKED ALONG, sometimes at a pace faster than Mara could keep up with, sometimes crawling. When Clint mentioned that the balky loaner wasn't running right again, she snapped that she had more important things to do. Clint stared but said nothing about her uncharacteristic show of temper.

During her lunch break she put in a call to the police station. Detective Kline was eating at his desk. Between bites he told her there was nothing on his desk to indicate she'd called last night. He was glad she'd insisted on having someone come out. "We take on these college kids who get class credit for helping out the department. Sometimes they know what they're doing and other times... Have you had calls like this before?''

Mara explained that she'd had her share of wrong numbers. It happened occasionally with a business. "But this time I know someone was on the other end. If this is someone's idea of a joke..."

The detective offered a couple of possibilities. The only one she really heard was that it might have been her attacker. If that was the case, Kline suggested strongly that Mara either move or find someone to stay with her. If nothing else, Mara should get her number changed. She couldn't, she reminded him. This was both her home and business phone.

"Let me know if it happens again," the detective finished. "I don't want to blow things out of proportion. But neither do I want to make light of it."

MARA TOOK TIME for a shower after work and then drove herself to distraction trying to decide what to wear. In the end she chose a dress because she needed to feel feminine. The skirt of the pale yellow summerweight cotton was full and draped loosely around her legs. She didn't bother with pantyhose. Her sandals were a few ounces of white leather. A thin gold chain accented her throat and hid the mark left by the knife point.

The Hotel Corinthian was at least forty years old and spoke of a timeless elegance. Mara thought the presence of a doorman and the grandeur of the lobby a little much, but if this was where Reed needed to be seen, she would accept it. Because Reed had suggested it, she made a show of asking the man at the front desk for directions to Lane Reaves's room. After an appreciative appraisal of the woman asking after one of their longtime guests, the concierge directed Mara to the eleventh floor. She barely heard the muted music in the elevator and paid scant attention to the middle-aged woman fiddling with her pearls who shared the ride with her. Only one thing mattered: Reed.

"You're here."

His eyes said so much. His hands stretching toward her were life giving. His words made everything right. Mara had no memory of which of them closed the door.

"Too long," Reed muttered with his body pressed against hers and his strength becoming hers. "Too long without you."

"I missed you."

"I hate being apart."

She hated it, too. Now, with his mouth tight against hers and the world painted in shades of love, everything was right in her world. "You're all right?" Reed asked.

"We're together," she said by way of answer.

"I know." He held her so tightly that Mara grew alarmed. She leaned back, searching his gaze. Whatever he was thinking was hidden behind dark lashes and blue eyes sliding into dusky slate. "But you haven't answered my question. Are you all right?"

"Why shouldn't I be?"

"You're the only one who can answer that, Mara. I'm sorry," he went on when she remained silent. "I shouldn't keep questioning you like that. It's the things I've been doing. The people I have to deal with."

"Don't. Reed, just don't," Mara whispered. "If that's what you're going to talk about..."

"No. It isn't," Reed whispered back.

Mara wasn't enough weight in his arms. The ease with which he carried her into the bedroom shocked him. She should have more substance to her. This woman, who'd taken possession of parts of him he hadn't known he had, was so light. So easily lost.

But Reed refused to think about the painful leavetaking that would punctuate the end of their night together. She'd come to him, willingly, freely, because she, he hoped, wanted him as much as he needed her.

He would use these hours together to come to grips with her impact on him.

"Is this too soon?" They stood at the entrance to the bedroom. "Maybe... If I'm rushing..."

"No. We can talk later."

"Later," Reed repeated as he lay her on the bed. "Later."

Mara shuddered. Reed stroked her shoulders, pressing her against the sheet, stilling the movement. She wore a dress. It was pale yellow, an illusion of fabric that could be destroyed if he wasn't careful. But it was so damn hard not to rush the disrobing when there was so much he needed from her, so little he had a right to ask for.

She lay quiet and ready, her eyes huge, making new inroads into his heart. His body became an electric current pulsing with need and want, but if he simply tapped that, if he ignored everything else, their lovemaking would touch only one dimension. Yes, he wanted her, to feel her hot response, to push both of them as far and fast as they could go. She would let him do that; her hands and lips and body would help rush the journey.

But the texture of their lovemaking should be full and rich, a blending of everything.

A transcending of the hard fact that until he was free of this commitment, all he could give her were stolen moments.

Reed kicked off his shoes and sat beside her. He leaned forward, in awe of the fragile gift of her body. He felt her fingers on his back drawing him even closer, and then covered her breasts, one with his hand, the other with his mouth. He felt the hard points, in his palm and against his tongue.

His fingers told the story Reed didn't have words for. His lips and tongue painted a silent picture. If he searched for words, they might not be enough, or they might be too much. He might wind up bringing both of them face to face with how much more he wanted to give her of himself, how little control he had over that. But he could touch and taste and worship silently. She wore nothing but a shimmer of gold around her throat. Reed concentrated on that. It became his focal point, his contact with sanity.

Slowly, beautifully, Mara did for him what he'd done for her. First his shirt went. She reared up and ran her tongue down his chest before falling back on the bed. She tugged at his jeans. He moved quickly, awkwardly, helping her. And then while he lay beside her she slipped his briefs down over his hips, and he gave up what was left of him.

MARA WAS CRYING. Because she couldn't keep her tears from him, because in her honest vulnerability she didn't want to, she gave him the only explanation that made sense. Still, the darkened room helped.

"I love you, Reed," she said softly into the night. "I don't know how it happened. I don't know what I'm going to do about it, but I love you."

"You do?"

Mara hesitated. "You have to ask?"

"I don't know what to say," Reed whispered. He rose on his elbow. Reverently he ran his free hand through her hair and then to the slender gold cord around her throat. She heard him take a deep, unsteady breath. "No one's ever said that to me. Not like this."

"I can't think when I'm around you," Mara admitted, her words of love still echoing through her. "I feel. But I can't think."

"Maybe, if either of us knew what we were doing, we wouldn't be here."

Although Mara hated the idea of their being apart, she understood what he was saying. If either of them could, they would step back, set a slower pace. But she'd opened her heart to him, and it was too late. "Is that what you think?"

"Maybe."

Mara rolled away. She lay with her arm under her cheek and focused her eyes on the blank wall. "Don't say that. Just . . . don't."

Reed ran his fingers down her spine, then touched his mouth to the back of her neck, the gesture incredibly gentle. She shuddered; she couldn't stop herself. "I want tonight," she whispered with her back still to him. "That's all I'm asking for. Tonight." Her lie echoed against the wall and slammed back into her.

"And I want more than that. If only I could give it to you."

HOURS LATER Reed woke up hungry. They'd made love again and fallen asleep with their heads on the same pillow. Now, however, his stomach was growling. "There's nothing open at this hour," Mara pointed out when his movements woke her.

"The restaurant downstairs never closes. They cater to insomniacs and lovers."

Although she wanted to talk about what she'd told him earlier, needed to know if he felt the same, Mara nodded. Her time with Reed was so short; whatever he wanted, she wanted as well.

To her surprise she found a half dozen people in the quiet room. Mara was a little taken aback by the size of the breakfast Reed ordered, but the waitress, who obviously knew him, only smiled.

While she sipped coffee, watching his every movement, Reed told her of five-course meals served by women with more than waitressing on their minds. "It's a monied world," he said of his whirlwind trip to Reno. "I've been there before. At least I knew my way around the place."

Mara tensed. "The women with other things on their minds. Did they offer them to you?"

"I think you know the answer to that. But I didn't accept the offer." Before Mara could speak, Reed went on. The display at the private club had been orchestrated to impress several automobile collectors, Reed among them. The women were part of the package. Zack wined and dined; he expected his guests to partake of what was offered. Reed concentrated his "interest" on a woman who'd had too much to drink. He'd spent the night in a chair while she snored on the bed.

"Will you have to do that again?"

"I don't think so. The net is tighter than those characters know."

"You're sure?" Mara kept her voice so low that even the waitress moving near their table couldn't hear. "I mean, are you sure they don't suspect you?"

"There's no way I can be sure of that, Mara."

She felt cold. "But you must think about it."

"I can't. Not if I'm going to do my job."

There it was. The difference between them. Mara had wanted to believe they could get through their night together without having to touch the vast canyon that stretched between them. It was impossible. "Maybe it's your ego, Reed. You will not back down, will you?"

"What are you getting at?"

Fear in the guise of anger guided her. "I'm getting at this unholy alliance you have with Jack. Sometimes I wonder if your thinking is so distorted that you can't see what you've gotten yourself into."

"You really think that?"

"Maybe."

Reed spread his hand over his napkin and crumpled it. "I need more than that from you, Mara. If you can't handle what I'm doing, I need to hear that."

"Do you? If I asked you to walk away from this, would you?" Mara waved away what Reed might have said. "But I can't ask that, can I? Jack got in line before me."

Reed pushed aside his half-finished meal and reached for Mara's hand. She let him take it, and he pressed his lips to her fingers. "He isn't more important than you. Believe that."

With his words making their impact, Mara knew she wouldn't tell him about the terrifying phone calls. She would if she could keep her fear out of her voice, but around him she was all emotion. "I do," she whispered. *Just tell me you love me.*

REED HAD TOLD Mara he didn't think he'd be able to get in touch with her for at least a couple of days, but she'd no more than finished with her class the next day when her secretary announced she had a call and did she want Mr. Steward to call back. Mara hurried into her office and closed the door behind her.

"Where are you?" she asked.

"Why didn't you tell me?"

Mara went cold. "Why didn't I tell you what?"

"About the phone calls. Damn it. Didn't you think I'd want to know?"

Despite what Reed's anger was doing to her, Mara managed to keep her voice strong. She matched him, hard words to hard words. "Maybe I thought it was something I could handle on my own. Just like you handle drunken call girls and men who use bodyguards."

"What are you saying?"

I don't know. "Tell me something, Reed. How would you react if I jumped all over you because I didn't like what you're doing?"

"You already did."

He was right. "I told you how I feel," she countered. "There's a difference. How...who told you?"

"I'm at the police station."

Mara leaned heavily against the desk. Relief flowed through her. He was with the police. Maybe it was all over; maybe he wouldn't be disappearing into any more shadows. "What are you doing there?"

"Passing on some information. How are you doing?"

"Fine. What kind of information?"

"Where I've been. Where I still have to go. You could have told me."

"I could," Mara said with her eyes closed and her body hot and cold by turns. He wasn't through after all. Soon he would be back in the shadows, and he might never tell her what she'd told him. She might never know if he loved her. "But you couldn't do anything about it. Reed, I didn't come to the hotel so we could talk about some damn phone calls."

"Mara." Her name, carried along by his deep tones, faded. She waited, not breathing, for him to continue. When he finally did, he was whispering. "If you're upset because they had to let him go, because you couldn't identify—"

"That's not it."

"I'm listening. Whatever it is, I want to hear it."

Could she tell him about feeling as if she'd grown too large for her body? "I wasn't the only one there, remember? The other victim, she couldn't make an identification either."

"I know that."

"I want that animal behind bars, Reed. Things keep dragging on and I know so little about what's happening."

"There isn't much happening."

"Unfortunately. Reed, how far do you still have to go?"

"Not far. I'm into the final layer."

"You're sure? Of course you are. What . . . what happens now?"

Reed tried to keep the telling brief, but Mara pushed for details. By the time he finished, she understood that the time for springing the trap was drawing close. As soon as it could be arranged, a couple of undercover cops would pose as would-be customers. Their requests would call for the involvement of everyone involved in the ring. Reed would act as go-between.

"It's your basic sting operation," he finished. "If things come down the way we want them to, no one's going to escape."

"When is it going to happen?"

"I'm not sure. A few more days."

A few more days. At the end of that time Reed could put down the burden he'd assumed for Jack. If he was still alive.

"Mara?" Reed asked. "Are you there?"

"Yes," she told him around the fear. "You're sure? This sting, it's going to work?"

"There aren't any guarantees."

No guarantees. "You'll be careful?"

"I will. Mara? Afterward, we have to talk."

"About what?"

"I think you know."

THE PHONE RANG twice that night. Each time, Mara prayed it would be Reed. Both times whoever was on the other end said nothing.

The other night fear had overcome her. Tonight, though, Reed's example guided her. "Listen," she said the second time the phone rang. She kept her voice calm, speaking as Reed made her believe she could. "You are a sick man. Sad. Disgusting. You live in the dark and take your sickness out on people who can't defend themselves. If you were half a man, you'd stop playing these stupid games."

Mara had almost hung up when she heard the voice. It growled and rumbled. "Nice tits. Smooth long legs. I haven't forgotten that, Mara."

She knew the voice. "What do you want?"

"You. I want you."

Mara slammed the receiver. Trembling, she stumbled to her feet and jammed her fingers through her hair. Lobo looked at her in sympathy. Dialing the police should have been a simple matter, but it took three tries before Mara managed to make the connection. She explained what had happened and the officer promised he would have a patrol car out.

"Thank you," she managed and hung up. For some reason she suddenly felt like laughing. Lobo was staring up at her. She touched the doberman but didn't try to pull him close. The touch helped. She'd been calm before her attacker spoke. She could regain that emotion. She would!

Reed was out in the night somewhere, tightening a net. He might be with men with guns, with the capacity for violence. Certainly she could handle a simple phone call.

Certainly.

DETECTIVE KLINE called a little after eight the next morning. He'd found a note about last night's incident on his desk. "Mara, let's get a tap on your line. If he's calling from his place, we'll be able to trace him. In the meantime, you've got to get someone to stay with you."

An image of Reed came to mind. He was setting traps so the police could capture criminals. When it was over, he would come back to her. She would be worthy of him.

"If I do that," Mara started slowly, "he's going to back off. He might go after another victim."

"What are you saying?"

"I'm saying I don't want him going after any more teenage girls—putting any more women in the hospital. If he's concentrating on me, other women will be safe."

"I won't have you taking chances."

"I have a gun. I know how to use it. There's my dog. You can tap the phone so you'll know when the man calls. You— This won't get lost on some desk, will it?"

"No. Believe me, it won't."

"Good." Mara avoided looking out at her empty acreage. She would think of nothing except saving another woman from having to go through this and, somehow, becoming someone Reed would want in his life. Someone he could love. All she asked was that the police be ready when she needed them.

"This might not lead to anything, you know," she was told. "I've dealt with my share of rapists. Most are cowards. They love being in a position of power. Knowing they can intimidate and control. If he thinks he can't do that with you anymore, chances are he will find someone else."

"I understand."

"You're a brave woman, Mara."

Mara wasn't sure she would say that about herself, but knowing she was finally doing more than simply being a victim helped. It gave her the courage to weather the relentless question of what Reed was doing, and wonder when or if she'd hear from him again.

She told Clint everything.

"That bastard. You're sure you won't come stay with me?"

"I can't. Not if we're going to put him behind bars."

"I still say that it isn't your job."

"Isn't it?" Mara countered and repeated the arguments she'd used with Kline.

Finally Clint gave up. "I still don't like this. The things he's put you through. Does Reed know?"

"Some of it, but not everything. I can't get in touch with him. Maybe no one can."

"Look, I've seen that man around you. As soon as he can, he'll contact you."

But Reed didn't call. What Mara did get was a visit from the detective and someone from the telephone company so the tap could be placed on her line. A little after five the last of the students left. A couple of minutes later her secretary drove off. Only Clint was left. "My folks and I are going to be home tonight," he explained. "If you hear anything, see anything, I want you to call."

"I will."

Mara stood on the path between her house and the graveled parking lot, watching Clint leave. He waved; she waved back, forcing a smile.

The loneliness was coming. The safe, secure daytime sounds no longer enveloped her. There was only another night of darkness before her, waiting for the telephone to ring.

And not knowing whether Reed was safe.

Chapter Fourteen

The man was breathing, a hard ragged sound that vibrated through Mara and threatened to take over everything. "You've been waiting for me," he was saying. "Waiting and wanting."

"Yes." Mara sank to the floor, wanting to keep him on the line so the police would have a record of the call. A kitchen wall propped her up. Whether she closed her eyes or not made no difference. Either way she carried the image of a man sitting beside her in her Corvette. An insane, dominating man with a knife. Rage stirred and formed her words. "Waiting to tell you what a disgusting creature you are. You aren't a man. Do you hear me? You aren't a man."

"The hell. You want names. I'll give you the names of all the women who know I'm a man."

"Because you forced yourself on them?" Lobo was crouched nearby, growling. Mara reached out to quiet him. Electricity leapt from owner to animal and Lobo kept on growling. "That's not what a man does."

"How the hell would you know? I haven't gotten to you yet."

Was she saying the right things? Was there a line between making this monster believe she could no longer be intimidated and degraded, and pushing him over the edge? "Let me tell you something. A real man doesn't sneak around in the dark. He doesn't use the phone to make threats he can't follow up. A telephone call can't hurt me. Do you hear that?'' Mara inched along the floor until she could wrap her arm around Lobo. ''I'm tired of your sick game.''

A string of oaths followed Mara's words. She wasn't shocked; she hadn't expected anything different. The truth was, she was numb.

''Are you through?'' she interrupted as he was pointing out, in sickening detail, what he would do if he got her alone again. The words were pulling at her, drawing her back to that night. She fought them. ''This is boring me.''

''Boring! You won't be bored. You'll be dead. Nothing you say, nothing you do, will change that.''

Mara closed her eyes and counted to ten. Then to twenty. Finally, her mouth dry and her fingers nerveless, she dropped her head onto Lobo's back. ''He hung up,'' she whispered. ''Thank God. He hung up.'' Soon Detective Kline would let her know whether they'd been able to trace the call. In the meantime she'd let Lobo out so he could keep an eye on the property.

So he might keep her safe, because she knew this wasn't the end of it.

SWEAT RAN DOWN Reed's back. He was still breathing heavily from the last-minute chase but unaware of that. At the moment he was sitting in a patrol car on its way to the Harbor Island Police Department because the Jag had a flat. Beside him Captain Bistron laughed. ''I thought you weren't going to get involved in the physical stuff. You're supposed to be the brains, not the brawn of this investigation.''

Reed tried to turn his head and received a shot of pain through his neck for his troubles. Whiplash. ''Reflex action,'' he explained. At the moment he felt on top of the world. ''When I saw that slime try to take off, the only thing that mattered was making sure he didn't get away.''

''That was some fancy driving. Too bad you couldn't get him off the road without putting the Jag in a ditch.''

The Jag was the least of Reed's concerns. Laughter fed by adrenaline bubbled inside him. He'd taken Mara's course in order to learn defensive driving, but he'd been the one who'd wound up on the attack. That didn't matter. What did was knowing he wouldn't have been able to stop Zack if he hadn't been so confident behind the wheel. "We had to have the head man. His lawyer's going to have his work cut out for him, trying to get him out of this mess."

"You'd make a good cop."

"I don't wear uniforms."

"Not a uniform." Captain Bistron turned to make sure the three police cars containing the captured members of the gang were still following them. "I'm talking about getting into investigations on a local level. We could use you."

Reed couldn't concentrate on that. His heart was still beating double time, but it was more from excitement than exertion. The operation couldn't have gone better if he'd written the outcome himself. When it came time to write up his report, he would put things in simple terms. Mix equal parts of greed with the temptation of easy money and eventually someone made a slip. It had taken longer than he'd hoped, and there'd been times when he wasn't sure his cover would hold, but it had worked out. A gang that had thought it had Southern California in its pockets no longer existed. Not only that, the fingers reaching out to Reno and points east had been tracked, too. By this time tomorrow there should be seventeen men in custody.

Jack hadn't almost lost his life for nothing.

"I feel as if I'm about to explode," Reed admitted. "Whew! I'll never be able to watch a cops and robbers show the same way again." Ignoring his neck, Reed slid low in the seat. How long had he been working on this case? It wouldn't be until he went back over his daily log that he'd be able to recreate the events. It was only now, afterward, that the question of "what if" reared its head.

"You should feel good," the captain said. Like Reed he spoke quickly. "That was a damned good piece of work. If only we didn't still have all the paperwork ahead of us."

"You get started on the paperwork." Reed pushed himself upright. He was tired. Maybe more exhausted than he'd ever been. "The only thing I want right now is access to a telephone."

"When did you last talk to her?"

Reed was hard-pressed to remember what day it was. "Too long."

"You haven't seen her in the past couple of days?"

"I couldn't, damn it. She knows that."

"Maybe." Captain Bistron shifted position. "And maybe she doesn't. It hasn't been easy for her."

"What are you talking about?"

By the time they reached the station, Reed had been told about the continuing phone calls, the tap and Mara's decision to keep the rapist's attention focused on her. "Why didn't she tell me?" Reed's hands were knotted, his exhaustion forgotten.

"You ask her."

Reed sagged. Mara had told him she was all right. She'd handled herself like someone in control, and he'd believed her. Now, maybe, he'd learned everything she'd told him had been a lie. "I don't understand."

"She's a brave woman, Reed. She's weathered what she's been through incredibly well. I just hope—"

"You just hope what?"

"I'm saying this animal's been playing with her for a long time. I wouldn't think I'd have to tell you what that may have done to her."

"She'll tell me, if I have to drag it out of her."

"Don't push it, Reed. You don't know everything. Sometimes things happen between a criminal and his victim that can be as bad if not worse than rape."

Worse than rape. "Such as?"

"Such as one person's domination of another. Things no one wants to repeat."

"I don't understand."

"Don't you?" Captain Bistron asked and turned toward Reed. "No, I guess you don't."

Reed blinked. He felt at least a thousand years old. "Tell me," he ordered.

THE HARBOR ISLAND Police Department was a madhouse s prisoners were photographed, fingerprinted and allowed heir phone calls—all of them to lawyers. A couple of lawers from the district attorney's office were already there sking questions. Several reporters pushed their way in, too.

Reed ignored everything. Mara wasn't answering her phone. It was almost midnight. Maybe she was asleep, but he should be expecting a call from him. Wouldn't she answer it?

But maybe she was anticipating a very different call.

"You're out on your feet," Captain Bistron tried to point out when Reed dropped the phone back in its cradle. "Why don't you grab yourself some sleep?"

Reed shook his head, feeling sick. "She won't answer her phone."

The captain stiffened. "Damn. This bust, it took most of ur manpower. I'm sending a patrol out there right now."

"Don't bother. I'll go. If something happened to her—" He broke off, unable to voice his greatest fear.

Captain Bistron had arranged to have the Jag brought in. The dents were still there, but the flat had been changed. He handed Reed the keys. "If you see anything, anything at all, call us."

The night slashed past Reed. He cursed the traffic, the ag, Jack, Zack, his knotted stomach. Most of his real aner was self-directed. He'd let dedication and loyalty consume him because his job had long been the only true focus n his life. He'd done everything he could to keep abreast of what was known about the rapist, but in the end it hadn't been enough. He'd assumed Mara would tell him if anything changed. She hadn't. She'd been going through who knew what, for a long time. Their moments together had been too few. Too precious. They'd let—*he'd* let the passion he felt for her dull the reality of her pain.

What kept his foot pressed to the accelerator and his head pounding was gut-level fear for her life, and the realization that, when all was said and done, he didn't know Mara Curtis after all.

If only it wasn't too late for that to change.

THE PHONE HAD RUNG at least a dozen times; Mara was a breath away from throwing the instrument through the nearest window. Each time she'd answered she'd prayed it would be Reed. But it hadn't been him. Only once had the man on the other end of the line spoken and when he did, their conversation was over in less than a minute. Barely enough time for the monster to stretch his net over her. Barely enough time for her to be tangled in his sick game. According to Detective Kline, the calls were made from public phones, a different one each time.

Mara accepted that fact and others. He'd said he'd been out to her place several times, both at night while she slept and when she wasn't there. It was amazing what could be seen with a powerful set of binoculars, he'd told her. He'd described Lobo perfectly. He'd said he appreciated Mara keeping the dog in at night. His final words had been that a well-aimed bullet would put an end to the doberman.

And once the dog was out of the way, it would be party time.

At the sound of a car approaching, Lobo rose and slipped over to the window. He didn't growl. Instead, almost imperceptibly, he began waving his tail.

Mara didn't have to be told. Reed had come back to her.

Reed was walking toward the house with slow, measured steps. Mara stood at the door and leaned against her dead bolt. She felt both more alive and more terrified than she had in her entire life.

His eyes telegraphed that what he was going to say tonight hadn't been said before.

"It's over?" Mara whispered when he finally stood beside her. It was a moonless night. The desert felt lifeless.

"Over. Can I come in?"

He shouldn't have had to ask. Wordlessly, Mara stepped back. Reed entered the house, filling it. His clothes were limp and wrinkled. Dark hollows lay under his eyes, his wonderful cobalt-blue eyes. He moved his neck stiffly. "When?" she asked.

"Tonight."

Mara nodded. The need to touch him pressed against her, but because he hadn't reached for her, she stood where she was. Behind Reed, a fern, too long without water, drooped. Lobo moved forward and sniffed Reed's hand. Reed ran his hand over Lobo's head. "What happens now?" she thought to ask.

"Now we get ready to go to court."

"That's going to take all your time."

"No. Not all of it."

"You'll be taking another assignment?" Who was this man? She knew his body but not his words, his emotions.

"If I don't— Mara, I've been talking to the captain. He told me there's been a lot more going on out here than I knew. Things like calling the police to come out, threatening phone calls."

"Oh."

"Why didn't you say something?"

Mara felt hot and cold. Her thoughts went no further than the man in front of her. The man she'd made love to and loved. "When? How?" Mara challenged. "When we were together, or you managed to find a way to call me, all I could think about was you, what you were facing."

"I don't believe you."

"Don't. I don't care."

"I don't believe that, either."

Mara couldn't take much more of this insane argument. She felt too raw. Reed was the last person in the world she wanted to fight with, but he evoked responses in her no one else could, and she had no control over those feelings. "What did you want me to do? I told the police. I have a tap on the phone. It—"

"You didn't tell me."

"When? You were never here." The words came from that place called pain. "You showed me how to use a gun. You were there for the lineup. But you had no idea how incredibly hard that was for me. You didn't know what I was going through. When I needed you, you weren't here."

"You mean that, don't you?"

"Oh yes, Reed," Mara said, glaring at him. "I mean it."

Reed couldn't keep his eyes locked on hers, fighting this battle he couldn't win. It was easier to drop to his knees in front of Lobo and run his hands over the animal's lean back.

He hadn't been there for Mara. He hadn't sensed her turmoil during the lineup. He'd done that to her, to the woman he loved! "That's it?" he asked even though her answer might destroy him. "You didn't tell me because you believed all we had were phone calls?"

"I couldn't reach you during the past few days. You were out somewhere, maybe getting yourself killed. The last thing you told me was that you were about to throw a net over those crooks. What was I supposed to do? Tell you I'd gotten some damn phone calls, that someone left ice cream on my car? I had to listen to a voice on a line. That's all. A voice. You were risking your life."

Reed stood. "Ice cream?"

"Yes. Ice cream. You don't get hysterical over melted ice cream, do you? No one does. Only me."

Reed wanted to know what Mara was talking about, but her tautly strung body told him she'd said all she could on the subject. She couldn't depend on him; she really believed that.

Until this moment Reed hadn't known self-hate could feel like this. With everything in him, he wanted to hold her. But he had no right. Somehow he would have to find words, the right words to heal the damage he'd done. "I want to say something," he managed. "When I'm done, you can tell me what we're going to do."

Mara walked over to her couch and sat. A throw pillow fell to the floor. She ignored it. She was wearing her nightshirt. The hem crept upward when she sat, but that didn't matter. Reed took the chair opposite her, reminding her of a diver tensed on the edge of an impossibly high board. She could have lost him today. Today could have been the end of him. This distance was better. Safer.

"A few days ago you told me you loved me," he began. "I didn't say anything then. I didn't know how. But, Mara, I love you, too."

"That's what you want to talk about?"

"That's part of it. But no matter what else we say, I don't want either of us to forget that."

Mara nodded.

"Maybe . . . maybe love isn't enough."

Mara died a little. "Maybe."

Something that might have been pain flashed in Reed's eyes, but it was quickly gone. "Every time I got in touch with you I was taking risks," he said. "Risks that might endanger you as much as me. I didn't want that. I needed to believe you were someplace safe. You must know that."

"Yes." He was strength. Nothing but strength. Even if she didn't know who or what else he was, she could still want that part of him.

Reed ran a hand over his red-rimmed eyes. "This case— what I was doing—it was total for me. I didn't dare make the mistakes Jack did. But, Mara, I fell in love with you despite that and I was so damn torn between wanting to be with you and keeping my promise to Jack."

"I understand." Mara couldn't think of anything to say that wouldn't reduce her to nothing.

"You understand? Is that all?"

"You know what I mean."

"No. I don't."

His words undid her. They were getting at a truth. His truth. Maybe hers as well. "What do you want me to say?"

"Nothing. Everything. That monster is out there, stalking you."

"Yes."

Reed blinked, a slow covering, a slow return to their uneasy gaze. "When I called earlier you didn't answer. It's because you thought it might be him, isn't it?"

There was no reason for Mara to lie about that. She might not be strong enough to lay herself open and admit her inadequacies before this courageous man, but she would be as honest as she could. "He keeps calling. He says things . . ."

"What kind of things?"

"Does it matter?"

"You know the answer to that. Why didn't you tell me? I—"

"You what?" Mara interrupted. "You would have dropped what you were doing to run out here and answer the phone for me? We both know your case had to come first."

"That isn't true."

"Isn't it?" When Reed had walked in the door, Mara hadn't known what she was going to say. She was still taking the conversation one step at a time. Her turmoil fed the words. She didn't understand her need to hurt him, only that it had something to do with preventing him from getting too close and discovering her flaws. "You slip in and out of my life. Don't," she warned when he tried to stop her, when his wounded eyes stayed on hers. "The times we were together? They were wonderful. Becoming lovers . . . When we were together, you became the only thing in my life."

"I wish you hadn't let that happen."

He was right. So right she could hate him for it. "I don't know what I'm saying," she told him. "I don't understand what you're saying."

"Try. Why didn't you tell me what you were going through? Why?"

"That works two ways, Reed." She wanted to ask him to stop looking at her, but maybe she didn't. "Do you have any idea the hell I went through waiting to hear from you?"

"No. I don't."

"You . . . don't?"

His features were darkening, turning him into even more of a stranger. "Mara, I've never had to balance a private life against what I do. This is so new for me."

He had to stop wounding her. Otherwise... "Is that it? You just didn't know how to spit it out? I know you. You wouldn't do that."

She'd waited a long, long time to say these words. To take this step. And now it nearly killed her. "You're wrong, Reed. You don't know me."

"You think—"

"Don't. Don't interrupt me," she said even though she was the one doing the interrupting. "We don't know each other. The hell of it is, it's too late."

"You believe that?"

Mara couldn't sit. She surged to her feet and then didn't know what to do with herself. Somehow she wound up looking out the window, seeing nothing out there except the night. Once Reed had stood here, telling her about the sounds of silence. "I don't know anything," she whispered, "except that this is getting us nowhere."

WHEN HAD HE LEFT? Sometime while the world waited suspended for the next day to begin. They'd said things. Things about both of them needing to sleep and more words having to be said, but not while they were this raw. Then Reed had gotten up and walked out the door. Mara hadn't gone after him. She hadn't tried to make him understand that if she said anything, anything at all, she would wind up admitting things that would destroy everything he believed about her.

It didn't matter. Until dawn it simply didn't matter.

And then the sun came and the earth warmed and Mara began to cry and Reed's absence mattered much too much.

AFTER SPENDING THE NIGHT in his car on the road leading to her place because he couldn't leave her out there alone, Reed returned to his hotel to shower and change clothes. His first move was to call Detective Kline. No. There wasn't anything more the detective could tell him about the rapist case. Yes. Kline had talked to Mara this morning. Her calls would continue to be monitored, and Kline had cleared his desk so this would remain his priority. Reed was welcome to drop by the station whenever he wanted. He'd be there soon, Reed told him, as soon as he was done at the hospital.

Jack was sitting by the side of his bed, knobby knees extending below the faded hospital gown. "It's about time you showed up," the older man growled when Reed entered. "A phone call. I get one stinking phone call from some character I've never heard of, telling me I'm going to be testifying one of these days. That doesn't tell me a damn thing."

Reed shook his head. If he'd been able to concentrate more, he would have needled Jack about the return of his acid tongue. But this morning Reed was incapable of thinking beyond the tangle of his own mind. "I was busy. The captain gave you the details, didn't he? He said he was going to."

"How should I know? I'm stuck in here."

"Don't go milking me for sympathy," Reed said. He sat. The plastic chair didn't fit his contours, but he would survive. "I talked to one of the nurses. You're getting out tomorrow."

"It might as well be next month. You look like hell."

"Thanks." Reed shifted position. "I hope your sister brought you some pants. I don't think they're going to let you take that outfit with you."

"She did. I'm not kidding, Reed. You look like something that should have been thrown out with the trash."

That was the trouble with Jack; the old bum knew him too well. For a few minutes Reed filled the air with talk about the case. Jack pumped him for details, showing at least some of his old enthusiasm. Despite what he'd said about being in the dark, Jack had already talked to the D.A.'s office. His testimony would be a valuable part of the prosecution's case. "Maybe I won't be retiring right away after all. The bureau, I've been talking to them about my staying on to do some consulting work, training wet-behind-the-ears kids like you."

"You'd be good at it."

"Hm." Jack slid out of bed, gripped the back of his gown, and walked over to the window. Suddenly he turned. "Are you going to tell me what's wrong?"

Reed did. He hadn't wanted to; his inner turmoil was none of Jack's business. But maybe he spilled everything because Jack was the only one who might possibly understand.

Reed sighed. "I don't know what to call it. If I say smoke screen, it sounds as if she deliberately kept things from me. I don't think it was like that. Or if it was, it was because too many things were going on inside her. Things she couldn't share with me."

"Why do you think she couldn't?"

"I don't know—" Reed started to say, but stopped himself. He wasn't going to throw up a smoke screen of his own. Jack would see through it. And more important, so would he. "I'm no good at knowing what's going on inside people, Jack. I wasn't what my mother needed. She needed so damn much. I couldn't give it to her. And then Mara— She knew. She got close to me and then she knew."

"This is gibberish."

Was it? "What good am I for her?" Reed moaned, pain filling him. "I should have known. She went through a nightmare. I should have known it wasn't over when she couldn't identify her attacker. But I couldn't get into her head." He sagged. "I've never been in anyone's head."

"Yeah." Jack erased the distance separating the two men. "Just like you weren't rummaging around in my brain."

"What are you talking about?"

"Figure it out. Think about getting my sister out here and bringing me roses and not leaving me to rot in self-pity, and then tell me about not knowing anything about someone else's head."

REED SPENT a couple of necessary hours with the district attorney reconstructing the gang's organization. But despite the need for concentration, his mind drifted constantly to Mara. He knew what pleased her in bed. He knew she loved the beat of the ocean and the silence of the desert. Her home meant a great deal to her. She loved her family and shared a special relationship with Clint.

He'd given her more of himself than he'd ever given another human being. Not as much as he now wanted to turn over to her, but a start. Only, he hadn't gotten enough in return.

Why?

She had to give him answers, and maybe once he had those answers, he'd know whether Jack was right.

MARA RECEIVED an invitation to have dinner with Frank and Rennie Chambers. She tried to beg off, but Rennie wouldn't take no for an answer. The lineup was still on Rennie's mind, and she wanted to talk to Mara about it. "I know we can't change what happened," Rennie pointed out. "But I'll feel better after I've talked it out."

Mara wasn't sure anything would help her, but the alternative was to sit home waiting for the phone to ring and the wrong man to be on the line. She wouldn't be gone long. She could leave Lobo inside where he'd be safe, turn on her answering machine. If that animal called, maybe a trace could still be attempted.

Mara didn't take the Corvette. Instead she picked up the keys to one of the loaners and called Detective Kline to let him know she wouldn't be home for the next couple of hours.

Mara had barely stepped inside the Chamberses' house when she was handed a glass of wine. "Rennie's been chewing over that blasted lineup since it happened," Frank explained. "She keeps saying that if she'd been more observant, she would have been able to make an identification. I've told her and told her, the only thing I care about is that she's alive."

Rennie leaned against her husband, her eyes glistening. "I don't know how many men would have hung in there the way Frank has. Some couldn't handle knowing what had happened to their wife."

"Don't," Frank warned. "Don't ever think that."

Rennie blinked away tears. "I was a basket case when I got out of the hospital. I couldn't sleep. I wanted to move, to get a gun, to put bars on the windows. It wasn't just the rape. It was . . . the other things."

"Past tense, sweetheart. We're putting this behind us, remember," Frank soothed his wife while Mara's loneliness sliced into her and left her breathless.

The dinner conversation began tentatively, but before it was over Rennie had told Mara everything she'd been subjected to. Mara kept looking at Frank, searching for any sign that he wasn't handling this. But what he said was that his wife had done what was necessary to stay alive. She was still the woman he loved; nothing that animal had done could change that.

Mara's eyes were hot and dry. Rennie had Frank and a close, concerned family. Mara had lost Reed.

She hadn't been able to talk to him and she'd lost him.

"Mara? Have you . . . Do you feel different now?"

"What do you mean, different?" Mara asked.

"The way you look at life. The way you feel about yourself."

"I'm not sure. So much has been happening."

"What kind of things?"

Mara breathed deeply and willed herself to plunge on. "I met a man right after I was abducted. Our relationship . . . There were times when it was wonderful. But I didn't see enough of him." No. That wasn't the truth. "He's a brave and committed man. I tried to be like that—"

"You're speaking in the past tense," Rennie said gently.

Past tense. Two horrible, horrible words. "What do you want me to say?"

"To me, nothing. What makes you think things can't be right for you and this man?"

"Because—" Mara was crying, silent, unspent tears. "It's too late."

"It's never too late."

"I lied to him."

STRANGELY Mara felt a little better by the time she returned home. She hadn't expected to cave in around Frank and Rennie, but once the emotions broke free, she hadn't had any control over them. She desperately needed to believe that things weren't over between her and Reed, that it wasn't too late for them. But Reed had fallen in love with a woman who didn't exist. There were so many hard truths to be faced.

Mara knew how to admit them to herself; hadn't she stepped back from her family's life and created one that worked for her? But she'd never told her family how she felt, and now she'd extended that self-protective silence to Reed, and it was ruining something precious.

At least she'd come to grips with that reality, Mara thought as she headed down the long drive leading to her mobile home. She and Reed had had a wonderful relationship, one built on wind and waves. It might be over, but she would always have the memory.

Even if the memory would have to last her for the rest of her life.

Mara parked close to the front door and, aided by the porch light she'd left on, walked quickly to the front door. The moment she unlocked it, Lobo barreled past her. The hackles at the back of his neck stood up. He was panting, his legs trembling in excitement. He divided his attention between her and their surroundings, his low growl a song of warning.

"There's someone here?"

Lobo continued to growl.

Mara turned and faced the night. She reached down and touched the top of Lobo's head, taking comfort from the animal's presence.

Her attacker had said he'd kill Lobo.

But Lobo wasn't dead.

A week ago, maybe no more than a day ago, Mara wouldn't have been standing in the dark, facing the night. But changes were taking place inside her; a certain commitment had been made. Instead of getting in her car and runing away, she held her house door open and stepped back, etting Lobo go inside first. She heard the dog moving about and then slid forward and snapped on the light.

Five minutes later Mara was convinced that no one was or had been inside. Then she picked up the phone and dialed he police. "I know who you are," the man on the other end of the line assured her. "Detective Kline said I was to act, pronto, on any call from you. It's going to take us a while to get out there. Is there anyone close by?"

There was a man. But they couldn't speak to each other.

Mara poured herself a glass of water and walked into the living room. Her shoes pinched and she kicked them off. She didn't bother with turning on the TV because she needed to listen to the night.

When she heard the car coming down the drive, Mara jumped to her feet and pulled aside the curtain. The vehicle was a bloodred Jag.

Chapter Fifteen

Mara stepped outside. She met Reed before he was halfway to the house. "Did the police call you?" She kept her voice neutral.

"The police? No. Should they have?"

The porch light was strong. Mara noted that the weariness hadn't left his eyes, but he had changed his clothes. There was a small hole in the left knee of his jeans. His T-shirt looked as if it had lain in the dryer too long. She shouldn't feel like this. A wise woman would be able to look at a man without what they'd almost been to each other undermining everything. "What are you doing here?"

"Not out here. I want to go inside."

"I don't remember inviting you."

Reed pushed past her. "I think we've gone beyond waiting for invitations, Mara."

Mara stared as he walked through the open door and into her mobile home. She wanted to run. If she'd been wearing shoes, she'd have darted into the night and let the desert surround her. She wouldn't return until Reed was gone.

No, the pocket of sanity left in her insisted. She wouldn't run from Reed.

Confused, Mara could only follow after him. He hadn't sat. Instead he waited for her to close the door. Absently he patted Lobo. "He's inside again."

"Yes." Reed had done more than walk into her house. He'd once again taken it over, and now he was trying to take her over, too. If she wasn't careful, he might succeed.

"Did you think I'd come back?"

Mara had no idea how she was supposed to answer that question. If she said nothing he might read too much into her silence. If she said the wrong thing, he could turn her words against her. "You walked out on me last night. I didn't know what to think."

"You wanted me to leave, remember. There wasn't anything to say. Then."

"And there is now?"

"Yeah. Are you going to sit down?"

"Are you?"

Reed's laugh carried no warmth. "I think I'm going to have to."

Not want, have to. Was it possible that this wasn't any easier on him than it was on her? Mara perched on the arm of the couch, ready to jump if his words became something she couldn't handle. For so long that she could barely handle it, Reed remained silent. Slowly, so slowly that it nearly undid her, the tight line of his mouth eased. She'd seen him smile so little. She wondered what it took to make him laugh. "It's after midnight," he said. "You aren't ready for bed."

"What?"

"You asked if the police sent me out here."

"And you said they hadn't."

"I'm going to have to drag it out of you, aren't I?"

She could tell him yes, but to what purpose? Mara was incredibly weary of trying to walk a line between what she was and what Reed needed her to be. She'd learned a great deal since last night. The most important was that she couldn't be anything except what she was, for anyone. With emotion riding the crest of her words, she told him about coming home from an evening with another victim and finding Lobo upset.

"I don't have any proof he was here," she said with her hands wrapped around her knees. She felt small. Small and yet somehow safe. "But it isn't like Lobo to act like that. And there have been threats. Maybe that man's playing with me."

"I know about the threats."

Of course he did. Some she'd told him about; the others she was sure he'd learned of from Detective Kline. "And you expect me to cope with them, just cope with them, don't you?"

Reed touched a forefinger to the ragged denim at his knee. "I never said you weren't coping, and incredibly well."

"Didn't you?" Mara challenged. "Never mind. It doesn't matter."

He wanted to shake the truth out of her. That irrational need had ruled Reed during the drive out here, but he couldn't do that to any woman, especially the woman he loved. The knuckles of her hands clutching her knees were white. Her eyes, her huge, open eyes belonged to someone without enough support under her.

He hadn't seen that vulnerability before. Damn it, he hadn't wanted to.

"It does matter," he told her. "Maybe not right now, but it's going to before we're through."

"We are through."

She couldn't mean that. "You believe that?"

"You don't?"

"I don't know what I believe," he told her honestly. This journey was so new. He had only the instincts of a man in love to guide him. He wasn't sure that was enough. "Don't you want to know why I'm here?" he asked, hoping he was saying the right thing.

Mara shrugged. Reed didn't know what to read into the gesture, only that he wasn't immune to it. Or to her. "I've been thinking, asking myself questions."

"What kind of questions?"

"The kind that might help me better understand what you've been going through. Only, I don't have the answers. And I don't know if you'll give them to me."

Mara swung to her feet. She sensed where the conversation was going. Despite the danger, she no longer fought it. Yet, how was either of them going to survive what had to be said? "Go on. Ask me," she challenged.

"Ask you? You don't know what I'm going to say."

"I know." The living room was so small. Why hadn't she been aware of that before?

"Maybe, no matter what I say, you'll go on telling me what you think I want to hear."

"Don't make the blame all mine," Mara countered. She hadn't been given enough time to prepare for this, to plan what she was going to say. "You fly into my life. A few hours later you fly out of it. When we were together—you know what we wound up doing."

"Yes. We made love. At least making love was part of it."

Mara sat back down. "Only part?"

"You know the answer to that."

It was late. Somewhere in Germany her family was preparing for another race. A sixteen-year-old San Diego girl might be sitting in her room doing her homework, still innocent because she'd run. "You don't know what it's been like for me."

"That's why I'm here. Tell me."

Tell him. Where would she begin; would there ever be an end? "You don't know what it feels like to fail."

"What have you failed at, Mara?"

He was making her name a song. How was she going to see this through if he did that? "At being what you wanted me to be." That wasn't enough. In truth, that wasn't what this was about.

"Tell me about it."

"Tell...Reed, there have been so many changes in me, so little that's the same."

Reed leaned forward. For the first time since they'd sat down he erased a little of the space separating them. "I've seen a few of them. You hardly ever drive the Corvette."

"That isn't true. I—"

"Maybe you've forced yourself behind the wheel, but it hasn't been the same. Mara, if I asked you to get in it now, what would you say?"

Mara wrapped her arms around her middle. It wasn't until the gesture was finished that she realized what she'd done.

She didn't have to explain herself. Not now. Lobo's growl gave warning of an approaching vehicle. Reed was on his feet first. He strode to the door and opened it. "The police," he said.

Mara had forgotten that they were going to come out. She walked to the door, herself, careful not to come close to Reed. The young, blond policeman was one she'd never seen, but he was obviously aware of the situation. "I'm not expecting to find anything in the dark," he told her. "But if there is someone out there, I'm hoping they'll see the patrol car and back off."

The thought that someone might be out in the desert, watching, no longer unnerved her. "He's been playing with me," Mara said with a calm that would have been beyond her a week ago. "He threatened—"

"He threatened you?" Reed's voice was too controlled.

The porch light wasn't doing enough to ease the shadows surrounding him, and yet, those very shadows drew her to him. "He said he was going to kill Lobo."

"The hell he is." Reed snapped his fingers and Lobo, who'd been watching the policeman, stepped to his side. "This has gone far enough. Something has to be done."

The officer nodded. "That joker's making a real game out of this, all right. You're sure there was no one in the house?"

Mara nodded and explained that Lobo had been inside which had made searching the house easy. She'd checked the closets, under her bed, made sure none of the windows had been broken.

"Damn it," Reed interrupted. "That wasn't safe."

"That's my decision, Reed," Mara said around lips that barely moved. "I knew he couldn't have gotten in. I left every door and window locked."

"Wonderful. Do you see what that animal has done to you? You're turning your place into a fortress."

Because she couldn't deal with him right now, Mara ignored Reed. She asked the policeman to start with the detached and locked garage and moved as if to follow him.

"Mara." Reed touched her shoulder. She tried to ignore him. "You could have turned around and left when you saw Lobo's reaction. Why did you stay?"

"I don't know."

Reed muttered something she couldn't hear before setting off with the policeman. She and Lobo walked inside.

Inside. She really had unlocked the door and walked into her house when there was the possibility that her abductor was on the property. Had wanting to be there for Reed, if he contacted her, been that strong?

Yes. And yet that was only part of the answer.

TEN MINUTES LATER Reed returned. The policeman, convinced that no one was around, had left. "He's going to report back to Kline. He'd like to come back in the morning and see if there are any footprints around the house. The rapist, he didn't call you tonight?"

Mara repeated that she hadn't been home. Then she remembered she'd left her recorder on. Wordlessly she walked into the spare bedroom, Reed following, and punched the Play button. There were five messages. One was from her parents saying they'd try again in the morning. Twice no one had spoken. The final two messages echoed through the room.

"I know you're there, Mara. You just don't want to talk to me. That's a mistake. Talking's easier than what I have in mind.

"You'll never know when I'm going to show up. Maybe tomorrow. Maybe next week. Maybe tonight. When I do, it's going to be party time."

Reed glared at the machine. "Damn! How long has this been going on?"

Mara leaned over the machine, her finger poised over the delete button. But she couldn't erase his horrible words. The police would need to hear what he'd said. "Days. At first no one was on the line. But this— He's getting bold."

Reed turned to face Mara. He expected her to be trembling. If she was he'd know what his role should be. But she wasn't, and he had no place to put his hands. "And the police haven't done anything?"

"What?" Mara asked impatiently. She wiped the top of the machine with the back of her hand, ineffectively dusting it. "Slap him with a restraining order? We don't know who he is. He calls from pay phones so the tap hasn't worked."

"You could have let me know."

"Why do you keep saying that?" Mara's hands became fists. She didn't try to hide that from him. "I couldn't give a blow-by-blow to someone who's never here."

She knew how to hurt him. Reed had to hand her that. "That's not it," he told her softly. "That's not what I'm talking about."

Mara headed back into the living room, turning off the light as she went. "Then what?" she asked without looking at him. She was already perched on the couch when he joined her.

Maybe touching her wouldn't break through the barrier she'd thrown up, but Reed needed to take the chance. Still, he waited until he was standing over her, with his body inches from hers, and she'd looked up at him. It was then that he reached out and placed a forefinger on her throat. The scar barely registered. "I'm talking about emotional release."

"I couldn't."

"Why not, Mara?"

Reed had spoken her name in that way only he could. He'd touched his finger to her throat, acknowledging what her attacker had left as his calling card. That simple gesture broke down her barriers. Despite Lobo's warning that it might not be safe, she'd walked into the house and convinced herself that her attacker hadn't invaded it. Drawing on that same strength, she could speak and let emotion guide the words. "I've never been in hell before."

"Hell. Oh Mara, why didn't you want me to know?"

"You wouldn't understand."

"Wouldn't I?" Reed grabbed her hands, sustaining her. "Why didn't you give me the chance? What was it? You didn't love me enough? You didn't think I had a right to know?"

"Damn you, Reed."

"Yeah." He touched his mouth to her knuckles. "Damn me."

He'd touched her again. That was all; he'd touched her. No. It was a great deal more than that. "I don't know what you want me to say."

"Everything. Tell me about the hell you've been through."

"Everything?" The word sounded bitter, but Mara couldn't help it. Although she knew she wouldn't be able to do it much longer, she was still fighting to protect herself. To protect both of them from the truth of her cowardice. "You don't know what's going on inside me. Doesn't that bother you?"

Reed released her. Heavy-footed, he made his way to the window and stared out at the night. Mara read the end to everything in that gesture. Why had she attacked him when what she needed was his warmth? When he was everything to her. She found her feet and trailed after him. Still, she wasn't brave enough to do anything but stand beside him, feeling the night. Feeling him.

"Reed?" she began. "The night I was abducted I was forced to deal with something I thought was behind me."

"What?"

He'd asked the hardest question of all, and now, standing next to him, she had to tell him. "I'm a Curtis," she tried. "That's supposed to mean something. The rest of my family, they're so brave. Not me. I can't even watch them race. Not after seeing my father almost kill himself. But..." Reed wasn't speaking. She would have to go on. "I faced that about myself, admitted it. I made my own life. I accepted what I wasn't and became proud of what I am. I built this business using what I'd learned from my father. And then...*he* took that from me."

Reed wasn't interested in the night. Even if the physical distance between them remained, she knew he was listening to her every word. "You're so strong," she told him as her head pounded. "There isn't anything you can't handle. Nothing that scares you. I wanted to match that."

"I, what?"

She had to go on speaking. As before, emotion carved the words out of her. "I have to have pride in myself. Without that I'm nothing."

"No." His single word stopped her. "Don't say nothing frightens me. Do you have any idea what I've been going through?"

"Of course. Your job—"

"This has nothing to do with my job." Reed turned. He touched his fingers gently to her cheek and then let his hand drop. "Nothing I can't handle? You really believe that?"

"You're self-reliant."

"Self-reliant? Mara, I want to tell you something. Maybe it doesn't have enough to do with what's happening between us. Maybe it does. I believe it does."

Mara waited.

Reed glanced down at his hands pressed tightly against his thighs. When he looked back up at her, his eyes were so dark that she felt herself tumbling into their depths. "I told you what it was like with my parents. The lack of any real bonding. I think maybe when that happens, a child draws back. Insulates himself."

"Reed."

"But insulating myself doesn't mean things don't reach me." Reed didn't blink; there was no way she could pull free. "I've been going crazy worrying about you, not knowing whether you were safe. When I couldn't get in touch with you—when I was in Reno and when the net was being stretched—I thought about that monster getting to you. I told myself I was thinking crazy thoughts, that he wasn't interested in you."

Reed blinked. It didn't help. "That's what you wanted me to believe, isn't it? Only, that didn't stop the thoughts. Maybe I'd never see you again. There wasn't a thing I could do about it. Not a damn thing, except deal with that emotion."

"You didn't say anything."

"What? That I wanted you to pick up and move? That I wanted you to close the business and go somewhere safe? If I'd done that, you wouldn't have had anything to do with me."

Those were the words she'd given him. "You—how can you say that?"

"How can I not? You'd put the attack behind you. When you went to that lineup, you gave every impression of having things under control. You couldn't make an identification because it had been dark, but looking at those men was no big deal for you. I believed that, then. I couldn't match your emotions. That's why I didn't say anything."

No. That wasn't the man Mara knew, or, maybe the truth was, that wasn't the man she had created. "You aren't supposed to be afraid."

"Why not? I'm human."

Human. "But your job. How could you do what you did if you were afraid?"

"How? Mara, I grew up knowing there wasn't anyone for me, telling myself I didn't need anyone. And then Jack came along. He gave my life focus and meaning. There probably isn't anything I wouldn't do for him."

"Even if it means risking your life?"

"Yeah. But it backfired. In the end it made me hurt the woman I love."

Mara swayed. "Love?"

"I don't understand you," he whispered. His fingers were points of warmth on her throat. "I don't understand where we're going. But yes. I love you."

"Even—"

"Don't," he told her with a wisdom that took her from everything except him. "I love you. I believe you feel the same about me. Only, right now we're talking in circles. We hurt each other, when that's what neither of us wants."

"Yes."

"When we should be learning why neither of us can walk away from this."

"Yes," Mara repeated. His fingers were trailing lower. Lower.

MARA WAS SITTING in the living room when Reed woke, a little after dawn. They'd remained silent and let need do the speaking for them. But now, even after a night together, Mara couldn't dismiss how far they still had to go.

"Did I rush things again?" Reed asked as he joined her on the couch.

"No."

"Then what?"

"I don't know," she told him, although she did. "I don't know where we're heading. If the other thing was resolved, maybe I could concentrate on us. That man. I want him behind bars."

"It's going to happen."

"I want to believe you."

"So do I," Reed said. He rested his hand on her knee. "I want to give you back everything you had."

Mara took a moment to release her breath. Even after a night devoted to easing hunger, his touch showed her how quickly hunger could return. "You can't. Reed, I have to do this by myself. For myself."

"I don't think so."

"You don't know what I'm talking about. That man—I can't even drive my car anymore."

"I know."

"I could sell it. I've been thinking about that."

"Yes, you could."

No, she couldn't. Selling the Corvette was an admission of failure. And in the end that would undermine what she and Reed were fighting for. What she needed to believe about herself. "I have to try to face— I want my car back. It's only a little thing. It isn't everything, but I want it to be my car. Not his."

"We can try."

We. "How?"

"By getting behind the wheel of the damn thing and driving it into the ground."

So simple. So incredibly simple. "You'll be sitting next to me?"

Reed nodded. "But you have to do the driving."

"I did, a couple of times," she told him. "But that was before I was sure he was after me. Even then it was as if he'd left some residue of himself behind. Does that make sense?"

"Yeah. It does."

Ten minutes later they were on the track. The man in the passenger's seat was the one she loved, not a dehumanizing criminal. That thought sustained Mara through the first couple of turns while she warmed the engine. Then she pressed down on the accelerator, remembering the last time she'd tried to do this, and the phone calls and threats that had come since.

It was easier than she'd thought it would be. The Corvette responded like a race horse kept too long in the barn. Mara gripped the wheel and watched the needle inch forward until she was going over eighty miles an hour.

Reed nodded approval. "Keep it going. Come out of the curves as fast as you can."

She'd said much the same to Reed when he was the pupil and she the teacher. If she could advise, surely she could learn.

Ninety. A quick glance at Reed. He was still there, shutting out the other presence. A little more pressure. Yes. She could do that. Then they were into a turn. Mara held steady, accelerating as she came out of the turn. One hundred. She'd never taken it that fast.

"A little more. Just a little more."

Reed trusted her. She couldn't fail, either him or herself. Another turn, a quick stab of the accelerator as she hit the straightaway. Nerves wired, everything blocked out except the effort of controlling the vehicle, Mara breathed in Reed's essence and pushed.

"One hundred ten," he read for her.

Mara took her foot off the accelerator and let the Corvette slow. She was aware of her tension but waited until they were back at the starting position before relaxing her grip on the wheel. Her palms were sweating, and she wiped them on her jeans. "I did it. We did it."

"No." Reed stopped her when she reached for the key. "You aren't done."

"What? Reed, my students are going to be here soon."

"Now do it alone."

Mara froze. "I don't know."

"You never will if you don't try."

"I'll do it later."

"Not later." Reed unfastened his shoulder harness and stepped out. "Your dad got back in a car after his accident. You can do the same."

Mara thought of Reed's hands on her in the night, his whispered words of love that took the place of what still stood between them and wondered if he truly knew what he was asking her to do. It didn't matter. He was right and she couldn't fail herself in this thing. Mara eased back to the spot she'd left a few minutes ago. Part of Reed had remained in the Corvette. Would it be enough?

The day was going to be hot. There wasn't much of a breeze. Mara sensed only Reed. Remembered only Reed. And then she took her foot off the brake and acknowledged the emptiness to her right. She shook that off. She was going to hit the track and duplicate what she'd accomplished with Reed beside her. That was the only thing in the world she had to do.

Bringing the Corvette up to ninety miles an hour was the easy part. She concentrated on the smooth movement of the needle, the hum of wheels. But now she was going too fast to take her eyes off the road. She would have to let the Corvette tell her when she'd reached the ultimate speed.

"I love you," Reed had told her.

And then *it* was there, pressing, making its presence known.

There wasn't enough room in the Corvette. She wasn't alone, and the man riding with her wasn't the one she needed.

"Say it. Tell me you're going to enjoy this."

"No."

"Say it. If you want to live, say it."

"I'm—"

He'd laughed, touched her, held that damnable knife. Forced her to say things that made her want to vomit. Made her hate herself even more than she hated him.

"I love you." She heard Reed's voice in her mind, and drew strength from it.

She bit her lip, drawing blood. The needle touched one hundred.

But the animal was still there. His knife glistened, touched her blouse and ripped through fragile fabric. His words were obscene, his orders enough to make her gag. What she'd said, what had been forced out of her, echoed despite the sound of tires and engine. Once again the Corvette slowed.

"I love you, Mara." Her foot came down on the accelerator again.

One hundred and five. Steady through the turn. Straightening out.

"Party time." A knife on her leg. Foot off the accelerator. A scream crawling higher, higher, slicing off into the desert morning. "Party time. Say it. Party time."

"I love you, Mara."

One hundred and five again. Another turn. Another challenging straight stretch. The knife. Where was the knife? Her father would have pulled the key if he'd seen her take her eyes off the road, but then her father didn't know what she was going through.

Mara had a passenger. A man. He represented either sanity or insanity. A promise met, or failure.

"I love you, Mara."

One hundred fifteen miles an hour.

The knowledge brought Mara no joy. It should have. What she felt for Reed, what he'd given her, had made it possible for her to drive this vehicle. But all she'd really done was match something her father had been doing all his life.

She still didn't know if she had the courage to tell Reed everything.

Chapter Sixteen

"You don't have to do this."

Mara wasn't surprised to hear Reed say that; she probably would have done the same thing if the circumstances were reversed. But that didn't make dealing with him any easier. She waited until Detective Kline was out of the room before responding. She hadn't noticed before how small and cramped the detective's office was. She'd have to ask him how he managed to work in it without feeling claustrophobic. "Yes, I do."

Reed had been studying what could be seen of the department's parking lot from the small window. Now he turned. "Maybe you do." The words came out on a sigh. "But do you understand what Kline is saying?"

"I'm supposed to try to draw *him* to me," Mara began. "Make him believe I'm terrified and vulnerable so he believes he has the upper hand."

"Do you think you can do that?"

"Do I think I can act frightened?" Mara laughed; there was no warmth in the sound. "The only doubt I have is, is he going to believe me?"

"We can only hope."

"We?" She caught on the word, needing to believe him, knowing what still remained to be said once this other thing was behind them. "Reed, this is a police job, and you aren't a policeman. You heard the detective. It's going to be a stakeout of sorts. Someone will always be with me."

"Are you saying you don't want me there?"

She could wait until they were back at her place, but maybe by then she would have retreated into silence again. "I don't know how I feel. This morning, with the Corvette, I relied on you. If you hadn't been beside me, I wouldn't have been able to do what I did."

"You did it again when I wasn't there."

Mara hadn't told him about his memory making the battle with her attacker possible. She did now, revealing everything except the words that her attacker's spirit presence had used to make the test so hard. "I used your strength," she admitted. "If you're there when he comes, I might never know whether it's me or you standing up to him."

"No one is asking you to be Superwoman."

"I know that. The police are going to be there." To Mara, the police were simply tools, the physical force capable of putting her attacker behind bars. "I don't know if I can explain it." She was back to whispering. "I've been trying to deal with this for so long. Sometimes I feel like a Ping-Pong ball. My moods are driving me crazy. When we're together, I feel as if nothing can touch me. That isn't the way I want it. I want... There have to be certain things inside me."

Reed ran his hands down his thighs, feeling his physical strength. What he felt inside was far different. Wondering if he'd lost Mara had nearly undone him. Even making love and sitting beside her in the Corvette hadn't eased the knot that had become part of him. He accepted Mara for what she was, a fallible and wonderful human being. He wished she could accept herself.

"I don't know what to do with my emotions," she said. "You have no idea what it feels like to be paralyzed."

Didn't he? "Do you feel paralyzed now?"

Mara swept her arm to take in her surroundings. "I'm sitting in a police station. It's hard not to feel safe, to tell myself it's all been a nightmare. But it was real. It still is. That isn't going to change until he's behind bars."

Real. For a moment Reed was once again a child, face to face with a world he couldn't control or understand. His universe consisted of an absent parent and another whose needs were beyond his comprehension.

But he wasn't a child. Life was what it was. One took reality and carved out a life. Sometimes that life was full. Sometimes it wasn't. And sometimes someone else entered that private world and made it rich. Mara had done that for him. In turn, in gratitude, he wanted to help her put aside her own demons.

But she was the only one who could do that. "Mara? I understand what you're saying. You want to face him, and what you've been going through. But you're dealing with a madman. Mara? I *need* to be there with you. Do you understand that? I'd lose my mind worrying about you."

Mara blinked. "You— Oh, Reed. I'm sorry. I don't want to do that to you. I want you there. Only, please, don't play rescuer. Don't try to insulate me."

BECAUSE HER ATTACKER obviously watched the mobile home from a distance, Reed and two policemen came in early in the day, crouched in the back of Clint's car the way they had for the past two days, since the decision had been made to try to draw the rapist to Mara. Now it was dark, and the three men were sitting in Mara's living room, waiting for the phone to ring. Mara had run out of conversation last night while the phone remained silent. Tonight she tried to read the newspaper. The police officers watched TV. Reed sat. He hadn't said more than a half dozen words since the evening began.

Clint had called a half hour before, causing a flurry of activity until Mara recognized his voice. Clint passed on a message from his parents. They were praying for her. If there was anything they could do, all she had to do was ask. "Where are you?" she'd asked.

"We just left the realtor. My folks put down earnest money on a place about a mile from here."

"Your dad? How is he feeling?"

"Tired. But I've got him resting. Mom and I are making chili. We'll save you and Reed some. I'll be here. Call me."

"I will," Mara whispered and hung up. For a moment she struggled to bring back those innocent days when she and Clint had had nothing to talk about except their students' diverse personalities. But that was the past.

"Do you like chili?" she asked.

Reed didn't say anything, but Detective Kline pointed out that his wife was one of the world's great chili cooks. Her success had something to do with just enough beer for the liquid and some other ingredients he wasn't too sure about. Chili, Kline maintained, was always better the second time around.

Then the phone rang again. Pretending a casualness she didn't feel, Mara picked up the receiver. For a few seconds she didn't think anyone was on the other end of the line. Then: "Did you miss me? I've been gone. A little business I had to attend to, but I'm back. Back and thinking about you. What happened to your boyfriend? The one with the hot car? He leave you?"

Mara jerked her head at the men. The voice, that painfully rasping voice prodded at her, but she hardened herself against its impact. She would play her role, nothing more. "Stop calling me," she began. "Please stop calling me."

"I can't do that, Mara. I keep thinking about you. About the unfinished business we have."

"No!" Her voice rose. Kline nodded encouragement. Reed stared. "Please leave me alone. I just want you to leave me alone."

"What's the trouble, Mara? I thought you were looking forward to this. That's what you said. Remember."

"No! I didn't mean it. I thought— What do you want out of me?"

"Everything. You figure out what that means."

Mara moaned. She let the sound waver, weak and airy. She closed her eyes, shutting out Reed's comforting image. Nothing existed except the monster on the other end of the line. The only thing she wanted in life was to reach out and pull him into the net. But if she wasn't careful, if she didn't say the right words, the net would tear and he'd escape.

If he did, she'd spend her life knowing that.

He laughed. It sounded as if laughing hurt him. "What happened, party girl? You sounded pretty sure of yourself the other day."

Party girl. "I keep having nightmares. I heard you on my answering machine. Just go away."

"I can't do that. We have things left to share, like strawberry ice cream."

There was nothing of the actress in Mara now. "You..."

"Couldn't you figure it out?" he asked. He sounded so pleased with himself. "Did you get your purse back? That was a nice touch, if I do say so myself. The cone I left on the Corvette. Masterful. I was just going to watch you that day, but then you took off, and I followed. I waited until you and that kid left the Corvette in the parking lot and then— Masterful."

"You're sick."

"I had another word in mind."

Mara wasn't sure what she said after that. Her abductor made a few suggestions that made her want to gag. It took every ounce of strength in her not to slam down the receiver until she believed she'd gotten across the message that she lived in terror of him. Her abductor laughed and threatened by turn. His moods made her skin crawl, and yet part of her felt suspended over what was being said, listening, assessing. She hadn't been losing her mind after all. Her purse and the ice-cream cone had been threats, not coincidences.

"I'm coming for you, party girl. Maybe tonight. Maybe in five years. You'll never know. Where's that mutt of yours? Afraid he isn't safe outside? You know, maybe you're right."

"Don't do this to me," Mara whimpered. "Please." She hung up, wondering how much of her final words were staged and how much had been wrung out of some gut-honest core of her being.

"Are you all right?"

Mara didn't open her eyes until Reed pulled her fingers off the receiver. She blinked, waiting for him to come into focus. Where had he come from? The police. Had they been there the whole time? "I think so. He's sick. Sick and dangerous."

"He loves what he's doing to you."

Mara had to agree. She calmed a little. "He sounded so sure of himself."

"So in control?"

"So in control." Reed stood nearby. Every fiber in her ached with the desire to be in his arms. To let him tell her she was safe. But she'd agreed to set herself up as bait, in part because she needed to learn certain things about herself. That job hadn't been completed. "I just hope he wants more. He said I'll never know when he'll show. It might be years."

"He's aggressive," Detective Kline reminded Mara. "He believes he holds the upper hand, that he can do whatever he wants with you. That gives him an incredible sense of power. He doesn't impress me as a man with much control. If we're right, he's going to want more than what he can get over the phone. Soon."

"Hopefully tonight."

"Tonight?" Mara asked.

"Call it a hunch," the detective explained. "My hunches are wrong as much as they're right, but the last thing I'm going to do is leave you alone now. Mara, I don't want you touching your gun. Leave the use of a weapon up to us. I'm going to have enough to think about without worrying you might hit the wrong person."

Mara nodded.

Reed faced the detective. "Until he's caught, she isn't going to be safe," he said sharply. "This damn plan of yours is jeopardizing her life."

"It isn't his plan," Mara reminded Reed. "I agreed to it."

"Yeah. I know."

There'd been times when Mara had felt as if she could each out and touch the energy in Reed. Tonight he was iet, lost in moods she couldn't fathom.

She didn't believe concern for her safety, at least tonight, as the reason. With three trained men in the house, cerinly she wasn't in any real danger. What then had stripped m of the electricity that was so much a part of him?

The TV was turned off, the house silent. Fifteen minutes assed. Mara's nerves felt stretched and frayed. She could ily wait. For what and for how long she didn't know.

Lobo had been curled at her feet. Twenty minutes after ie call, he rose and padded to the door. He cocked his ead, his ears pricked. His growl was more feeling than und. Wordlessly Reed and the other men got to their feet.

The doberman's growl grew. Mara dropped to her knees id clamped her hand over his muzzle until he quieted. His ody remained ripcord taut.

A minute later the men had slipped out a window at the ar of the house, leaving Mara alone.

Lobo continued to stand by the front door, a silent arning vibrating through him. Mara stayed where she was. he felt nothing.

There was a sound; she was sure of it. Lobo didn't bark, ut the hairs stiffened on his back. The muffled sound was peated. Lobo rose on his hind legs, and before she could op him, began clawing at the window near the front door.

Something—Mara had no idea what the force was—proelled her to her feet. She stood beside Lobo, her heart udding. This was it. She knew it. Weeks of waiting, of nly half-living were drawing to an end. *He* had come for er. If only she had her gun in her hand. But the detective as right. She'd never forgive herself if she shot a policean, or Reed.

With a recklessness she would never try to explain, to erself or anyone else, Mara pulled back the curtain—and ooked into the face of her nightmare.

He needed a shave. He'd dressed in dark clothes. And he arried a handgun. The weapon was aimed at Lobo.

In the split second before the gun exploded, Mar smashed into her dog, knocking both of them off their feet She landed on top of Lobo as a bullet shattered the win dow.

Mara didn't wait to see if Reed and the police were there That monster had tried to kill Lobo! He would have don the same to her with as little remorse!

The dead bolt gave way under her fingers. With n thought to her safety, with no thought beyond hot fury Mara stepped into the night. Five feet away stood the ma who'd turned her life into hell.

He still held the gun, but it wasn't aimed at her. Instea it dangled from his fingers. Victory was plastered on hi features. "Mara Curtis. You've been waiting for me."

"Damn you. Damn you!" Weeks of fear and hatred and self-doubt spurred her on. Mara cared nothing for the pis tol. He wouldn't kill her; not yet. Not until he was done with her. Good. Mara had unfinished business of her own Nothing mattered except sinking her nails in that mocking face and inflicting pain. What he'd done to her, and to other women was over. As long as she lived, he'd never do tha again. "Damn you to hell!"

Her attacker opened his mouth. An oath cut the night, almost burying Mara's words. He took a step toward her.

A moment later he lay sprawled on his belly with his face in the grass. Reed straddled his body.

"WHAT DID YOU do that for?" Reed demanded once the rapist was in the house, handcuffed. "My God, he could have killed you."

Mara didn't look at her attacker. She'd seen the hatred in his eyes as Reed wrenched the gun from him. She had no doubt that he would kill her if he could. It didn't matter; the man would never have the opportunity.

"He wanted to kill Lobo," was all she said.

"Lobo? We were there. You knew the plan. Your job was to draw him to you, nothing else."

Mara couldn't remember making the decision to face the man. Everything happened so fast. A face in the window. Her dog's life in danger. A gun that could, in a heartbeat, be turned on her.

And anger. Anger far stronger than any fear she'd ever experienced. "I had to. I thought about the women he raped, that girl whose life he could have destroyed. Everything he put me through."

"He could have killed you."

Mara shook her head. She waited for aftershock to set in. So far it hadn't come. "He didn't want me dead. Not yet anyway," she told Reed in a tone she could take pride in. "There wouldn't be any game. He needed to be the dominant one."

"You're crazy." Detective Kline had called for a patrol car and was off the phone. Reed didn't give a damn what the other men heard. For as long as he lived, he would never forget the sight of the woman he loved facing down an armed man.

He hoped he'd never experience fear like that again.

"No Reed," she said. "I'm not crazy. Maybe I did everything the wrong way. But I faced him. I stepped out into the night and faced him. Do you have any idea how incredibly good that makes me feel?"

She smiled. Reed hadn't expected that.

But, maybe he had. Maybe her confident smile was what both of them needed.

"And you're proud of yourself, aren't you?" His heart was still beating out of control, and he seemed to have forgotten how to breathe without having to think about it, but those reactions would wear themselves out. The woman who'd shown him he was capable of giving and receiving love was safe. That was all that mattered.

"Yes. I am." Mara took his hands, her steady small warm ones wrapped around bone and muscle without enough warmth in them. "I'm sorry," she told him honestly. "I know what it feels like to have things you don't have control over happen. But if I had it to do over..." She glanced at the rapist. Then, feeling the finality of the act, she dismissed him. "I wouldn't change anything.

"I did it," she continued with what she'd learned about herself directing the words. "I saw him, and everything sick and demeaning he represented, and instinct took over. I made it past my fear because this other emotion got in the way. I acted. Finally I did something."

Reed pulled his hands out of Mara's and touched the vein pulsing at the side of her throat. He felt her warmth. He sensed the life in her. She'd scared the hell out of him, but he would go through that again a hundred times if it meant having her smiling up at him with her pulse calm and easy.

He wanted to promise her a lifetime of smiles. He wanted to give her his strength and love and believe that would be enough.

But his strength couldn't be hers. Just as hers couldn't become his.

They might love. They did love. That didn't mean either of them could complete the other. And until Mara found all of herself, or failed, the only thing he could do was love her. And wait.

Or did he? Tonight she ran on pure energy. If he tapped that force and guided it in the right direction, she might find that vital and necessary acceptance of herself. "We need to talk," he whispered.

"About…"

"About what happens now."

Reed wasn't talking about making sure the man sitting in her living room paid for what he'd done to her and other women. He wasn't talking about the trial he'd be testifying in. "What does happen now?" Mara asked.

Ignoring the police, Reed led Mara into her bedroom and closed the door. "You said something the other day," he began. "About my not being there when you needed me."

"I'm sorry." Mara touched her fingers to Reed's waist and drew closer. His breathing was back to normal. The depth and dark was still in his eyes. And, she knew, in hers as well.

It would remain like that until she told him about forced words and self disgust. She'd done an incredibly brave and insane thing tonight. The question was, could she draw on that now? Would it give her the courage to do something far more difficult? "I was hurting when I said that," Mara whispered. "It didn't make sense. It was crazy. But I wanted to hurt you, too. I'm sorry, so sorry."

Reed shook his head. Just the faintest hint of a smile played at the corners of his mouth. "Don't apologize. I needed to hear it."

"Oh, Reed."

His smile took on more definition. "I learned something when you said that. Maybe I already knew it and just hadn't faced it. I don't want to be away from you ever again. Ever." He touched his lips to the tip of her nose. "To not know what you're doing—to not be able to talk, to touch. I want to make love whenever we want and need."

"Reed . . ."

"To reach for the woman I love and know she's there."

Mara waited. His smile was an incredible thing. She lost herself in it.

"I've been offered a job. Doing investigations for the San Diego Police."

"Have you?" Her phone rang. She ignored it. A moment later she heard Detective Kline speaking in the other room. "You'd stay here? You'd quit the bureau?"

"I can always get another job."

He was offering her everything, and her heart wanted to sing. There was incredible richness in his eyes. That kind of light could give her life definition. But not yet. Not until he knew. "Reed? Please let me say this. It's hard, but I have to. I think I know why I protected Lobo. Why I went out to face that man."

"Why?"

"I had myself to face." She wasn't going to drop her eyes. Whatever his reaction, even if his eyes became dark and distant, she'd brave that. "I haven't told you everything.

Not yet. When I was with him... When he thought he owned me... He made me say things.''

"What kind of things, Mara?"

He shouldn't have spoken. He should have let her do the talking. "It was a sick game," Mara began and then stopped. But she no longer wanted or knew how to hide. "He made me say I wanted him. I did that. I would have done more. I said—those things. I would have said, done, anything if it meant staying alive."

"I know."

He knew? No. That was impossible. "You don't understand," Mara pressed on. "He was talking about a party. About the two of us having a party. Because he demanded it, I—I told him that's what I wanted, too."

"I know."

"Don't." Mara tried to wave away Reed's incomprehensible words. "No one knew. For a long time I didn't tell anyone. I didn't know how. I couldn't. And then I told another victim."

Reed's gentle, loving smile returned. It drew Mara away from words and into the warmth and wonder of emotion. "Detective Kline knew, sweetheart," he said so softly that she didn't need to defend herself against what he was saying. "He's spent years going after men like that. He knows how they operate. The kind of things they do."

"He told you?" Reed had taken her hands; why hadn't she been aware of his touch before this moment? "You knew and you aren't disgusted? You aren't repulsed?"

"Why? Because you have the instinct for survival? Mara, sweetheart, if you hadn't gone along with him then, you might not be here now. That's the bottom line."

"I couldn't talk about it," she whispered. "Just like the way I feel about what my family does, I kept it inside."

"But not anymore. I don't ever want you to do that again with me."

Cobalt was hard and brittle. Reed's eyes were hardly that. "You want me to tell you ... everything?"

"I think you need to be able to," he told her and tightened his grip. Tightened his hold on her heart. "Me and your family. And then we'll all put it behind us. Do you understand?"

They would do this, just as they'd taken the Corvette out on the track and made it hers again. Together.

The bedroom window where the men had exited a few minutes ago was still open. Through it Mara could smell her roses and the desert. Those were the scents of promise. Of tomorrow.

HARLEQUIN

Romance®

**This September, travel to England
with Harlequin Romance
FIRST CLASS title #3149,
ROSES HAVE THORNS
by Betty Neels**

It was Radolf Nauta's fault that Sarah lost her job at the hospital and was forced to look elsewhere for a living. So she wasn't particulary pleased to meet him again in a totally different environment. Not that he seemed disposed to be gracious to her: arrogant, opinionated and entirely too sure of himself, Radolf was just the sort of man Sarah disliked most. And yet, the more she saw of him, the more she found herself wondering what he really thought about her—which was stupid, because he was the last man on earth she could ever love....
